THE FORMATION OF CALCIUM

M. S. Coe

T0300638

SPURL EDITIONS

Published by Spurl Editions

ISBN: 978-1-943679-15-7

Spurl Editions
www.spurleditions.com
spurlcontact@gmail.com

THE FORMATION OF CALCIUM

UPHOLSTERY FOR DUMMIES

I did something and it's done and there's no going back at this point. Now and then I imagine that there is – some going back, I mean – but really there's not unless God or someone has a way to make time work that I haven't figured out yet.

My name is Mary Ellen Washie, I am fifty-four years old, born in the great small state of Delaware and formerly a resident of Chautauqua County, New York, but no longer because I had to leave that place fast on account of what I've done. My family is left there, though, my daughter Sallie and her girl Mae and a few no-count cousins, but no longer my husband as he is departed, a recent development.

Things happened in Chautauqua County which I would prefer to forget but instead I need to record them here just as they were, and once that's done, I will be able to put them out of my mind forever, because they will be preserved and safe in a different place, on an actual tiny cassette tape. I thought about recording on my cell phone or somewhere digital, but I don't trust that medium. With all the hackers and floating clouds of information, might be someone could get to them.

I suppose the best moment to start is on the day my dear departed husband and I married. Still I think of him that way, as dear, even after all that happened between us.

On that date of our marriage I was already pregnant with Sallie, but it's not what you might think, I was no knocked-up teenage bride marched into a shotgun wedding, but a full-blown woman of thirty-two who had, in fact, been married once before, and who knew her own mind as well as she knew which shoe was left.

But sometimes a woman like me rubs up against a hard time. Not my wedding day, only later, from the thing that prompted all this soliloquizing.

My wedding was planned for a Tuesday, as Jim Dave had Tuesdays off, and I worked only part-time in the front office of the same mechanic shop where Jim Dave changed oil. You would think that the two of us had met there in our place of business, but the truth was we had met before that and then Jim Dave had asked his uncle, who owned the car shop, to hand me the job. I figured it was pure security, right there, to have a man who could work for his family and deal out jobs as he pleased. Man like that wouldn't ever be laid off.

I had been sitting at the shop's front desk about seven months, I think, before we decided to get married. This was springtime and we wanted a woodsy sort of thing under this tree out back of Jim Dave's pa's property, but when the day came, the sky poured rain, and so we all of us had to cramp into my new in-laws' living room.

His ma hugged me and said, "Never have I seen such a prettier bride and gracing my own house, too."

That made me feel warm, at least until Jim Dave's pa started to complain about all the people tracking mud inside. He couldn't believe his son was so popular, is what I think, and felt put out about it, since he and Jim Dave never did get along, and so his pa thought that Jim Dave oughtn't get along with anyone else, either.

Overall, I felt glad we had the wedding the way we did, and even having to help clean up the tracked-in mud while wearing my dress didn't dampen my mood. Back then, Jim Dave looked like Elvis, just a heap more like Elvis than any man I'd ever seen around, with loads of dark hair only gray just a bit in the back, and big blue eyes and strong eyebrows and a soft, cute belly I wanted to press my face into straight off, and as soon as we got to our hotel suite, well, I jumped

Jim Dave's bones so's he fell straight to sleep after. But I stayed wide awake in that big bed and planned our future, the way we would raise a mess of kids and they'd all fight over who got to take care of us in our old age, and we'd take trips down to tropical islands on fancy boats stocked with caviar and champagne – but of course newlyweds are especially prone to silly dreams.

Sallie's first word was *booby*, and this sure made Jim Dave mad; he wanted it to be *dada*. She was an okay baby, I suppose – only one I ever had, so's I got nothing to compare her with. She did not like eating or sleeping or being quiet, so I had to force her into everything good, since Jim Dave was the typical father who sat back and watched me at it. Sure seems funny how a man who gets dirty every morning, noon, and night working on gritty cars grows squeamish when asked to work on a dirty baby.

On that day Sallie said *booby*, I carted her out to the garage to show her daddy she could speak. We had moved into the apartment attached to the back of the garage, a rent-free wedding present from Jim Dave's uncle, who'd kicked out the alky tire dealer who'd lived there before, and so's we were always around the place.

Jim Dave was down in the pit under a car, and I held Sallie in the gap where he could see. "She can talk!" I said. "This baby has started talking."

Naturally he wanted to know what she'd said, but all the other guys were in there, and I felt shy saying *booby* in front of them, especially with my own so unwieldy and leaking, so I told Jim Dave to come on home so's I could show him.

"Be there at lunch," he said and told me to have him a pork chop.

He came in when the food was cold, and before he could sit down, I told him, "Baby said booby!"

He made me repeat it twice over because he pretty much couldn't believe it.

"You teach her that word?" he asked me, and I said that maybe I had, though not on purpose.

I looked down at my chest. "She eats out of them, after all."

He goes, "Seems a dirty word for a little girl baby to be saying." He mopped up ketchup with his chop and then bloodied the corners of his mouth with the stuff. "Hope this ain't a sign she turns out bad."

Now I know that this is when we started to split, me and Jim Dave. We never got a divorce – I don't mean in that sense – but we grew apart, gradual like, over Sallie. I always figured she was a pretty good kid, and he thought she was pulling one over on us. Plus the idea of her growing up never seemed to fit soundly in his mind, so when she would ask for, say, his signature on a field trip slip over to the lake, he would harangue her about wearing a one-piece and staying away from the boys. Look how well that turned out.

But hey, enough about the past: I made a new friend today down here in Florida, where I thought maybe no one would ever cozy up to me seeing as they all look like tropical birds and I'm this dreary farmer who's never before heard of the Art Basel. But they say that you get along with people who are like you, and I'm thinking this must be the case, since my new friend and I resemble one another so much that someone asked if we were sisters.

Her name is Natalie, and we met at bingo this very afternoon, so's I guess you could say it's a fast friendship. The bingo hall was in a church and seemed to me the cheapest fun you could get on a weekday afternoon at a quarter a card and free snacks set out on a table. Natalie liked my setup of gold-rimmed sunglasses, snow globe burying Elvis in flakes, fuzzy keychain, et cetera, and we got to talking. I gave her my name, or rather, my Florida name, which is Deedee, seeing as I have always been fond of the way it sounds, and she said she was more than glad to meet me, which was maybe the first real pleasantry anyone has offered me since I moved down here, and then right away we found out we'd been born not only in the same year but the same month, too, September, which meant our parents had been ringing in the new year in a special kind of way, and she laughed her hat off when I said that.

It's true she started asking everyone around her – after she'd sipped quite a bit from her to-go cup which I doubt was purely soda pop, if you know what I mean – about their interest in a special bingo investment, starting at two grand with the possibility to double their money in a week, but as soon as I told her how I was saving up because I was hunting for a place of my own, she dropped it. She's not the pushy type.

When I stood up and shouted, "Bingo!" she was so happy for me: she told me I was lucky.

"Deedee," she said and grabbed my hand, "I think we should be friends. Don't you agree?"

Of course I took her up on it, and when she invited me over for cocktails this very evening, I said I wanted to, but I felt poorly because I couldn't reciprocate, seeing as I'd moved to town not long before and was still looking for the right kind of place.

She wanted to know where I was staying, and when I told her the Marriott Residence Inn, she said, "Well, how dreadful. Why don't we extend cocktails into dinner so you can get a home-cooked meal, too?"

"I'd be grateful," I said, trying not to get too weepy, but not wanting to hold it all back, either, because one thing I've realized is how much people like to see you going googly over them and their generosity and such.

Last night, Natalie opened two whole bottles of wine over supper, and that was after gin and tonics at the cocktail hour, all of which seemed to make her sweeter until just at the very end when she started complaining bitterly and unintelligibly about her homeowners association, which apparently is made up of several recycling

Nazis all named Cheryl. I worked my charms on her best as I could, and I even tucked her into her bed, though I doubt she'd be able to remember that last bit.

Her hospitality and kindness got me to thinking back to the time when I last felt close to someone, when someone was last sweet to me. And I've been leading up to tell about this, anyhow, since it is pretty much what you might call the crux of the matter, the reason I started recording this tape in the first place.

There came a time when I grew so fed up with Jim Dave I could spit. Sure I still brought him meals, but on purpose I didn't season them the way he liked, and if we'd been able to afford a bigger place I wouldn't have slept in the same bed he snored away in, but we were poor as snot ever since Jim Dave had given up his work ethic and quit his uncle's mechanic shop, which then of course forced us out of the garage's free apartment. He wouldn't seek out other work as he claimed his hernia was killing him, though I saw him lift what he wanted to lift when he wanted to lift it, which was a thirty-pack of beer about three every Sunday.

Our world became my responsibility. Where we lived, what we ate, and of course how to pay for it all. I did my best. Quit the part-time work – Jim Dave's uncle was mad at me, anyhow, for not being able to get Jim Dave back in the ring, especially considering that we had lost Jim Dave's coworker Squirrel and the shop was seriously understaffed – for two full-time jobs, or near enough, because you see they keep you just under to avoid paying benefits. One was cleaning houses and the other was cashiering at the grocery store, which turned out convenient enough seeing as I got a discount and never had to make an extra trip for milk. What chews me up is, I paid attention in school because no one told me it was a waste of time. Being able to recite the presidents or do long division does not get you any kind of good job – what gets you a good job is having money or connections in the first place.

As you could imagine, the responsibility wore on me hard, and so I admit it was near enough a relief when, a week before turning seventeen, Sallie announced that she was moving out and going to live with her boyfriend. She didn't mention anything about being pregnant at the time, but we had our suspicions.

Only, with Sallie gone, still nothing got better for me, except of course for the fact that Jim Dave took over Sallie's old room, which wasn't much bigger than a broom closet. Straight off it filled up with his smells and his toenail peelings, but thanks be at least I could cordon him off. Jim Dave's attitude got worse. When Sallie's little girl was born, he got so mad at all the time I spent up at the hospital that he hid a leg of chicken in my bed.

"What's this nasty thing?" I asked him when I found that old chicken leg tangled up with my sheets.

"That's your dried-up old nose," he said, "gramma."

Now he knew I was sensitive about being a gramma at an age much earlier than I had expected, not yet fifty, and that just pushed me over the top, so's I said, "No, it's your dried-up old sausage, is what it is."

Then he pulled my hair until a chunk came out, and right after I'd finally taken the trouble to dye it a nice red, too. I had to dye it again when I skedaddled, of course, and now it's blond, the same beachy shade of hair as Natalie and most of the women here in Florida.

"You'll never see my dick again," is what Jim Dave said, and he stuck to his word. This, when he used to be my Bubbles, an endearment come about in the unfolding of nicknames, he was my Bubba, then Bubba Butt, then Bubble Butt, then Bubbles.

Sex was never a preoccupation of mine, I think because my no-good cat-scratching first husband had problems in that department. Still, it's lonely to be a woman without any man, most especially in Chautauqua County, where what all the folks do at night is eat a home-cooked meat-and-potatoes meal and the women bring beers to their hubbies in front of the tube. Or maybe they go down the road for a barbecue and then peel off into groups – husbands in one, wives in another. And so's I got to feeling isolated and lonely and real down about myself, down about everything, and I lost one of my jobs, the cashiering one, seeing as I could not concentrate and likely looked dishwater dirty. Getting myself up in the morning to shower became too much of an effort.

But I'm doing better now, as Deedee; you ought to see me. I slap on a gold eye shadow and a pink lip every time before I leave the house, and my hair's not as fried as when I first bleached it, and I'm making over my personality, too, with smiling and talking nice. In fact, that is working, and I have concrete proof: Natalie invited me back to her house a day from now. She wants to see me again, which means she likes me, which means I don't scare off every single soul I meet, as Jim Dave claimed.

Last night I grew sleepy and distracted and never got to the part about the last time I felt close to someone, much less the main point of recording here in the first place. Well that someone was Jim Dave, my husband himself, approximately four years ago – what made it all the more bitter when he was never sweet to me for even a moment since. During that day, he stayed sober as a Mormon, and he drove me to this place where the river cascaded into a little falls, and he set up chairs for us out there and we sat and talked over things like what we wanted out of life and whether we ought to move to Nashville. Jim Dave had always had a thing for Nashville, even though he'd never been. He said that if he won the lottery, we'd move there in a squirrel's shit. We held hands and actually enjoyed one another's company and not even the feasting mosquitoes ruined the sunset for me.

What did ruin it, after, was the next day, when Jim Dave went back to being himself. I asked him what had happened, why he'd acted so different, why he'd done something nice for me. He said, "I had this feeling like you were fixing to leave me, and I don't want you to: it's the truth." I thought over this. I hadn't considered leaving him, but the more I mulled it, the more it seemed a fine idea. Only the whole prospect felt overwhelming, and I wasn't sure I could do it without finding myself worse off. Jim Dave must have read my mind, because he said, "I love you, Mary Ellen; you're the only thing keeping me together."

Cleaning houses the next day, I brought up my dilemma to my friend and coworker, Minnie Pearson.

"You're saying he took you on a date out to a waterfall?" she asked as she scrubbed furiously at the bathtub. "And this makes you want to leave him? Looks to me like your hair hasn't been washed in three days and your butt crack is hanging out of your pants. Just saying, he sounds like a gem." She went on to ask me if I'd ever thought about the other prospects in Chautauqua County. "Even the gross ones are hitched up," she said, "and the single ones, there's got to be a reason, one you don't want to find out."

Minnie's own husband was a big man who knew it, who stomped around so's you could feel the quake of the earth under him. Some-times Minnie wore sunglasses, even inside, for days on end.

"Maybe I want to be just alone," I said. Fed up with scrubbing the faucet of its calcium deposits that somehow grew as fast as green on cheese, I tossed down my brush. "Just me."

Minnie goes, "Not here, you don't," and I have to admit that she was right. But somewhere else, somewhere like Florida, ladies own condos and talk about bingo strategies and the best way to spend fifty bucks on themselves.

"You just got to keep the right kind of loyalty," I remember Minnie telling me. "Showy enough, but it can't overwhelm you. Keep a little something for yourself; there are ways."

I remember looking down at my wedding ring that felt like a big joke to me. Well, a little joke, considering its size. The problem was,

Jim Dave hadn't been a husband to me for years, and one day at a waterfall wasn't enough to change the fact.

My reverie was broken just now by a knock at the door, and I had to interrupt my recounting to deal with the proprietor of this junk-hole place, the Flamingo Motel.

Soon as I open the door, she says to me, "Next week's rent is due." No hi hello nothing.

I go, "If I have to live here one more week, I might as well cut off my own nose." And then I pinched my nostrils shut to show her what I meant.

She held out her hand right there like she wanted to show me she knew that I was bullshitting, and I was going to be in purgatory at this stinkhole place for ages.

The people in Florida are the opposite of country kindness and discretion. I had to wait ten minutes after slamming the door before I could start recording again just to make sure my voice wouldn't be corrupted by anger. It's people like that think they run the world. When all she runs is this bunk establishment tricked out with chests of drawers that don't open and sinks clogged by old hairs. I bet she's never got her cherry popped and never will, sour as she smells.

Anyhoo, back to what I was trying to say: after the waterfall, Jim Dave grew lots more maudlin. He'd been dragging chains ever since he'd quit working, but those chains started to wrap him up tight right about the time Squirrel's kid invited Jim Dave to his graduation. Jim Dave started to ask me things like what was the point of life when everything felt so sad and how could I not find myself abandoned by my country and God and all else? He put on weight; he stopped brushing his teeth. Everything to him became morbid, down to the way a can of Genny looked like an urn. Though he never mentioned Squirrel's name, Jim Dave seemed to be experiencing a delayed reaction to the man's death, which had happened right in front of him, after all, in the mechanic shop, and though everyone said that it would have been impossible for Jim Dave alone to lift that truck up off of Squirrel's chest, I'm sure that, deep down, Jim Dave blamed himself. Plus it couldn't help that the hernia he got while straining to save his friend grew more and more painful over the years, but Jim Dave refused to have it repaired, as if he wanted to punish himself. Or maybe keeping hurt was the perfect excuse to avoid work. His deepening despair threw me; for the first time, he started to visit Squirrel's grave; he was so unlike the man I'd married, who had not ever approached these grim topics. And I don't feel bad admitting that I preferred it that way.

NATURAL RESOURCES OF DELAWARE COUNTIES

I can't believe I've started another tape, but an incredible thing has happened, more than I could have hoped for myself. Life is finally starting to go a little bit right for me after all the sorrows I've drowned in and so maybe I deserve this contentment now: Natalie asked me, Deedee, to move in with her!

It all started like this: she called me up to check if I'd like to come to supper again, she'd had such fun with me before, and of course I accepted. Then, without thinking much about it, I decided to try and whip up a little magic, a little bit of good juju to take with me along to her house the next night. At the witching hour, I opened the left-overs that she'd sent me home with after our first dinner and arranged the deviled eggs into a five-point star on my fold-up card table. In my mind's eye, I pictured her home, the clean carpet, the hallway that led to her two spare bedrooms and guest bath, the stain-less steel fridge. I concentrated on spending more time there – I wasn't even thinking about moving in, just about stretching out on the overstuffed couch while we watched a movie, or being welcome to help myself to the olives in the fridge. I didn't realize how power-ful of a reaction this little spell that I'd made up as I went along might have. Finally, I ate all of the deviled eggs.

And the next evening at her condo, which anyone would admit is large for just one, it's a three bed one-point-seven-five bath in a tony complex with tropical landscaping, we opened a bottle of wine. She asked me how I was doing, and I threw her some story about not being able to sleep, as there were too many kids running wild through the hotel hallways, even though I've always been an ace sleeper and kids wouldn't have bothered me, but of course Natalie doesn't know that, and she said she felt awful for me stuck in a hotel and she knows how hard it is to get a place here with the market so tight.

I told her, "You wouldn't believe the things people think to do in a hotel. Leaving their old Chinese food to rot in the hallways. Making bedroom noises as if they were the only ones for miles. And my 'kitchen' – it's just a microwave and mini fridge! I sure miss the comforts of home." I let out a big sigh as I sipped Natalie's fancy wine and popped a cheese puff into my mouth. "I can't wait to get back to having a place of my own," I said. "A place like this."

And then she said a line that gave me hope: "As a good Christian woman, I love opening my home, especially to those who need a real meal once in a while."

Of course I had to tread very carefully – at least at first. But I thought about those deviled eggs that were still churning around inside me as I said, "And that's another thing! I can't even get it together enough to go to church like I normally would; I'm all over the place, my poor routine . . . "

Natalie comforted me, and I let the conversation drift onto other topics – the crocodile nest found inside a five-year-old's playhouse, the man who got arrested for soliciting and eating dirty undies, the other man who fed his neighbors' dogs and cats to his illegal pet tiger, until I told her that I'd best be shoving off, as I felt exhausted. "The bed is far too soft in that place," I told her, "and no regular person could ever sleep a full night, what with all the door slammings and loud music."

"Oh, don't go!" Natalie said and poured more wine into my glass. "It's early."

I told her that I could barely keep my eyes open. "You know, sleep affects everything about a life. I feel more sad, like my immune system is down, all that stuff – though maybe it's only because I've been moving around."

Natalie tilted her head side to side like a curious bird. She gulped the wine that she'd been steadily drinking throughout the meal. And she goes, "This is a touch impulsive, but the thing is, I have plenty of room here – you might as well be comfortable while house hunting. Besides, yours is the worst Marriott I've ever heard of."

The deviled eggs somersaulted in my guts; I had not been expecting such a windfall. To seal the deal, of course I had to tell her that was a generosity too much to bear, that I couldn't possibly. She was in the process of opening wine bottle number two, and maybe that was the reason she felt so bighearted, or maybe it was because my witching-hour juju had willed her generosity into existence: she said oh no no no you are not putting me out I want you here.

And I accepted.

And she said, just one tiny thing, I am hoping you might be open to a small favor in return.

A jolt of worry zipped through my arms, leaving them weak; I set my wineglass down on the table. "What is it?" I asked, imagining sponge bathing her or feeding baby mice to a creepy pet, or maybe some kind of weird sex thing.

She goes, "Well, honestly, I hate to drive, I just really don't like it, and so I am thinking that it might be nice if you would be willing to take me around sometimes, to different places."

This was so much simpler than anything I had imagined that I agreed straightaway. We clinked our glasses, and then we started planning.

To have such a pal is really quite the scoop in my cup. I can't remember the last time I had a true friend. Maybe my sister. And to think, Rosie died back when I was twenty.

I've got to pack my motel room, but I don't have much. Just a few things from the house – picture of Sallie and my grandbaby, favorite spoon with the yellow porcelain handle, a key printed with hearts that opens my old front door – that I figured the police would never know were missing, and a few more I bought along the way, like Bermuda shorts, wedges, pink-tinted sunglasses with golden rims. In fact, I ought to acquire a few more things so that Natalie doesn't find it suspicious, how little I moved with, but the problem with buying things is money. Sometimes I wonder what the people back home think happened. Hopefully they figure I'm dead; it would be easier for us all if they did.

Bottom line is, I'm moving, and not a moment too soon. I've got to figure a way to get back at this pesky motel proprietor before I go. Demanding money from me when her water wouldn't turn hot if you whipped it. Hers is the kind of junked-up office that posts bogus signs everywhere about the security system, though there isn't a camera in sight, so's I have an idea or a few about how to get some pocket money before I decamp.

I know! I'll just move a few empty boxes into Natalie's place along with my other stuff. That'll cost nothing and make it look like I own three times as much.

But before packing up, I need to focus on recording all I meant to say. The truth is, I need to stop dillydallying. Where was I? That's right: Jim Dave started asking me to off him. And not in some sly way that meant he wanted sex, but in a genuine, I-want-to-be-a-corpse kind of way that really brought me down. We wore out our tongues over this, conversations like:

Jim Dave: "There's nothing for me, nothing."

Me: "You could go get a job, go see your daughter, go plant a garden in the yard."

Jim Dave: "I truly cannot unpeel myself from this chair."

Me: "You can; it is physically possible."

Jim Dave: "You don't understand that I feel like a thousand weights are tied to my body. Please, please, please leave me alone to rot."

He'd been a couch potato for years, and I'd resolved myself to the undeniable truth: he was never going back to work. One of his chief complaints was that all the good jobs in our county had dried up, the President had forgotten us, wanted us to die because we didn't vote anyhow. Of course his other complaint was his hernia, though he would pooh-pooh my suggestion to see a doctor. As a point of pride, he had not been to one since the age of fourteen. Mostly Jim Dave stayed home, moping every morning, noon, and night. Sometimes he wouldn't get up from the bed, Sallie's old twin mattress. It made sense he wanted to die, seeing as he wasn't really living. Only place he ever got off to was the roadhouse every couple weeks. When he rallied like that, I'd have to drive him, seeing as we only had one car, we were so poor, and I'd pick him up again before close, by which time he would have spent two days' worth of my wages on beer and lotto tickets.

I knew that this could not be my life forever. Living with him was like keeping a cow plop in the middle of the room.

Before Jim Dave, I swear, I was an interesting kind of person. I was destined for great things, I truly was, and then Jim Dave came along and squashed me like a pug's nose. For example, when I was a child, I had a dollhouse that looked very much like the real house we lived in. One day, playing with it in the yard, I made a little airplane with sticks and had it zoom over the house, again and again, until my make-believe pilot finally got so dizzy that his plane plunged straight into the roof of my dollhouse. A minute later, a crop duster did the same thing to my real house, thirty yards away. I stood and stared at the smoke billowing from the destruction and felt the power swell inside of me, felt it rise up and overtake the blood in my veins and beat in me like a drum heard for miles. I knew that I had special powers, that I was a witch, probably, like the ones I'd seen on TV.

When my family came home from the market, I told them what I had done. I pointed at my little stick plane and the pilot's feet dangling out of my parents' bedroom window and said, "I made this happen." My ma put me to bed for a week, and when she thought I was asleep, I saw her praying over me, trying to cast out my witchiness with a rosary that she must have dug up from one of the boxes of my dead gramma's things. Maybe her prayers worked, and she really had cast it out, and Jim Dave was able to make me feel like nothing for all those years because inside me was a yawning hole where my witchiness ought to have been.

But back to what I really want to talk about, the whole reason I am making these tapes. I swear I've been as distractable as a kitten, I suppose because things are finally happening in my life. The matter is, in his final two years, Jim Dave was wildly depressed. Life was not all butter and bread for me either. Sometimes at night I cried and I cried. Or I liked to cry in the car, driving home from a shift, thinking over things, because oftentimes my work friend Minnie Pearson would corner me to discuss the curse of husbands. Minnie's was bad in a different way than mine; I liked to hear her stories over him busting his hand when he punched the wall. It was interesting to think about a man so full of passion, when the biggest gesture Jim Dave made was lifting a beer can to his lips.

Now and then I wonder what happened to Minnie. She left the job about a year before I did, and even though we had been friends, I didn't see her past then. In Chautauqua County, you had to make a real effort; you had to visit at each other's homes, unless you had the money to go out to eat. I wasn't too comfortable with letting people into my home, and I had the feeling that Minnie was the same way, that she wanted to hide her dirty dishes and shabby couch and the overall veneer of despair that probably clung to every surface.

But I am not the kind of person who can lay low forever; I wasn't going to let life wipe me out. And I think that I realized what I needed to do one day when I clipped a deer on my long, empty drive home from work. I pulled over and scooched out of the car to check on her. Soon as she saw me coming, she struggled to her feet and launched off into the trees, her hind leg buckling under every step. She stared back at me over her shoulder as if I were the devil come to claim her soul. Her rolling glass eyes jarred me back: survival was the most important thing, escape, no matter how painful it might be, and if I were going to survive, I needed to cut Jim Dave out of the picture.

Back at the house, the lump of him moldered in his chair. I nuked a potpie, his favorite, and then stood over him, waiting until he looked up from his food.

He goes, "You want something?"

My whole body felt like a balloon as I said, "Things have not worked out between us for quite some time, and I need to sever myself from the anchor of you: let's have a divorce."

His body kind of shook, maybe laughing, maybe crying, and he said, "Marriage is forever; I know you been taught that, too." A bite of potpie fell into his lap.

"Then what makes this worth it?" I asked him, and he shrugged like a little boy.

Instead of eating he sat there, his eyes like the unmilked teats of a cow, hangdog low and dripping, his posture old-man hunched. He said the world was out to get him, he had proof that I was cheating on him with another man, that was the only reasonable explanation for why I'd leave a marriage: I was a hussy.

I remember very clearly how Jim Dave said, "Till death – remember when we promised that?" He choked on his potpie. "Till death do we part."

The saddest bit was, Jim Dave was already half-dead, and he wanted to off me as well – but sure as shit I didn't plan to let him. Once I'd asked him what he thought people found in the afterlife, and he'd scoffed that it would be a big warm pillow of cherry bourbon pie he could eat his way through like a worm. And then he'd said that he'd never make it there, of course – he'd be seeing me in hell. He'd always been a goat whenever I asked him something serious.

We'd had some good times, once, but I felt certain that we never would again, not even if the both of us lived to a hundred. There'd been that one time we drove all the way to Pittsburgh for a weekend, and we took a tour of the national aviary. The birds flew all around, right alongside you in a huge open room, and I kept fretting that one might land on my head. Jim Dave walked the whole time with me tucked under his arm, to protect me, and so I thought it was pretty alright. We ate Mexican food after and the color of the salsas, red and green, reminded me of the parrots.

Us two hadn't gone on a trip together for twelve years.

Now this next part I promise to tell the truth the whole truth and nothing but.

I planned Jim Dave's peaceful departure from this earth for three days. Of course, it took me a hundred times that number to come to my decision, but those last three days were crucial. The whole while, I gave him chances. *Easy* chances. *If he passes me the butter without complaining, I won't. If he applies for one single job, I won't. If he only drinks three beers tonight, I won't. If he smiles at the TV, or hums along to a song on the radio, or takes a stroll in the sunshine, I won't.* Every single chance, he missed.

I even tried a compromise: "Jim Dave," I said, "you don't want to divorce me, but what if we just lived separate?" After I heard it out loud, I knew how silly it sounded: what would Jim Dave do for money? Where would he live, and how would he eat?

"We can't live separate," he said. "We're a married couple."

"Well," I go, "what if I left you? What if I went and lived some-where else?"

"I could find you," Jim Dave said. "If you were fool enough to do that, I could track you, no doubt. I could hunt you down and we'd be together again as intended."

The funny thing was, it was clear as creek water that he didn't really want me, but even so, he wouldn't let me go. He'd fixed his mind and backed me into a corner. But I was the one with more left to live, and Jim Dave wanted it all to end. He told me so, over and over again.

On the night in question I snuck Jim Dave's pistol out from the old biscuit canister up on top of the fridge and hid the thing inside my purse. Then I told him that I'd heard a mooing down by the pond behind our place. One of our neighbors owned the roadhouse and also some cows and when they got loose, they liked to wander over to this big sludge pond a quarter mile off from us where sweetgrass grew. For every cow that Jim Dave brought back, the roadhouse owner gave him a free pitcher.

Jim Dave was slumped in his armchair, feet propped, TV blasting, popped beer in his hand, but still he had this sour old look on his face, and I couldn't remember the last time I'd seen him happy. I was putting him out of his misery, just the way he'd asked me to.

"Cow's off down to the pond?" he said as he struggled to rise, one hand pressed to his stomach.

"That's right. I'll show you. Might be a whole mess of them."

"I don't need you," he said, glaring over his shoulder at me as he shoved on his shoes.

One last chance, I thought. "If you don't need me, let me go. It's just a little paperwork."

He glared at me like I was a shit stuck to his shoe, but he hated himself so much that he would never scrape me off. He said, "Leave it alone."

And so he slammed out the door.

And, stealthily, I followed.

The night smelled of fresh-cut grass and cow farts, and the frogs were going crazy, which nicely covered up the fall of my footsteps. Jim Dave ambled along, oblivious of me, pausing every now and again to pick up a stick, what might be good for poking the cows back home. I'd known there was no way for dragging his big body out here, and so I'd needed to get him to the site first.

Jim Dave walked around the pond with his stick, mooing and burping. "Moooo," he'd go, "where are you, you bitches? Ain't got all night. Mooooo."

The tenderness I'd once felt for my husband had melted out of me, and I won't pretend like I took no pleasure in stalking him. The adrenaline pumped through my veins, drenching me with power. I kept imagining a hole in him from which blood would pour out like a tiny, mysterious fountain. The part of the bullet and my finger on the trigger didn't figure into this daydream. As we walked in tandem around the pond, frogs screamed excitedly as they plopped into the musty water and a few birds twittered their goodnight calls and I breathed the shallow breath of a hunter, a woodsmoke scent in my nose.

When he got tired of searching for the cows, he sat on a boulder at the edge of the pond and slapped his stick against the water, which fanned out in ripples highlighted by moonlight. He bent down and scooped up a few rocks and tossed them out where a rusted wheelbarrow stuck up from the depths. I watched him until the agitation behind my heart settled into a steady thumping, giving me strength, and then I reached into my purse for the gun and leveled it.

I can't be sure if Jim Dave heard one of my movements or just sensed me, but he turned to look over his shoulder and saw me. I braced myself for him to lunge, come at me, spit out foul names, but instead he stayed there, slumped.

"Go ahead," he told me, trailing his hand through the air like he was helping to disperse a cloud. "Go on and do it; I don't mind. I want you to. I ain't here to stop you. I ain't even surprised."

I promise you that's what he said, word for word, right before I shot him.

The bullet zipped through his neck, and though I would have preferred a bit higher or lower, that's what I got. It came out the other side and lodged itself in some tree along with the countless other bullets and buckshot from hunters. I didn't sense any passing of life from Jim Dave, no last heave of air, no brush against my face as his soul fled his body. It occurred to me that maybe he hadn't been kidding in his hope that heaven was a giant cherry bourbon pie.

When Jim Dave fell back and I looked at him, his inflated body that had bumped up against mine so often, the inevitable supper stain on his pants leg that was now disappearing beneath the black lava of blood gushing from his wound, I thought over this story they'd made me read in school. "The Scarlet Ibis." And somehow this got mixed up with the trip to the aviary, and I had to sit down for a minute to regain my wits and banish the image of all them bright red-necked birds.

Once my head had stopped spinning without any movement from me, I rolled Jim Dave to the end of a big old oak log fallen partways into the pond. His clammy flesh moved too freely over his bones, as if already the bits of muscle that had animated him in life had started to unravel, to untether him from the earth. The blood felt sticky and smelled almost sweet, and I recalled how Jim Dave had told me once, a long time ago, that in black-and-white movies they used chocolate syrup for the blood. For a bewildering moment I had the urge to dip my finger into his neck and taste it, to prove to myself that the blood was real, that I hadn't fallen unawares into some cinematic trap, that this was my life and now I was free. Instead of licking the blood, I shook my head, hard. And funnily enough, I'm doing the same thing right now as I make this tape. Let's get on with it; I won't dwell.

I got right wet and muddy lugging Jim Dave out to his final resting place. Once he was to the end of the log, I weighed him down with the cinder blocks I'd hauled out earlier, and then I pushed him off and he sunk. He wasn't but three feet from the surface. Still, you'd never be able to see him through the black muck of that water. I hoped that fish and birds and such would pick at him and, not too slowly, he'd disappear. I wasn't overly worried about the blood gleaming on the log since a hard rain was near. And so, then, I was ready to get on with it.

It might seem crazy that I recorded a tape of my confession, but when you really think about it, setting what happened down permanent is the smartest move I could make: memories are fickle things, and already the reasons I had to do what I done have started to shift: was it for Jim Dave's sake, or for my own survival? I need to remember – for myself. Anyhoo, I keep these tapes in a locked metal box underneath my bed, and label them all with the dullest titles you could imagine, "Upholstery for Dummies" and whatnot, just in case I would need to throw off any snoopers, so it all feels safe enough.

For the record, I'm not a monster. I listened to Jim Dave, and I gave him what he wanted.

That same night, after cleaning up from the cow pond, I executed the second part of my plan: the escape. My idea was for the both of us, me and Jim Dave, to disappear. I didn't want it to look like a break-in or anything, just maybe like we'd hightailed it for greener pastures. I figured it would take a couple months, at least, before someone got serious about searching us out, seeing as our landlord was used to unregular payments of rent and our daughter came around about never and all our friends had abandoned us years before and so forth. I had to stop for gas just a few miles from the house, and while the tank was filling, I worried and worried that already the police had started their hunt for me, and I was a sitting duck on the side of the road. Before the tank was even full, I skedaddled. At night in the motels, I'd turn on the news to check for anything about me, but there never was.

The quick-passing road – what's in front of you slips behind unnaturally fast – is an excellent place to think. I wish I'd been able to make some of my recordings in the car, but I'm the safe sort of driver who keeps both hands on the wheel. Always I knew that I was headed towards Florida, land of warmth, ocean, and lots of older middle-aged people who'd been able to retire, always a dream of mine. I would fit right in; it would be as if I'd retired myself.

And now I've left forever the crappy Flamingo Motel and found my place here in Florida, freshly installed in Natalie's spare bedroom. From time to time it feels I'm in a dream. I've never had nothing, and it was almost better than I'd imagined to step into an instantly hot shower, or have padded hangers so my blouses don't crease on the shoulder, or an actual tissue box right there on the bedside table so's I don't even need to blow my nose with toilet paper. I think it must've been God's idea, to put me here. He made me suffer, and now I'm set to live in comfort. I don't want to suffer a drop more, I've decided. Not if I can help it.

My bed is a queen size, all that for little old me, with a puffy pink comforter and not one, not two, but three decorative pillows. My daughter Sallie would call a setup like this "the bomb" – the slang of youth just confuses me. We were all afraid of bombs when I was a kid. Though I guess I oughtn't call my Sallie a kid anymore, seeing as she has one of her own.

Before Sallie's pregnancy, we were close. She was my little girl, my one and only child. She loved overalls, I think because her daddy wore them and told her about how useful they could be. She filled all those pockets with hair ribbons, My Little Ponies, pictures torn from magazines – stuff that wasn't useful at all. Every Tuesday, I would pick her up from school so's she didn't have to take the bus and we would go to the ice cream store run by the Amish girl. Sallie always picked cotton candy as her flavor, though she would taste-test a different sort of flavor first, maybe chocolate, maybe moose tracks. But she always ended up with cotton candy. It turned her lips blue, and then she'd do a monster impression, fee-fi-fo-fum, which cracked me up every time and caused the Amish girl to turn red with anxiety.

She grew out of me, though, like I was a too tiny pair of overalls, and she replaced our Tuesday afternoons with chasing boys, which is how she got into the situation of being a teenaged mother. I think she sensed my disapproval of her boyfriend, or probably it was that he put a wedge between us. Sallie started staying away and spending more and more time at his house, until it got so's I hardly ever saw her. When she was pregnant, though, I went back to bringing her cotton candy ice cream on Tuesday afternoons, when her boyfriend was away at work, and she seemed to like that, she really did. She'd sit right there in her boyfriend's living room and let me braid her hair while she ate. Her hair was the same as my hair, back when I was her age: fine and prone to static so that, sometimes, it crackled while I braided. I wonder how her and butterball Mae are doing right this very minute. I wasn't too concerned about off and leaving them; Sallie's got her own life that didn't much involve me, and I can't remember the last time she'd talked with her father. She must still be in ignorance that she'll never talk with him again.

Look at me, rambling on to the end of the tape. This about Sallie wasn't what I set out to say, but here we are plenty of words later. Pretty much I've gotten down all I meant to, so's it might be time to hide these tapes until I ever find the need of them. It's comforting, to have this physical reminder of my recent past. It means I no longer have to harbor the memories, no longer have to hold onto them so's I don't forget. These tapes will remind me of what was my truth so that I can move into my future unburdened.

THE USES OF VINEGAR FOR COOKING AND CLEANING

Well, my, here it's been but two days since I've made a recording, which falsely I stated was my last. The problem is that I seem to have formed a habit. I rather enjoy talking into this little machine what makes a reproduction of my voice – I think maybe it's the act of creating something, putting it down and leaving it there so's my life becomes a sort of story I could open up and enjoy someday when I'm old. I didn't have much of a life for many, many years and now that things have ratcheted up, excitement-wise, I guess I want to tell the world, an impulse which, no doubt, would land me in jail, so's I'll just whisper it here into my little tapes.

Anyhoo, I suppose I'm back to it – recording, that is.

Lately, my senses have been on overload because of Natalie's antics. She might just turn out to be the best friend I ever had. She is a hot-damn type of friend, the sort where you're fine doing everything together and still somehow don't get on each other's nerves.

Though we have our alone time, of course, like right now: she's in the bath and I'm locked inside my room, what feels perfectly private.

Yesterday, us two decided to head down to a fish fry at the beach. Imagine – me living again in a place where you can just drive to the beach. When I moved from Delaware up to Chautauqua County, I figured I might never see the beach again. Natalie packed two beach chairs, one umbrella, and a cooler full of rosé. She let me try on three of her old swimsuits – they all fit perfect, seeing as we are the exact same size and both top-heavy. I settled on one with a royal blue diagonal stripe over a yellow background.

"It's accurate to say that you look like a beautiful, exotic bird," she told me and handed me a cover-up that matched the suit. Her closet is full of clothes with the tags still on, and her jewelry box could not fit one more earring. I don't know how she got all her money, and I won't ask – but I'm not above snooping a bit.

Natalie is the type of person who buys clothes and jewelry in sets: little dangling club earrings with a golf ball necklace, robe and slippers covered in the same floral pattern, pink rectangle studs with a bracelet of the same, lime-green blouse and culottes. Something about her always matching impresses me, maybe because I know I could never get it together enough to have my lime-green top and bottom washed at the same time, or because I come home with just one earring in my ears about once a week.

Natalie tucked all of her stuff into her car, tossed me the keys, and then we were off. The car felt luxurious, and I dropped my sunglasses over my nose so that I could watch the world pass through rosy lenses.

"Have you ever played poker?" Natalie asked as she fiddled with the radio. "Or the slots? Are you much of a gambling woman?"

"Well," I go, "I do like a riveting game of bingo, like the one we had when we first met. I think it is sure fun, daubing out all my squares and arranging my good-luck setup."

Natalie had this whole little speech prepared. She goes, "Bingo is fine, but honestly, it doesn't give you the intensity of *real* gambling, if you know what I mean. When you have high stakes, and you're playing for more than a one-night stay for two at Seashell Wineries, that's when you feel something I like to call exhilpation. It's like exhilaration and anticipation colliding down in your stomach, where everything real is felt."

"Sounds nice," I said, staring out at the ocean which shimmered on the other side of the road. It can be hard to concentrate when you're driving here in Florida.

She goes, "It's not, really. Not at all. But it's *addicting*, and that's what matters."

Somehow she said this without making me feel like a dummy, because she explained it like this: "Exhilpation should feel nice, you'd honestly think that it would, and so you keep trying, waiting for that feeling – and maybe it does come, every once in a while, when you win, and so you keep going because you just have to win again, and then before you know it, you're skipping church out of guilt and thinking about a second mortgage on the condo."

"Oh, no," I said, "you did that?"

She goes, "I am afraid that I did, once, when I was younger and reckless. But I turned things around."

I wanted to tell her that I knew what it was like, living without money, but I also wasn't sure if I ought to give her the impression that I was poor. I had the feeling that she wouldn't be as generous with a poor person, that she was helping me out because she thought we were equals, and off-balancing that dynamic wouldn't suit her.

But I wanted to give her something, a real tidbit about myself, so as we pulled into the parking lot, I said, "I have a daughter with money problems like that." I kept back the fact that this was because she'd never had any money in the first place.

As I clunked us into park, Natalie said, "Kids. I am grateful that I avoided that burden. They don't know how hard mothers work for them, just to get abandoned in the end. Well, at least we have each other." She got out of the car, but I stayed in it for a moment longer, savoring the fact of how much Natalie liked me: *at least we have each other*, she'd said.

The fish fry on the beach reminded me of picnics me and Jim Dave used to do on holidays at the lake – but a little bit wilder, with everybody drinking more than just beer and wearing less, too. I helped Natalie set up our lawn chairs in a spot with a good view of the grill and we sat there with our rosé in plastic cups and stared at the men flipping fish.

"Which one of them do you think is handsomest?" Natalie asked.

"This one in the palm-tree shorts has me fascinated," I said. "Look at those calves!"

"He has all his hair, too. Do you have a boyfriend?"

We both watched a shirtless young man jog by, kicking up sand. "At the moment I'm focusing on me," I said.

She goes, "Honestly? You're a smart woman. Unlike me."

And when I asked her if she had a boyfriend, she said, "I'll show him to you sometime." I'm pretty sure she winked behind her big, mirrored sunglasses.

I ate two whole fish. It was a great day, better than any old pic-nicking days with Jim Dave, which always started out promising, but then would dissolve into complaints about the food – flies in the mayo, not enough beers, soggy buns – and us in general, baby never stops bawling, white shorts make your ass look fat, et cetera.

I think the only thing me and Natalie complained about was that the water was such a perfect temperature, we wished we knew how to swim. I grew up near the ocean, but I'd never learned – my uncle drowned in a riptide when he was a boy, and so my ma told us we weren't allowed to set foot in the ocean. She thought that maybe her folk were incapable swimmers, a trait passed down like a crooked nose or buck teeth. My ma was a strange woman: once she fixed an idea in her head, it wouldn't shake. When we were kids, she started to believe that cobwebs were the source of colds, and then you ought to have seen how neat she had us keep the house from there on out. If one of us started sniffling, she would rally the whole family for a thorough scrub. Draperies, baseboards, everything. She told us that a ghost lived in our attic, and she spoke to him, sometimes; appar-ently he liked it when she cooked scrapple. And when I was about fifteen, she convinced herself that we had to eat one peach a week, or we'd be cursed. I can't tell you for how many years I ate one peach a week, even in winter when they were expensive. Sometimes, if our funds were low, we'd do peaches from the can, but fresh were better at preventing disaster. When I stopped eating my weekly peach, at first I knew I'd doomed myself. That very week I got into a car accident, a fender-bender that worried me endlessly as I'd skipped on insurance. But the second week of no peach, and the third, nothing happened. Then the fourth, I dropped a picture frame on my toe so hard the toenail turned black and fell off. Then the fifth, sixth, seventh, nothing – and so I decided that the car and the toe weren't curses, but just regular life, which I needed to get on with, peach or no.

Last night I had a horrible dream. Jim Dave came to me with his throat slit, which might have been funny, seeing as a bullet killed him, but instead fear filled me to the brim. I was in my room, my new room at Natalie's place, and everything was just the same. Jim Dave, his body blue, walked in dripping blood and immediately I dropped to all fours, scrubbing at the spots with an old sock. "Natalie won't like this on her pretty carpet," I said, "oh, no."

He sat in the fancy green chair by the window as the blood made purple patterns on his chest.

"Blue never was your color," I sassed him, but my throat had started to close up with the extreme sort of worry that is only possible in dreams, the sort of distress that radiates through the entire world.

His eyeball slowly squeezed itself out of its socket, and he poked it back, jamming a finger right into the pupil. He said, "You ever heard of haunting? It's mostly just hanging around. Real boring."

I asked him, then, why he hadn't just let me leave, let me run off away from our marriage and be done with it.

"You could have," he said. "You could have done, no problem. Lord knows why you made this choice instead." His blue hands waved around, encompassing his ghost body, which seemed to be decaying at the armpits.

"But you said you would track me down," I reminded him. "You wouldn't let me leave."

He fake-laughed. "That was a joke, Mary Ellen. A little scare tactic to keep you from doing something silly. But we can all see I wasn't able to knock that train off its rails."

The room felt intensely hot, and I waved at my sweating face with my hand. "You never wanted to pay the least attention to me," I said, "so this must be your hell, watching me this way. 'Hanging around.'"

"It's supposed to make me satisfied," he said. "I get satisfied that I've bothered you enough, and I'll move on. This is supposed to buoy me up into the afterlife."

"Into your cherry bourbon pie," I said, choking on my laugh.

Jim Dave said, "It's time for you to follow me," and those words quieted me; they covered my skin in evil little goosebumps. Then he sucked me into a memory, I swear my body felt like a piece of cooked spaghetti and he slurped me there into his mind, where I could sense the muscles of Jim Dave's face tightening into a smile. He was out back of our little house – I saw out his eyes – and he was happy, just watching the birds flit and the clouds crank across the sky.

Finally, he tilted his head, and I slithered out of his ear in a soggy spiral.

I asked his ghost, "Did you really want to die, then? I mean, when you were alive. You seemed happy for a moment, but you were always telling me you didn't want to live."

"Sometimes, around you, I didn't," he said, "but other times, I did. It's complicated, these things. It can come and go. When it comes on, it can be so powerful, it's hard to resist, but when it goes, the relief is huge. It's confusing." His ghost body shrunk a bit. "But now that I don't have the choice, it's sad. It's so sad."

Both before and after the fact of what I had done to Jim Dave, I'd told myself that it was a mercy, that he was like a dog whose owners were moving far away, and it was kinder for them to put him down rather than leave him to fend for himself. But if parts of his life made him want to live, parts I wasn't invited into, then I had been reassuring myself with a lie. Of course, that's where my thinking was wrong: I didn't need to reassure myself at all. What happened had happened because Jim Dave had let it happen. Around me, he'd stopped being any kind of person; he'd been more like a bona fide ghost.

Awaking this morning, I didn't feel rested. This dream has stayed smack-dab in my brain. The fog of Jim Dave in my head has kept me off-balance, like I'm a top spinning and tilting, spinning and tilting.

Today I drove Natalie all around to different suburbs, past countless pastel-pink stucco houses and skinny palm trees, to the homes of people she called her "Bingo Ladies." To each one she handed a box of fresh bingo cards, and she collected a check.

"Easy money," she said to me as I drove. "You're sure you don't want to invest?"

I told her that I couldn't have my money caught up in a new enterprise, not while I was house hunting.

"You're smarter with finances than me," Natalie said, and I had to keep from guffawing.

After the last Bingo Lady, and after I'd driven Natalie to the bank to deposit all her checks, I asked what, exactly, we were up to.

She goes, "I sell the Bingo Ladies their box of game sheets, and they can sell them to other people, or play the cards themselves, and then we have a big game once a month where the prize is based on how many cards were sold – it's usually a hefty pot, so you can make money both from selling your cards and from a potential win."

"Huh," I said, thinking about how many cards she'd just sold; at least a hundred to each house we'd hit.

"I created this business all myself," Natalie said proudly. "Well, I needed some help with the technology parts, of course."

On the way home, we stopped for a drink in a Tiki-themed bar. It's hard to explain how far my life has come, because it would seem just ordinary – right? – for a grown woman to sit underneath a palm-thatched roof in Florida and sip a mai tai through a swirly straw, but for me it was like my life had been returned to me, like I had been caught up in a tornado that finally set me down just where I wanted to be.

Natalie and I have just had ourselves a special girls' day for our birthdays; since we're both born in September, Natalie, the type who finds any excuse, figured we ought to celebrate. It reminded me of the time Minnie Pearson convinced me to knock off work with her on her birthday. This was before I figured out she was a klepto-maniac and an overall mess. Anyhoo, back when we were friends, me and Minnie went to this converted barn roadhouse to drink beer and play the jukebox, and then the owner, this craggy old woman, invited us into the secret part: a hidden basement. She said it had been made for the Underground Railroad and then converted into a bar during Prohibition. The bar was still down there, stacked with old bottles and everything. Minnie and I talked about that bar for months, about how much fun we'd had, until she turned on me and her true sour nature came out.

When I showed up in the kitchen this morning, Natalie declared happily, "Today is the day! Pampering day." She'd already made coffee and set out orange juice, which no one had done for me ever, not once, in my own household, so already I felt batted in the soft cotton of caring.

Once we finished breakfast, we went to get our toes done.

"I know this place," Natalie said as I used her car's fancy backup camera to scoot us out of the garage, "this exotic little place where they dip your feet in an aquarium with tiny fish who swim over and nibble the dead skin from your heels."

This disturbed me, and I told her so.

"Deedee, don't be a scaredy-cat," she said. "If you don't try new things in this life, when will you ever? Just see: you'll be reincarnated as a fly, and then you won't have any toes to paint at all."

Something about the way she said it struck me: if I hadn't tried to free myself from Jim Dave, where would I be now? Right back where I'd always been, that was where, but instead, I was zooming fast down a sun-filled highway with a comfy place to live and toes that were about to get nibbled by fish. If Natalie knew the truth, she'd be impressed.

"What do you believe happens when we die, anyhow?" Natalie asked. "Do you think we get reincarnated?"

The sunlight caught in the spiky leaves of a palm, making it hard to see the road. "I think heaven is a big old cherry bourbon pie," I said, "and hell is the oven it was baked in."

We were quiet for a second, riding, and then Natalie laughed into her hand. "Women like us," she said, "childless women, we never do believe in an afterlife, do we?"

I had mentioned Sallie to her, once, soon after we'd first met – I'm sure I told her about Sallie because I recorded it right here, on the tape – but Natalie had forgotten that in order to remake me in her image. I started to laugh along. Of course Deedee was a childless woman; she could up and leave wherever she'd been to come to Florida, after all. Only a woman without ties could do such a thing. Maybe it was a compliment, that Natalie had forgotten what I'd said so that she could turn me into a woman more like her – or maybe it was just a result of her martini habit.

At the salon, the fish against my feet tickled like flames on a spit, and Natalie kept poking me in the arm as I giggled, but in a friendly sort of way. We picked out the same color polish, electric blue, and I tried to recall but couldn't the last time anyone had massaged my feet. I melted into the feeling, pudding-like.

"Next we get tans," Natalie said as she paid the women for our toes – ninety dollars with tip, I could hardly believe it, the amount I'd spent on groceries for my family for half a month – "to set off our pretty new feet, and honestly, our color hair looks great with a tan."

Thanks be she'd already declared the day her treat, since my pocketbook wouldn't have stood for it.

We walked along the shaded strip mall sidewalk to the tanning place. Natalie gushed about the process: "You're isolated in this little box, like a glowing coffin, you go in pale and your skin looks rather purple from the lights, and then when you come out, you're a beautiful golden color, like a statue. You know, some celebrity moms, like Katherine Heigl, they have their children tan – those young skins aren't ready yet. But what are the children going to do? Tell their rich, famous mother no? Honestly, it is so difficult to stand up for yourself with a woman like that – believe me, I know."

In the tanning salon, they gave me goggles that made my eyes look like a chameleon's. I took off all my clothes except my underwear, which I bunched into a little string up my butt, and I rolled into my white coffin. The eerie, ultraviolet glow surrounded me, and all sense of time dissolved. My eyes moved back and forth, but I couldn't see anything; maybe they were closed. It started to feel like I was being crushed in there, under the weight of dirt, grave dirt piling over me, the bubbles of air inside my lungs popping flat, one by one, and for a second I thought that I ought to regret every single thing I'd ever done. But then the purple light receded and a woman was opening my coffin, and she was helping me out, saying, "Did you fall asleep in there? Lots of people do." And so I knew I was just like everyone else, all of us running scared there in our minds.

Next was lunch at the Mediterranean restaurant down the road. A few old men sat in the back dipping artichoke leaves into olive oil, and when Natalie burst in she said, "It's our birthday!" and ordered a bottle of wine without looking at the menu.

"Twins?" asked one of the old men, and Natalie told him yes. Of course I knew that she was joking with him, but still it made me feel nice, that she would want to associate herself with me so closely.

"You come here all the time?" I asked once we were seated at a table by the window.

She said the place was one of her favorites as she sniffed the cork the waitress held out to her. I wasn't sure why she would do that, but then, I don't know the rituals of wine, only of Genesee — Jim Dave taught me that you bought Genny in packs of thirty; then at home, you took them all out of the box and piled them in the vegetable crisper at the bottom of the fridge; and then at four-thirty, or three on a Sunday, you took them out two by two, popped them one at a time, and waterfalled them into your mouth in front of the tube.

Though Natalie's love affair with wine seemed a little bit classier than Jim Dave's with cheap beer, it ended in the same result: Natalie got drunk.

"Try the baba ghanoush," she said. "Try it!"

The bowl looked full of blended-up slugs, but I touched the tip of a triangle piece of bread to it and folded that into my mouth. "What is it?" I asked.

"Eggplant!" she said. "Isn't it amazing, what people have done with food? Who would ever have thought to eat an eggplant? Or a potato, coming out of the ground, all rooty? Or a lobster? But then, some people thought lobsters were giant cockroaches . . . "

I ate the triangles of bread plain while she rambled on and on. Like a good guest, I nodded and tried to mold my face into something other than utter boredom — she was, after all, paying.

She goes, "I often think that, if my mother had eaten a Mediterranean diet, she would still be alive today. Would probably have
lived to a hundred! She was from Greece, you know. Moved over
here at thirty-six. Didn't even have me until thirty-nine! And then I
only got her for eighteen years, eighteen short years, just long
enough to really know her and feel what I was missing when she
passed." Natalie stared down into her wineglass as if it held precious
drops from her mother's heart; then she stuck her tongue inside it
and lapped them up. The pink hunk of muscle was stained maroon
in parts, and pressed against the side of the wineglass, it looked like
a lewd worm, speckled with nodules, that someone had trapped
beneath a microscope slide. When she put it back into her mouth
where it belonged, I was grateful. She goes, "She was famous, you
know. My mother. She was so beautiful; most of my childhood was
spent watching her from afar, or watching her reproduction – on
television, or in magazines. Is your mother still alive?"

"No," I said, put on the spot to invent Deedee's story. "She died
not too long ago, now. She must've been eighty if she was a day." My
real ma died at sixty-six, just about a decade after my sister Rosie.

"You don't know for certain?" Natalie asked.

Real fast I go, "No, I do. I do. Eighty, it was. Kind of incredible
to think about." I needed to make sure that I was myself – Deedee,
Deedee, Deedee – always myself: beachy blond, light and carefree
past, and of course, now, childless.

"Our mortality," Natalie said, "is almost too much to contem-
plate."

Red veins started to thread her eyes; the bottom lids trembled
wetly. I sensed that we were veering into dangerous territory, but we
were in a restaurant, and I figured that, in public, she couldn't knock
too far off the trail.

Just then, the waiter came out carrying what looked like a giant
wonton with a candle stuck on top. "Happy birthday to you!" he said

and set the thing on the table between us.

"Baklava!" Natalie said, as if the wonton were pure gold.

Everyone in the restaurant sang us the whole birthday song, and at the end of it, the both of us blew out the one candle.

"Twins!" cheered the old men in the back, and Natalie replied, "Bingo!"

But I had lost the festive mood. I tried a bite of the wonton, which was filled with honey and chopped nuts, but it had no more taste than my napkin. When Natalie wasn't looking, I glared at her, which brought me a mite of comfort.

"Ready to go home?" I asked as soon as Natalie had paid the bill.

But she wanted to sit by the water and have a cocktail and watch the sun set.

"That won't be for another few hours," I reminded her as she started listing all the drinking establishments that were right on the beach. "I think I'm a little tired," I said. "A nap would be nice."

"Siesta," she slurred. "My mother, she liked to take a siesta. Her beauty rest. She was so beautiful. She did commercials for sponges; so many advertisements. They turned her hair into a work of art. Sooper Sponge."

"My ma, she never slept," I said. "She loved to stay up late watching the infomercials. She never bought anything, not once, but she loved to see what they were selling and tell us all why it was stupid or no-good." It gave me a mean little thrill to tell Natalie a tidbit that was from my actual life, while claiming the history as Deedee's. I was becoming and not becoming, moving ahead and reverting, and these contradictions pulled at me, like stretching a muscle that hurt. I'd never had time, before, to do much more than make it from one day to the next. But Deedee had time for beauty treatments, for recounting her every thought into a little tape record-er. And there was something about that process, about the time to think, that encouraged more thinking: I'd never done so much of it before. These thoughts are like bunnies, seeming to magically propagate themselves. And maybe that's why I was fuming, because all this thinking let me see how different me and Natalie's lives had been. She had it easy, a famous mother, she had money; no man had ever wrung her out like a rag. She celebrated her own birthday with food I couldn't even pronounce.

It should have made me happy to be included, but instead I felt miffed at everything in life I'd missed.

"Give me a cigarette," Natalie said. "I saw the pack in your purse."

I told her that I didn't smoke, and she said that she didn't either.

As I helped her to the car, already I was wondering how much she could become a problem. That was the thing with friends.

HOW TO REMOVE DRYER LINT

The one time I offered Minnie Pearson, a false friend if there ever was one, a true tidbit about myself, she threw it on the ground and heeled it to a pulp.

We'd gotten a new manager at work, and I thought he looked like James Dean turned Hells Angel, a combination which struck me right there in the low part of my belly. He drove a green motorcycle with handlebars like a steer's horns.

I told Minnie about my innocent crush.

"Well isn't that something," she said.

Wait, no, her voice was more uppity and rude, like: "Is that not *some*thing!"

Yes, she sounded snooty all the way to her boots, just like that.

At work the next day, it was as if I'd tattooed the new manager's name on my forehead inside of a heart. Everyone teased me about him mercilessly, saying grotesque things about his beard and how hard of a time he would have keeping it clean and that he ought to invest in a green sidecar for me. When I asked Minnie why she had betrayed my secret that way, she giggled and claimed that she hadn't known it was a secret in the first place.

I felt so angry that I couldn't even talk to her any longer; I marched off and made sure we weren't assigned to clean the same houses. For days I let my anger tremor beneath the surface, until the burly James Dean called me into his office.

My heart was running away, but not because I still tingled for the man. Minnie's betrayal and my ensuing fury had squashed my crush flat.

He'd been receiving a few complaints, he said. Things missing from clients' homes. I'd been working there longer than anyone else; did I know what might be happening?

Well, the tremors of anger I'd been carrying around with me became a volcano, and I told him with conviction how Minnie was a certified klepto, how I had noticed things in her purse after a job that seemingly had not been there before it, how she always had new earrings. I made sure not to implicate myself in any of this. If I had seen her swiping some perfume and failed to tell management, I would be guilty by association. So's I noted that these were only suspicions; I wouldn't be able to prove a thing.

"That won't be necessary," James Dean said to me in his gravelly voice. "You've been very helpful."

After speaking with him, I felt much better, and I'd come to an understanding, too: it was rarely a good idea to offer someone a true part of yourself. It only gave them ammunition with which to hurt you.

This is why I suspect that Natalie, despite her faults, might turn out to be the best friend I've ever had: she knows nothing real of me.

Vaguely, I've been keeping up with the Chautauqua County *Courier* to see if there's anything about Jim Dave or, for that matter, me, and I hadn't seen a single mention until today.

AREA COUPLE GOES MISSING, it read. I was using the free internet at the library, so's I figured no one could trace me; I was just like any other lady sitting there, scanning the news. Soon as I saw the headline, I knew it was about us: nothing ever happens in our county. Maybe the occasional break-in when there's a tiff over who inherited granny's coin collection, or every few years a kid or a prized dog is killed by a stray hunting bullet, but all in all, there isn't much crime or intrigue. And so's I knew that the missing couple was set to get a fair amount of attention.

I'm going to read the article here, so's it's recorded. I printed it out using someone else's library card that I found on the floor in the bathroom, so there's no way, no how they could know it was me.

Jim Dave Washie, fifty-seven, and Mary Ellen Washie, fifty-four – strange to see my own name in print like that when I haven't used it for so long – *have been missing from their Chautauqua area home for what could be up to two months.*

I wonder how they could time it so precise like that?

Authorities became aware of the situation after Franklin Dodds, their nearest neighbor one mile to the east and owner of a local roadhouse, mentioned to patrons of the bar that he hadn't seen Jim Dave Washie, a regular, in some time.

My that bothers me, that the person to set the call out for us was Frankie; I wonder if Sallie even noticed her parents were gone. I'd quit the cleaning job as part of my plan and it's true we didn't have much else in the way of connections, but Sallie, our own daughter, you would think she might get concerned.

Two patrons of the roadhouse decided to drive to the Washie residence and invite Jim Dave Washie out for a drink. "Place looked abandoned," said Milo Knox, one of those men. "Trash all over the stoop. Like a raccoon done took over." Still, the men waited several more days before reporting their findings to authorities. "My cousin is a cop," said Knox, "and I mentioned the situation to him when I saw him next."

And so the investigation began. Despite a thorough search of the house, police found no evidence of foul play. Jim Dave Washie owned several shotguns and a pistol, all of which were present and accounted for.

I wonder if they dusted the guns for fingerprints. I'd touched all of them, before I'd left, because once on a daytime show I'd seen a suspect do the same, so's on every gun they would find the finger-prints of me and Jim Dave – otherwise it would have been the single gun with both prints, which no doubt was more suspicious.

Knox stated that Jim Dave Washie had enjoyed playing the lottery, and their last conversation had been about Washie's certainty that he would win. "Don't make no sense to me that he would up and vanish this way, unless, maybe, he did hit the jackpot and moved to the Caribbean."

Other valuable property and family heirlooms remain in the house, and authorities are uncertain if the disappearance is a cause for concern.

I wonder what they meant by valuable? The TV, maybe?

Authorities request that anyone with information on the whereabouts of the Washies contact them immediately at this number blah blah blah . . .

Sounds to me like they have scat to go on; I hope that I'm fretting for nothing and this will all disappear.

Now that my living situation is easy, my mind has flipped hyperactive: I keep having these terrible dreams. Jim Dave is a ghost like that strange god the Indians have, the blue one, and he walks through the air leaving scraps of blue flesh suspended behind him. Last night, the night after I found that article in the paper, the ghost him said to me, "They're getting close, and I can help them catch you."

"Our police are a bunch of dummies," I told him. "You know all they do is pump iron at the Y and talk shit at the Chow House."

"I can put evidence in their path," he said, his tongue fraying at its edges. "I'm a ghost. I can float over there, soup them up, float back here, keep you from sleep . . . "

"I am sleeping," I said.

When he told me, "That's what you think," I awoke with a shuddering gasp and an ache like a walnut caught in my throat. I couldn't get back to sleep for the life of me, so I headed for the kitchen to pour a glass of water, but the blue glow of the computer in the den stopped me. The door was cracked and Natalie was in there, clicking away. Then I heard her speak: "Oh! There you are! I see your lips moving but I can't . . . there. Now I can hear. Stop making fun! You know I'm terrible with technology; that's why *you* made our website. Yes, hello, darling! How is your weather over there? Oh? Well, here it's the same. Except humid too. Hot, humid, sunny." She must've been wearing headphones, because I never heard the other person speak.

For twenty minutes, I stood in the hall while Natalie prattled, and I waited to hear a mention of me, but there wasn't one, not once. I figured on the other end of that chatroom was her boyfriend, or maybe they're not that serious, and he's just a guy she met on a dating site, somebody to give her attention and fill up her inbox.

While they were saying their goodnights, I returned to bed without my glass of water.

A couple of days have passed without my setting anything to these tapes because nothing much has happened, and maybe I've been feeling lackadaisical, but here is the place I feel most comfortable putting my thoughts, and I've had a thought: back when my sister Rosie died, I wanted her to be a ghost so badly. I fantasized about how she would float back to me, and we would talk, and she would tell me how to be – because after she died, I had this inspiration: I figured the best thing for me to do was to act like her. If I did that, then maybe no one would miss her too much, and my ma would stop bawling like a goat when you take away its feed, and my pops would actually get up from his La-Z-Boy, and my own heart wouldn't be fully pulverized within my chest. But it didn't work out that way: no one even noticed that I was taking Rosie's place. It didn't matter that I dropped sour cream in my chili, even though I loathed the stuff and Rosie loved it, and no one batted an eye when I sang her favorite songs while washing the dishes or when I started going to bed hours earlier than my normal. But anyhow, that's not the point – what I'm trying to say is, maybe all that wishing for her spirit opened me up to Jim Dave's ghost. If only I knew how to shake him: his barn-sized bother is the way he keeps me from any real rest; all the other stuff is little, but I *need* to sleep.

And the other thing on my mind: this here conversation with Natalie.

We were in what she calls the breakfast nook but is mostly just a narrow, awkward space beside the balcony, and she had mimosas in a pitcher and some little cookies she called madeleines. She makes me feel so fancy with the way she puts ordinary things like orange juice into a cut-glass pitcher, and real cloth napkins on the table, and music without lyrics trickling in the background of everything. I've always sort of looked down on fancy people, but with Natalie right here in front of me, I don't want to make fun, not one bit – in fact, I am filled with the desire to join her.

So I poured myself a mimosa and whipped the cloth napkin over my lap and nibbled at a seashell cookie and fell into the life Natalie had given me.

After some chitchat, Natalie set down her glass and said, "Have I ever told you about Thu? My boyfriend?"

"No," I said, figuring this memory lapse along with her others was a result of how much she liked booze.

And she goes, "Well, he is my boyfriend, but we haven't technically met. Everything between us has been virtual. He's such a computer whiz; he knows how to speak that language of all zeros and ones. The point is, we'll finally be together for the first time, six weeks from now. He's going to fly out from California to see me!"

"Congrats," I said, trying hard to look happy for her. "How exciting."

"I really want to make a good impression with him," she said as she poured us a refill. "And have some alone time, private time, to get to know him better. He'll be staying here, of course."

My stomach gurgled; I looked at the floor. I knew where this was going.

"And so I wanted to check in with you about your house hunt," she said.

For a while I babbled on about how I've been looking around, I had a few leads, just needed to pull the trigger. Of course this was complete bullshit. I had started to get my hopes up that Natalie and I could live together forever, we'd take care of each other, we'd have fun together and live out our days. I allowed myself to say this: "I've been dillydallying, I guess, seeing as we get along like ducks and geese."

"Well, try to find somewhere close to here, so we can have each other over all the time," she said. "He doesn't come until November second. You know, All Souls' Day. I really do feel like I'm following God's will, having him come that day – it's a saint day, of course, and we just might be soul mates, me and him." You wouldn't believe it, but she really does sound all pious like that, with her voice gone higher: "I'll bring him to church on Sunday and we can find out what he's all about, deep down." Looks like the arrival of this man means I can no longer sit here and pat my foot.

I haven't recorded anything for a week or so, and I thought maybe I was growing out of the habit, but the impulse is still there whenever any interesting little tidbit happens to me. It's like a diary, but so much faster, and more intimate, because you can hear the inflection in my voice; you can hear what really happened. You can hear everyone else's voices through me – can't you? – I've always been able to do a fine impression, I must say.

Anyhoo, it is a confoundment, what people blast onto the internet these days. While searching to see if anything new had popped up about us in the Chautauqua County paper, I ran across this sort of internet radio show, this *podcast*, on mepodcast.net. If you ask me, it sounds like a fetish site for cannibals, but it turns out that really it is a website where any old dope can make a show; it's all boring entertainment for pod people, stuff like their great-aunt's tuna casserole recipe or this weird dog training method called "Do It" or, as it so happens, a botched true crime deep dive about *me*.

I apologize in advance for recording the hogwash of this amateur here, what I first listened to through headphones at the library, but I can't help but think it is relevant, and so's I should set it down. I dropped Natalie off at the mall and she'll be hours before she calls me for a ride home, which means I am free to play this so-called podcast through my phone and pick it up with my tape recorder, let's see how it works . . .

Welcome to the first episode of NEXT TO MY NECK OF THE WOODS: THE MISSING COUPLE. I firstly became interested in this case when I read a recently published article about the missing couple, and I decided to try my hand at some investigative journalism. This is a new direction for me, so thank you for being here and, of course, subscribe, subscribe, subscribe! Oh, and I should add a warning, because I know that many of you may be familiar with my first podcast, HERE IN THE HIGH CHAIR, since it got so popular after it made the Top Two Hundred list of parenting podcasts in North America. Thanks again, ladies. But this new venture is me in my civvies, out of my mommy coveralls, so if I were you, I would shoo the little ones out of the room, or better yet just use earbuds. Alright, let's jump into our subject.

I tried to figure if this voice was known to me – the author was listed as *BakinMama4C* – but I couldn't be certain if there really was a twangy familiarity to the vowels, or if it was just my imagination. What I don't understand is how my life became of interest in the first place. Only must be because Chautauqua County has as much mystery as a canceled postage stamp.

The old house where the Washies used to live sits behind a thick stand of oaks run through with vines so that its worn, white siding is barely visible from the road. Junk scatters the yard here and there and it's hard to imagine that the pipes and electricity would function, even if the utilities were turned on. If you don't know already, your host is visiting the site of a disappearance: Jim Dave Washie, fifty-seven, and Mary Ellen Washie, fifty-four, who once lived at this residence, have not been seen for over two and a half months.

The local police seem disinclined to turn this into a full-fledged investigation. Your host spoke with one young deputy who asked to not be named or recorded. "We figure they might've skipped town, on account of unpaid bills and all." That's my brother doing his best impression. *"Lots of people do it. And we can't be using all our resources to hunt down someone who left of their own free will, now can we?" When your host questioned this deputy over the fact that the Washies' possessions were still in the house, and if they had moved, they would have taken their things with them, the deputy said, "Truth is, besides the guns, wasn't much in there worth a can of beans. No one has even bothered to B&E. Probably it was too much work, the packing."*

It is possible that the Washies are now living in an apartment in Boonville, sipping margaritas, but your host feels that something more sinister might be afoot.

"To me they seemed mismatched from the start." That's the voice of Milt Barnce, who knew the Washies as newlyweds.

Milt was the alky tire dealer who'd been kicked out of the garage's apartment so's me and Jim Dave could move in; he must've held a grudge all these years.

He worked in the auto repair shop where they both had been employed, as well. "Always carrying on inside their apartment and showing themselves only during shift time. I wouldn't be surprised one bit if he offed her. Or they robbed a bank, something like that."

Your host believes that our boys in blue may be missing many important leads, though she does not want to go so far yet as to speculate about what we call a DB — a dead body. When your host questioned the Washies' daughter, she claimed that she had never been contacted by anyone about the case.

"They are quiet people," Sallie Blackburn, née Washie, sa —

Hold on, I've got to pause it right there. Even the second time hearing it makes my stomach shrink up inside me. But most likely there is no way my little girl has married that fool of a boyfriend she'd moved in with. She probably used his name just so's they wouldn't catch any flack for living in sin, or maybe to keep their little girl Mae from confusion. How complicated it was, the raising of children. Maybe I was better off childless, as Deedee. Here we go, I'll rewind it a touch.

— burn, née Washie, said. "But a sort of quiet where you knew things were simmering just under. I hope they're okay, wherever they are. I wish that they would let me know they're okay."

Your host would like to move back in time, before all this, to the blissful early days, when the young Washie family was just starting out, when Mary Ellen, like any normal mother, would never dream of abandoning her daughter. The couple fell in love when they met at a baseball game in the local park.

Our dear host must have picked up this intel from Sallie, as it was the story we always told her. The truth is that we met when a mutual friend broke into one of the Institute people's houses during winter and threw a rager; both me and Jim Dave had holed up in the pantry, where a group of us was passing a blunt and raiding the cookie tin. The hidey-hole grew so thick with weed smoke that I couldn't see Jim Dave's face even though it was mashed onto mine.

They soon had one daughter, Sallie, and spent their days caring for her while working at a local mechanic shop. They enjoyed family picnics by the lake and eating pizza. Looking at them, no one would ever think that a tragedy would befall the family unit, that a mystery would break them apart and leave their daughter, for all intents and purposes, an orphan. But life can do incredible things to a person; it can spin your head around like a roulette wheel and set it down backwards; or it can fill you with longing to do something similar to the heads of the people closest to you, your family.

And we'll delve into that on my next episode. Be sure to tune in, and don't forget to hit subscribe!

Well, I certainly don't know what to make of a thing like that. Thanks be I can see at the bottom that this trash has had only fourteen listens – two of those being from me and likely at least one other from our little host. Why anyone would wish to babble on about my dull life with Jim Dave is a mystery, but still there it is, for all the world to see and judge. Oh – there's also a picture of us on the website page, this black-and-white thing I don't know how came to light. My hair looks stringy and Jim Dave's neck looks like a chicken leg – not at all what we look like today. Or, what I look like. Jim Dave likely looks the way a pig carcass does after it's been roasted on a spit for hours and chunks of it cut off. It might seem disgusting to think of him that way, but really, it doesn't bother me a touch.

COMPANION TAPE TO SPANISH FOR TRAVEL

Natalie dragged me to her church as soon as I couldn't make any more excuses – there are only so many fake real estate matters you can schedule for a Sunday morning. The thing is, I'm a spiritual person, but I never have much taken to the church setup: some man droning on at the front of a cold room, telling us all how to obey our men and keep our pantyhose out of a bunch.

Natalie's church is just like that, the sort of place where all the women wear hats and pumps and keep a tight grip on the upper arms of their grandkids. Natalie had me borrow an outfit from her wardrobe, and I felt pretty fancy until we came up on the place and I saw everyone staring. They were all gathered outside on the wide stone steps, gawking at each other and making small talk. I recognized a couple of them from the bingo hits we'd made all over town. Natalie introduced me as Deedee of course to about a hundred people, and my brain began to thud, thinking about all these people who would carry my false name away with them, and all the people they might tell, and how my lie would be ferried out into the world like that. Before, I'd kept it small. Just Natalie and a handful of others knew me as Deedee, the cashier at the 7-Eleven, the librarian, a man I got to chatting with on the street, but now it was practically the entire town.

I settled myself down a little by huffing deep breaths, and then I was okay for the service, though I couldn't pay much attention to the sermon about the sovereignty of God, because as soon as the pastor started in on how God is going to barrel ahead no matter what we do, I began thinking about my recordings and how they are rather like my own private sermons, special little sermons to myself. I admit that

I get a bit full of it when I'm making them, just the way you can tell the pastor feels up there on stage, in front of us, his captive audience.

Maybe that's why I chose tapes over a diary. When I first had the impulse to record the facts, I thought a diary might be the way to go – I could always deny my handwriting, if it came down to it – but writing is slow and dull. Instead I push record and say what I wish to say, and you can hear the truth in my voice, you can *hear* it, when writing just seems like a frigid way to tell the story, little black marks on a white page, nothing, really. That's why everyone threw down their books to listen to the radio when it was invented.

After the service, I headed to the toilet while Natalie waited in line to thank the pastor. From the hallway, I heard two women in the bathroom talking, their voices echoing off the tiles.

"Did you see what Bingo Queen was wearing?" one asked, and I knew immediately that they were gossiping about Natalie.

The other one said, "If she tries to sell me one more stupid bingo card, I will rip the plaid culottes right off her."

Then their voices got quiet, and I pressed myself against the hallway wall, listening. They go:

"Did you hear what happened with Sheree?"

"Tell me."

"Well, she bought the box – "

"Not the *big* box?"

"The big one, and when she couldn't sell even half the cards – "

"Because her whole church and neighborhood and everyone she knows has already been saturated with this bingo business – "

"She asks Bingo Queen if she can return it, she could really use the money back to buy Christmas presents for the grandchildren, and Bingo Queen says no way. Would not even consider the poor woman's circumstances. She told Sheree to play all the leftover cards herself, because with that many cards, she'd have a great chance of winning the big pot."

"And?"

"Santa is not coming for those children."

The two women cackled together, and I hid myself in the alcove of the men's bathroom entrance while they left.

Once Natalie and I were finally back in her car, after we'd run the gauntlet of churchgoers on the front steps, who somehow all remembered to call me Deedee, Natalie goes, "Wasn't that fantastic? I have to post about it."

"Post?" I said as she untucked her cell phone from her bra.

"On Twitter – you know – social media. Wait. You don't have Twitter?"

I told her no, and she goes, "Honestly, it's no wonder you don't have a boyfriend! Here, look."

She showed me her phone, and its tiny screen said, *Can't wait for @PreachItDan to awe us all with his insight. Not to mention that deep baritone! #godsplan #unicornfolly*

"Huh," was all I could think to say.

"And then look here." She pointed to a side column where there were more words next to tiny round pictures. "These are the people who 'like' me. *You go girl!* and *Wish I could be in that pew next to you haha I rimed* and *blessed* and things like that. You see? And men can communicate with you through here, through social media."

"Huh," I said again, "I never thought of it that way." I hadn't confided to Natalie that I'd pretty much sworn off men, after what had happened. It seemed smarter to keep that line open with her, for the gossip possibilities and such, and to avoid any awkward questions. But of course I couldn't join up on social media, not with my fake name and the dyed hair and the possibility that someone might recognize me. Besides, the whole business seemed a bit silly. "You already have a boyfriend," I reminded her.

"That's right," she said, "but you don't. Here, look, one of the Kardashians, the sock one, followed me back. Probably because I come from fame, too – my mother, you know. Don't you ever wonder about the children of celebrities, about how hard their lives must be? I remember waiting on set with my mother for hours, for ages and ages, and there was nothing to do but nibble the free food. Did you know there's always a table of food at every set? Honestly, it's sort of a bad idea. I feel for those Kardashians. Their lives must be such a travesty . . . "

I'm telling you, that is exactly how she sounded, all snobby and wistful and sad, and without the slightest idea of how mean everyone could be, or how fake it all was. A *travesty*, she'd said, dramatic like that. I hope to never attend a service at that church again, but Natalie's hospitality is tied in with her being a churchgoing woman, and I need to make sure that I fit the bill of her generosity.

This morning, Natalie decided that I ought to drive her down to the casino.

"I'm feeling lucky," she said, whirling around the condo, filling up her purse with sunglasses, keys, lipsticks, tiny airplane bottles of booze. She pressed a finger to her pursed lips and then touched the picture of a handsome Jesus that hangs beside the fridge.

"Me too," I said, though I couldn't remember the last time, if ever, that I'd felt lucky for certain, and lately I feel plain hard up. The money I'd sneaked from the Flamingo Motel's register upon my departure had dwindled to a couple of twenties. My deadline for finding a place to live is now a mere three weeks, and of course I have no leads. Without money, it's impossible even to look, and I can't get a job without documents to prove my name. Maybe I could go back to being Mary Ellen Washie, and in this state so far away no one would notice; or maybe I could find an under-the-table kind of job, like phone sex. Basically I'm biding my time, hoping that Natalie will forget about my move-out date, or maybe her boyfriend's plane will crash on the way over here, or she'll suddenly find me invaluable for all the runs to the grocery and liquor store that I make with her car and her credit card.

On the road to the casino, Natalie played the radio loud, and she sang along, getting about a third of the lyrics wrong. "I come home in the morning right/My mama says, when you gonna bide your time right/Oh Mama hey, we're undeniable scums . . . " like that, she sang, and so forcefully I figured maybe she never could hear the words to know that they were wrong in the first place. This particular song had been my ex-friend Minnie's favorite, and so I knew it front to back.

Natalie's casino was one giant aggressively air-conditioned room full of machines that reminded me of schools of tropical fish: the red and green ones would flash in unison, and it was like they shot their commotion over to the blue machines, and then that would spread to the pink machines, all like an underwater theater us landlubbers had been dropped into the middle of. And I felt as out of place in the casino as a mouth breather under the ocean, seeing as I had nothing in terms of money. I hadn't been in a bona fide casino for at least fifteen years, not since the time I took Jim Dave and Sallie down to Delaware to meet my family, and all of us headed to the Dover Downs for the buffet, and then we milled around the machines, dropping in a quarter here, a dollar there. That was back when we both had jobs and the free apartment, and these small luxuries were just regular. If I remember right, Jim Dave won twenty bucks off the *I Dream of Jeannie* slot, which he spent straightaway on a NASCAR t-shirt and ball cap.

That had been a funny trip. Both my parents were alive, which they aren't now, and seeing as Sallie was their first grandkid, they didn't seem to care for her much. My ma smiled at her vaguely and my pops ruffled her hair, but they were real distant, maybe since they knew the visit was only for a few days, and we didn't have plans yet when we could come again. Maybe they didn't want to let her in because they didn't want to miss her, or because she had the same brown eyes as my dead little sister.

Back when I'd brought home my first husband Jeremy, my parents had stuck to him like a pig to cheese. He often had this effect on people, seeing as he sported a big chin and wide blue eyes and a thick crop of hair. Soon as I'd seen him at the Wawa where I always got my coffee, I sidled over and made sure we both reached for the same carton of cream.

He spoke to me first, and I swear what he said was, "You come here often?"

I told him every morning, and he said he did too, but he was running late this day on account of the hot water going out at his apartment. I was nineteen and still lived at home, and a handsome man with his own apartment seemed like a dreamboat sort of catch. The men I had dated so far were a bar bouncer with huge arms and a huge mouth to match, a man who served fried shrimp down on the boardwalk at Lewes, and one from my high school who drove chickens to the slaughter. All of them lived with their parents, like me.

"You smoke?" he asked me. "I'm trying to quit."

I stood outside with him near the ashtray and we shared a single cigarette, his concession for quitting. I imagined it was like we were kissing, our mouths touching the same place, and now looking back I bet I was making some awful funny faces, pursing my lips around that Camel.

Straightaway after our first date I ran home and told my sister Rosie that I had a new boyfriend, but she was in one of her depressed moods, and then when she and Jeremy finally met, a funny thing happened: they realized that they knew each other.

Such a coincidence would be harder to come by these days, what with everyone taking pictures of every single thing and then presenting all those pictures to everyone they know on social media, but back then, it was possible to realize only at the point of meeting your sister's new fiancé that you had dated him before, albeit briefly, three years prior.

When she'd been fifteen.

And he'd been twenty-three.

And I'd been a naïve almost-seventeen, blissfully unaware of any of it.

After Jeremy had left that night, Rosie pulled me into our room. She said, "I think he's a rollercoaster sort of person; he's good at taking advantage; you think you know him well enough to get married?"

Of course this really choked my goat. Here was the first big decision I'd ever made in my life, and my little sister wanted to ruin it, just the way she did with everything good. Her high-swinging moods had always left a distance between us.

Jeremy and I got married seventeen weeks later, and my parents seemed prouder than when I got my first job, prouder than when I graduated high school. They treated Jeremy like a shiny treasure they could show off out in public, a fact that their family was worth something. He worked in a big bank and drove a shiny car and actually used his fancy gym membership. Leading up to the wedding, my ma burned sage. She dusted the baseboards daily. She made up little rituals, like cleaning out my hairbrush and saving the strands in a mahogany box. Maybe she was so intent on making sure the wedding went well because she was finally getting rid of me, and since my sister Rosie had moved out just a few weeks before, the moment she had turned eighteen, my parents would have the house to themselves. I see now that it was actually very stressful for my ma to live with me and my sister. She was constantly worrying over us, constantly structuring her life around little habits meant to protect us. It was a very hard time for me, what with the wedding, and my sister suddenly pulling out of my life, moving away for what she said was a new job.

Turns out, Jeremy and I divorced thirteen weeks after the I do's.

I might have gotten us annulled, is what I ought to have done, but I didn't even know that word back then. My goodness, I was a baby. It's incredible to think.

Luckily, the new me is an only child and never has to worry about her little sister carrying on an affair with her husband, because that would be a devastating revelation, let me tell you, even though it had happened so long ago, it would still be painful to carry in the back of the mind, nonetheless. But I am a new woman – Deedee, Deedee, Deedee – and it hadn't happened to me.

Back to my life now. Today was an interesting day. At the casino, Natalie and I had settled ourselves down in front of a couple of slots to warm up, but already it was an hour in and we hadn't moved. Very, very slowly I had dropped five dollars into my machine, and now I was down to just twenty cents. Natalie kept pouring the little vials of booze from her purse into the sodas that we got for free, and she was up, her machine beating out the high-pitched, happy sounds of a win, while all mine made were the baritone disappointments of loss. *Beep-boo*, my machine went, and then my funds were out.

"Come on," Natalie said, "put in some more. Keep me company."

But I didn't have anything left.

It's terrible to feel old and broke and unwanted, the way I felt then, and I started to wonder if this was how Jim Dave felt, there near the end, with no job and his little girl lost to another man and a wife who wished him dead. He seemed so content to sit there every morning, noon, and night like a tick on a hog, but inside he must've been ruined, and he'd told me himself that he wanted to die.

Anyhoo, I turned to Natalie and said I didn't much care for this sort of gambling, rather than admit that I was broke. I've figured out by now that people don't like to give you anything if they think you have nothing in the first place, because then they see that you're not worth anything, that you are a yawning pit of need, and there will be no return on their investment. But if you let them take you in, feed you, sponsor your spa day, all while pretending that you're looking to buy a place of your own, that you need help because you're new to town, they don't question their own generosity as much. They compute that the two of you are equals, and the give-take will even out in the end. I knew that Natalie expected we would be forever friends. I had the feeling that she'd scared off her previous friends, maybe through some silly drunk thing that she'd done, because she'd never introduced me to anyone except at church, never had anyone over. Maybe, if she was lonely for a friend, I was in a better position than I thought. Maybe she would change her mind and let me stay. It didn't seem right that I would figure below a man in her life, a man she'd only talked to through the computer.

Natalie loved gambling. She yanked down the handle of her slot machine with the vigor of a milkmaid milking. The light on its top twirled in delight, and coins jangled into the metal trough. She told me that in Vegas, they've stopped using real coins – everything is electronic now. They give you a little card, sort of like a credit card, and you add money to it, and you swipe the card at whatever machine you're playing. "They actually have a soundtrack like this," she said and scooped up a handful of coins, then let them fall – "that they play when you win, but it's not *real*. Still, they know people are addicted to the sound, so they pipe it in."

"Do you like Las Vegas?" I asked her. I've never been, though I want to see it; all the flashing lights and circus shows and people having fun appeals to me. I imagine it as one huge block party where children aren't allowed and that the police never shut down.

"I go there sometimes," she said. "I used to have this boyfriend who lived there, this was when I was in California, and he was the one who taught me how to gamble. He used to tell me that I should become a stripper there, that I'd make more money than I did at my office job and it'd be more fun, too. God, that used to make me so mad."

"I'm sure it was a compliment," I told her. "He knew that you're beautiful and that people would pay good money to admire you. I think it's sweet, him saying a thing like that."

"You didn't know this man," she said.

"That's right. Maybe he was a snake. I mean, men are snakes, generally." This was a refrain of ours, one we'd use right after judging a gaggle of men on their looks. "So why would this one be a mite different."

Natalie laughed into her hand, and then she told me to watch her machine while she headed to the bathroom. As soon as she was out of sight, I reached into her trough, pulled out a handful of coins, and fed them into my machine. I lost at every pull.

When she came back, she was ready to move on to poker. "Do you want to play?" she asked me. "Or should you watch?"

"Watch," I said.

"Well, since you'll be an observer . . . " She looked around and then – I could barely believe it – she explained about her plan for secret signals. She said that I would set up at a slot kind of adjacent to the poker table, and act like I was playing, but really I would be watching the cards of whoever Natalie was playing against. And if the cards were really good, a straight or a flush, or two pair, I would chunk down the slot machine handle real hard. And if the cards were okay, a pair or something, I would take a sip of my soda pop. And if they were nothing much, I would play my machine quietly, pushing buttons. Then, when Natalie was done, she'd leave the table, and I would wait at least five minutes before I'd come out after her, and we'd meet at the car.

This turn of events was like the time I realized chickens could still run after you'd cut off their heads. They became a whole different animal, sort of threatening and scary and fascinating. That was how Natalie looked to me now: a whole different animal. She scooped her winnings into a plastic cup, which she handed over to me.

"Do you really want to win that bad?" I asked her, and she said that no, she didn't.

She goes, "It's not about the winning: it's about adding another element. A layer of gambling on top of the gambling. That's what really gets you to the exhilpation."

My heart was buzzing so fast that I'd become exhausted by the time I sat down at a slot machine near to the poker tables. Natalie waited a bit on the outskirts of the game before she joined, and then she settled in among three men, one with a cowboy hat, one with thick-framed glasses, and one with huge earrings stretching his lobes. I only had an angle on Glasses and Earrings; Cowboy Hat was lost to me, but I figured two out of three was pretty good. I dropped a coin from Natalie's cup into the slot. My sweaty fingers left marks on the buttons. At first, following our secret signals left me as awkward as a cat at the beach, but pretty soon I got used to the routine, glancing about, not just at their table, but every which way, as if I were a fidgety sort of person. I did a couple of ker-klunks with the lever on my slot, had a few sips of my drink, but mostly I lazily dropped coins into the slot and tried to stop feeling flustered.

Whoops, my little tape is about to run –

TEN METHODS TO REMOVE MOLD

So anyhoo, I figured that Natalie was probably up, seeing as she kept yipping and wriggling down into her chair, and finally I was starting to get up, too. The little numbers on my screen kept blipping higher, and coins danced into my trough, so many I knew they wouldn't all fit back in my cup, and a nice warm wholesome feeling started to come over me as I played.

After maybe an hour, Natalie pushed back her chair and stood. She scooped up her chips and strutted over to the cashier while another man eagerly grabbed her lucky seat. People were like that in casinos, bestowing fortune on swatches of carpet or certain machines or leather still warmed by somebody else's butt.

Once Natalie had left, I filled her plastic cup with coins and scooped the excess into my purse, and then I headed to the cashier's desk. I figured that Natalie would never notice if I kept some of the cash that I'd earned fair and square on my machine; in fact, she probably hadn't even seen that I was winning. I dumped all of the coins in my purse and then about half of what was in the cup into the divot for the cashier to turn into bills, and when they handed me back a fifty, a five, and two ones, I felt really good about myself: I'd turned nothing into something. I rolled up the bills and tucked them deep inside my bag.

When I stepped out of the climate-controlled casino, the humid air rolled over me and immediately dampened my armpits. All of a sudden, I had this premonition that Natalie had left me. She'd figured out that I wasn't worth a cent, and she'd driven away – that was why she always tucked the keys into her purse after I parked us somewhere, so that she could leave me if she wanted – and I would never see her again. The air smelled like rain, which in Florida meant old gas fumes rising from the asphalt. In Chautauqua County, rain smelled like sweetly rotting cut grass and musty bark. As I walked to the car, I could see Natalie sitting in the passenger's seat, and I expanded with joy. She hadn't left me; she didn't know I was broke and a terrible wife and indifferent mother, she just thought I was her friend, a pretty good friend. I was near enough to touch the trunk when I felt a hand on my wrist. It's all so close in the front of my mind, I'm going to record it here, dramatic-like, just how it happened.

"I knew it," said Cowboy Hat.

Some of the coins in my cup spilled across the ground as I yanked my wrist from his grip, and the crash of the coins or maybe a sixth sense drew Natalie from the car.

"I knew the two of you were up to something," Cowboy Hat said. "You're so stupid, you look just alike. Anyone can tell you're sisters running a racket."

"What are you doing?" Natalie said, hanging onto the open car door.

"I *saw* you two," he said.

"Honestly, you don't know anything." Natalie came around to the back of the car and stood right next to me. The car beep-beep-beeped because she'd left her door open. "We didn't do anything wrong."

"Like hell you didn't." He crossed his arms over his broad chest. "You come with me. Back into the casino. And we have them review the security tapes and confirm what I know you did. Or, you refund me what I lost on that game, right here and now, and nobody else has to hear about it."

"Stop molesting us," Natalie said.

I was gobsmacked at her talking back that way to an angry man –

I'd always learned to let it alone, to shut up and give in and plot revenge in silence.

Cowboy Hat goes, "Two hundred and seventy-five bucks. But let's round it to an even three, to make up for the time I've spent dealing with you two. For my time and suffering. Come on – let's get this transaction over with pronto."

I started to turn away, but he grabbed my wrist again. His fingers were strong and sweaty and horrible, and for a startling moment, I succumbed to the sensation that his fist was as big as my body, or my body was as small as his thumb, and his fingers were pressing against every part of me, strangling.

Natalie caught my eye, which yanked my mind out of the massive fist and back into my unpleasant reality, and then I ratcheted up my foot and kicked the man in his junk. The thick seam of his Wranglers imprinted itself over top of my shin. He doubled over, releasing me, as Natalie hurried behind the wheel; I flung myself into the passenger seat. Luckily, there was no car in the parking spot directly in front of us, so we pulled through and were on our way. I wonder now if Natalie would have backed up over him if that had been our only escape.

"Oh my God!" we were both saying, passing the phrase back and forth. Natalie drummed against the wheel. "I can't believe he *did* that" and "I couldn't even see his cards! He was at a bad angle" and "What a handsome brute!" and "*Pronto*! What kind of TV word is that?" were some of the things we shouted into the wind rushing at us from the open car windows. As we drove straight towards the setting sun, I think we did start to feel like sisters, or at least I started to feel like she was one to me.

"We fixed him," I said, and then I told her I was sorry. "I lost all your coins. Dropped them in the fight. He felt so *squishy* before I hit the bone of his pelvis."

"You were amazing," she said. "I haven't been in a situation like that in *years*. That was true exhilpation. You really saved us. And guess what? I cleared almost five hundred bucks. We're heading straight to a fancy dinner. Oh shit." She pulled to the side of the road, and for a panicked second, I thought the cops had found us. But she only said, "You drive," and we switched seats.

I rolled up the windows and turned on the air conditioning, and I felt so good from the day that I didn't even try to brush away the rush of goose bumps up my arm, I just let them come on.

I am trying not to panic. They've found the body, Jim Dave's body, and so of course panic is trickling up and down my arms like a winter stream, steady and freezing, but I'm trying to banish it by talking plain here to say what I know, and that is mostly what I've found out from an article in the Chautauqua County *Courier*. It's called *AREA BODY IDENTIFIED*, which is one strange title, if you ask me, seeing as it is so matter-of-fact when such a thing is never stated in our county and therefore might be followed by an exclamation point at least.

I'll read it here: *On Tuesday morning, Chautauqua County police made a heartbreaking discovery regarding the disappearance of Jim Dave Washie, fifty-seven, and Mary Ellen Washie, fifty-four.*

After two hours of dredging a local farm pond, a crew discovered human remains, which the coroner would later confirm were those of Jim Dave Washie.

"Sometimes Jim Dave would go down to the cow pond," said Franklin Dodds, a neighbor, "and sure enough, they found him down there. When I heard all the sirens and the flashing lights were rushing by our living room window, I said to myself, I bet it's something to do with Jim Dave."

I'd never liked Frankie Dodds, if I do say so myself. He hung up the stupidest signs all over his bar, stuff like, "I love the sound you make when you shut up" and "You can do it with beer goggles." In my opinion, he was always overserving Jim Dave – one time Jim

Dave came back from that roadhouse more flagged than a vet on Memorial Day, and he'd dropped himself into a muck pond on his way home, then came inside like nothing at all had happened. Stunk up our couch for weeks. Anyhoo, I'll keep reading . . .

"We thought to try the pond," said Chautauqua County police chief Newman "Nuddie" Brown, "because the Washies lived so near to it and were sometimes spotted there, or at least the husband was, at times."

The remains were deposited at the county coroner, which has yet to release a full report on the cause of death.

"We can't rule out foul play," said an anonymous officer, "seeing as he'd been weighted down by cinder blocks, though parts have been unraveling from him like old onion skin so I'm not sure what all they can figure."

The county's investigation is ongoing, said police chief Brown. "We're hoping we don't find another corpse — I mean, anybody else — in that black water, but no one yet knows the whereabouts of [Mary Ellen Washie]. In a case like this, all you can do is pray for the best."

The police are requesting that anyone with information about the case contact – well, those were all the important parts.

Sometimes I think my body is out to kill me. My breath is short because my lungs seem crumpled up and my heart might shimmy itself apart and my stomach is so sour if I drank milk it would curdle right into cottage cheese. If I don't get ahold of myself soon, I might have to jump in my car and hightail it to Mexico, never look back. I could take Natalie's driver's license, I just bet I could.

Natalie is expecting me to help her with something in the kitchen in just a few minutes. I need to get it together – I'm Deedee, Deedee, Deedee – as the fun and carefree, freeloading roomie I wish that I could always be.

Well, maybe it's for the best that Natalie's internet boyfriend is coming to replace me. I feel like we're those two ladies barreling towards the Grand Canyon in their convertible, like if we stick together, something wild will happen. When I went to help her in the kitchen, she blindsided me with the announcement that the next day, that is, today, we were having over all the church ladies for an hors d'oeuvre get-together, and I needed to run to the store for the supplies and then be her sous-chef. All these foreign words for what was basically weenies on toothpicks. Even before this announcement, I was feeling like crap, what with Jim Dave's body looming over me and my impending homelessness. But thinking about spending a day with all the church ladies, their coordinated outfits, their little pinkies in the air, asking me where I planned to live and what I did and if I had kids and where was I from and God knows what else, boxed me into a dark mood.

Natalie directed me on what to chop and how fine to chop it while she sipped wine. She'd moved on to harder stuff by the time I was piling baking sheets into the oven, and I knew she was getting blotto when she unfolded her little step stool and took a pack of cigarettes down from the cupboard over the fridge. She cracked the window so that she could blow smoke outside and kept chattering about the church ladies and how the big bingo game was coming up in a couple of weeks, and so she wanted to make one last push to see who might want to get involved, and of course she'd save a spot for me, if I settled my other matters and decided to invest, or I could even simply buy just a few cards direct from her. All the while I imagined dripping oleander concentrate into their strawberry shortcake. Not enough to kill anyone, of course, just enough to make them sick. Or maybe I could smash the bottle of vodka that Natalie had already finished and sprinkle the ground-up glass bits into the couscous salad. I was entertaining myself with these sorts of thoughts when Natalie said, "Oh dear, I feel a little tired. Will you finish up here? I'll take myself off and lie down." This was her code for getting the spins, which meant her picture of the evening would be like a kid's watercolor, all nuance blurring together.

Alone in the kitchen, I stewed – and not weenies in barbecue sauce, the way Natalie had wanted. Here I was her chauffeur, her caterer, her sidekick, apparently the only person left for her to boss around after she'd scared off the others with drunk texts or pricey bingo cards, and yet she had not lifted a fingernail to help me prepare this charade of a party, even though the whole hog was her idea.

All this, for a get-together I dreaded. It is terrible to find yourself indebted to another person over the need for shelter. I have always found unbearable that burden of pleasing the person who *has*, so that I can have, too.

But then an idea occurred to me: if there were no hors d'oeuvres for tomorrow, there would be no event. It was as simple as saving a seed. And so's I began to dismantle all the work I had done, popping strawberries into my mouth and dumping cheese puffs into the trash, and of course pouring the bottles of wine and champagne down the drain, and then hauling the mess out to the communal trash cans that sat perpetually at the corner. When the plastic lid of the bin closed over what would have been our party, I felt relief. My dark mood, the one that could rile me into doing just about anything, floated off like a spiderweb on a breeze.

This morning, Natalie awoke bleary-eyed, with breath like a Doritos-loving dragon. She joined me in the kitchen.

"Where's all the hors d'oeuvres?" was the first thing she said to me, no hi hello nothing.

I gathered my breath for this crucial bit of my plan. "You ate the bunch last night," I said. "You made a real wreck of things, and after all the hard work I put into cooking."

She pressed a hand to her stomach. "I *ate* them?" she said.

"Well, not all of them. But enough. And the rest, none of them looked right; they were all picked over and gross." I knew how to say these things with conviction from all my time around Jim Dave. My only hope was that, unlike him, Natalie would feel a smidge of guilt for what she'd done.

She poked her head into the fridge. "Where're all the bottles? For mimosas? And wine spritzers?"

"Those were the first to go," I said.

She sat at the bartop and rubbed her temples as if my words had given her an instant hangover headache.

"Why didn't you try to stop me?" she asked, and I told her that I had, but she'd resisted, and it was her house – I didn't feel right forcing her into anything.

"This is awful," she said. "I haven't had a flare-up like this in ages. I wonder why now . . . what pressure . . . I don't have the slightest recollection . . . ."

"Don't you think we had better tell everyone not to come?" I said.

She groaned. "I'm so sorry," she said. "I thought that this would be a great new way for you to make friends. A little bingo business, a little pleasure. You'd get to know the ladies in a more . . . casual setting . . . "

I told her not to worry about it, that I didn't really care for these types of gatherings anyhow. When I said that, she looked at me funny for a moment, but I made my face as bland and blank as possible, and she took herself back to bed to make her calls and post her change of plans – she'd tell them she was sick.

Which is why I answered the door when there was a furious rapping on it an hour later. As soon as I cracked it, figuring that one of the church ladies had failed to get the memo, the red-faced woman on the other side began shaking an empty wine bottle and saying that she'd found it in the trash. "This is *recycling* material," she said, "recycling!"

I go, "Huh."

"But it's not fit for recycling since it obviously has not been rinsed. And your food waste was not properly bagged; it attracted some kind of animal! What a mess." As she went on about the rules of recycling, I realized that she must have mistook me for Natalie. She would have never spoken to a guest in such a haughty, superior way, but a neighbor, an absentee member of the HOA, sure. I stood a bit taller and pushed back my shoulders; I stepped closer to her, just to see what she would do, and she took a step back to accommodate me.

I said, "I will keep this information in mind," in the smooth, confident words of Natalie. They felt good in my throat, powerful.

"We all have to do our part," the woman said, "to keep our community the sort of place we want to live." She reached up and touched a wind chime, which tinkled against her palm.

Putting all my Natalie into it, I nodded sagely, already feeling a bit more proprietary about the place. When I shut the door, I was smiling; what a treat it had been, to leave myself and all the problems that came along with me behind for a few moments.

I find it amazing what a person is able to put into someone else's mind: ever since the hors d'oeuvre incident, Natalie has acted a bit sheepish, and she moves around me gingerly, almost as if she were the guest and I were the owner of the house. She closes doors quietly, sometimes eats out of sight in her room, and smiles at me whenever we pass in the hallway. We haven't spoken directly about my move-out, which she has scheduled in just a few days, but she's invited me to a special supper tonight. I'm feeling strange; I've been worrying over Jim Dave's body stretched out there in a morgue somewhere, and what secrets about me it might reveal, not to mention the more immediate misery that will overtake me if I have to go back to living in some pit stain like the Flamingo Motel. I don't know if I can hold it together. But Natalie is cooking me something fancy, one last special supper before I'm kicked to the curb by her internet boyfriend, so I need to pretend happiness. Oh, sure, I'll tell her, I've just put my down payment on a condo across town. Three bedrooms, just like this one, for little old me. My life is a joke; I can't believe it. Who would have ever thought I'd be an outlaw, don't know where I'm going to rest my head.

It has taken me some days to get to the point where I could talk about this. I think three – three days. It all started at supper, which Natalie was so proud over cooking: first she brought out what she called a Caprese salad, basically big slabs of cheese and tomatoes, which looked quite patriotic stacked there on the plate. Of course it came with wine, something Natalie called light and crisp with a refreshing apple bite, but to me it pretty much tasted like diet Mountain Dew without the bubbles. I figure it was this wine that loosened her up after all that tiptoeing around.

"To us," Natalie toasted. "Oh, my. We've had some times. Do you remember when you kicked that cowboy right in his package?" She talked like this had happened ages ago, when really it'd been just last week. "After that, I went out and bought a stun gun. It's this machine, this strange black machine that fits in your hand, and it sends an electrified wave through whoever you point it at. For example, an attacker." Natalie laughed, and I fake laughed along with her. "If I'd had it during our little tiff with that cowboy, we wouldn't have needed to get close. This thing is industrial strength."

"Wow," I said finally, thinking she might have been chattering on and on because she was waiting for me to reply.

She goes, "That was so fun. Those were such crazy times. I'm going to look back on these days when we lived together as some of the happiest in my life."

I wanted to tell her that we ought to keep up with the arrangement, then, but that would make me sound whiny, and I've learned from experience that whining never gets you what you want. I used to try it with Jim Dave, sometimes, moaning about how if he didn't get off his ass and get him a job, I'd quit working too, and then just see how fast we'd run out of beer money. Well all that got me was a beer can chucked at my head. So's I said all nice and sweet to Natalie, "That's right, I won't forget these weeks not so long as I live, and no doubt we'll keep in touch and they're more good times to come."

She liked that, I could tell. She wiggled a little in her seat and poured us both refills of the Mountain Dew wine. But I had been feeling melancholy and still shook up from the thought of Jim Dave's body being fished from the depths. Probably his eyeballs were nibbled by carp and half his skin had sloughed off and his mouth was like a gaping hole down into hell, and I just knew that when I closed my eyes that night, his ghost would vex me, and this time its nose would be hanging by a strip of flesh or it would have frog eggs spilling off its tongue or some such awfulness. But one good thing is, I haven't slept since that supper, so his ghost hasn't got the chance yet.

When Natalie brought out the main course, chicken parm, she got down to the nitty-gritty. "Well," she said, "tell me about the new place. You find a nice condo or a townhouse, or maybe you're going farther out, to a stand-alone with a yard? Though I've always wondered what people want with yards."

I stared down, hard, at my plate, the chicken covered in red sauce beating like a heart as it shimmered in the tears dripping from my eyes. I was too weak; even though I'd practiced what I'd say to her, I'd failed myself.

"Oh my God," Natalie said, "oh no, what's wrong? You don't have a place yet, is that it?"

"I'll be fine," I said. "I'm completely fine. It's hard out there." I wasn't looking at her, but I could hear the click-click of her nails against her glass, a sound with a strange frequency that fell crookedly inside my ears.

"No one will give you a loan," Natalie said. "I understand. I think I know about you."

Fear chilled me further as a cold drop of sweat slid its way down my spine. I felt like a puddle. "What do you mean?" I said down into my plate.

She goes, "I have an inkling of what you might have done. I felt it right when I first met you, that us two were kindred spirits. I did something awful, too, a long time ago, and after it happened, I ran away to Florida, just like you."

"You did?" I said. "What did you do?"

She asked if I remembered that she'd had a boyfriend in Las Vegas. I nodded, still not looking at her.

She said, "Well, I derailed his life, just like that, without really thinking about what I was doing. I mean, I was angry at him, livid, and so I acted out of impulse."

"What did he do to you?" I asked, and she told me the story. She'd been positive that he had been living with this stripper, called herself Fanny Bleu, but later what she heard from friends and other people was that he actually really did love her, Natalie, and he'd put Fanny out after only a couple of days, she grated on his nerves so badly, and that short time with the stripper had convinced him that Natalie was the love of his life and they should move together to a farm in Vermont.

Oh no, wait, my tape is –

IMPORTANCE OF EXACT MEASUREMENTS IN BAKING

Starting now I'll pay more attention to the tape recorder; I hate it when I reach the end of a spool without noticing. I had to change the tape right in the middle of setting the scene for such a momentous night in my life. But I'll get back into it, here, we were talking at the supper table . . .

What I did then was I asked Natalie, "But he *was* with her? With Fanny?"

"Just for a blip," Natalie said, "one of those little blips in relationships that ultimately show you who the other person is to you, and you realize how completely you should be together, and you give up all the silly things you thought you wanted in order to make that happen."

Whatever she was talking about sounded like some fairy-tale fantasy to me, but I nodded because I knew that would encourage her to go on, which she did: "Before I talked to his friends, though, and figured this out, I let my anger get the best of me. I could not stand the thought of him and Fanny; it made me sick deep inside, as if he'd violated me, and I was pregnant at the time, too, early-pregnant, the hormones, honestly."

I looked up sharply.

"But there's lots of ways to get rid of a baby," she said. "Only, right then, I was entirely focused on getting rid of him, so what I did was I tipped off the police that he would have drugs in his pocket when we went to a particular club that night." She had this gleam in her eyes, as if what she'd done gave her a thrill even still. "I watched him being hauled away. They'd been wanting him for some time; the casinos hated him, because he was running cards and other things, and this was the perfect excuse. He went into the bathroom in the Stardust, and then they went into the bathroom, and then pretty soon they all came out of the bathroom, only he was cuffed and stumbling and a little corner of his shirt was poking out of his fly."

I asked her if she felt bad, and she said, "Not in the moment. I was young and didn't understand the magnitude of what I'd done. In the moment I felt powerful, like I could make anything in the whole world happen. Right then and there, as soon as they disappeared from sight, I sat down at a slot because I was feeling lucky. I won, too, I remember."

I understood: her inner witchiness had been unleashed, that realization that you were powerful, even when no one else figured you so. Ever since what happened that night, I've been feeling that way more and more: I can change the universe, I truly can.

I wanted to know how long he was in for.

She goes, "They were crazy about drugs back then, with the first lady and everyone acting as if drugs would be the downfall of society. He got eight years – eight! Only, three years in, he was shanked. He bled to death in a corner of the rec yard. When he first went in, he tried to blame me for things, and he claimed that I was in on running the cards, that I got a cut of his profits, but of course there was no evidence. After he'd gotten over his angry phase and recanted what he'd said about me, I started visiting him now and then, and we sometimes talked about when he would get out, and how we'd go ahead and move to that farm in Vermont. Some days, if the weather was just right and the awful smells weren't wafting in from the cafeteria, I could look out the window in the visiting room and believe it."

"But it wasn't your fault," I said, "that he died in jail."

Only, she disagreed on account of it being her fault he was *in* jail. "It's my biggest regret," she said, "but I've never told that to anyone."

Natalie was trying to put us on equal footing, here, so that I would feel compelled to spill my guts to her, but she didn't understand how impossible that was because she didn't know the vast and entirely unfair difference in our circumstances.

I bit into my chicken. As I chewed, I wondered if a heart would taste like this, sort of sad and raw, and the food caught in my throat.

"What I think," Natalie said, "is that you've come here because you're running from the same sort of thing. The same sentiment. I have this whole theory worked out, a special theory about you."

I was truly interested to hear what depths she had given me.

She wiggled around in her seat, excited to tell me, to hear her own voice expand into a story. "I think that you were one of those human traffickers. I saw a documentary about them once. You lived up there near the border with Canada, didn't you?" I'd told her that I'd come from Cleveland. "And I think that you must have been the lady waiting on the other side, the other side of that huge lake, and they would smuggle the women in from Canada on boats. They needed somebody to meet them and take them to their drop houses and give them food and clothes and things like that. I bet it was lucrative for you. But then you felt bad for one of the girls. She reminded you of the daughter you never had. And so you decided to help her out, get her away from there so that she could have whatever future she wanted. Only of course they found you out, the people in charge, and they stripped you of all your money and threatened your life, so you had to come down here, fast." She sat back, looking satisfied, and sipped at her wine. "Am I right? Or anywhere close? The gambler with the cowboy hat reminded you of one of the smugglers you used to work with, and that's why you kicked him in between the legs, almost without thinking: because you wanted revenge on someone like that. Even if you'd had a stun gun, you wanted contact."

"Wow," I said, "who knew you had such an imagination?"

She wanted to know, though, if she was at least a little bit right.

She goes, "You don't have some boring backstory, I can tell. You're an *interesting* woman, I just know it. When you moved in, half the boxes you brought were empty."

"You went through my stuff?" I asked her.

She goes, "Because you hardly say a word about your past; I had to see who I was getting."

And here I'd thought of her as incurious.

She said, "It made me think: what kind of woman would move with empty boxes?" Natalie's face was friendly, open, like usual. Thanks be she hadn't stumbled upon you tapes, or if she had, your dull labels did their job.

I said, "I guess I might have . . . done something bad. But it was a long time ago."

Natalie poured the last of the wine into our cups, which meant she was happily anticipating a good story. In our time living together, I'd started to recognize her habits and moods. And I wanted to give her something: all of a sudden, I felt like she would understand my plight; after all, she felt responsible for the death of the man she'd put in jail. If I told her, then ghost Jim Dave would disappear from my dreams, and reading the newspaper articles wouldn't make me feel like baby snakes were crawling up my throat, and she would take pity on me and let me stay even during her internet boyfriend's visit, or she'd at least let me come back after he'd left. Thanks to our secrets, we'd be fettered together for life.

Maybe I just needed to talk to a person instead of a recording machine.

And so I said: "I was married, once." Natalie gasped and then nodded, like she was shocked and yet knew it all along. "He was a terrible husband. The kind that made you his slave, pretty much. He wouldn't work, wouldn't lift a finger to do a single thing around the house. So I had a couple jobs, gave him all the money, he used it on beer."

"Did he . . . do things to you?" Natalie set down her glass, which meant she was especially concerned. "What did he do?"

I said, "I mean, he wasn't the worst of the worst. He would just . . . when he was drinking, you know . . . he would yank my hair, maybe. Or trip me on purpose. Spill beer on me and tell me I looked like corn smut."

"Oh my God," Natalie said, hand to her mouth.

I wondered if maybe it was possible to translate what I'd done into a language Natalie could understand. She'd never had a husband; she didn't know how an existence alongside someone else could mangle your life. I tried to explain to her how I'd got to a breaking point: "I thought I would go crazy if I had to spend another day with him. And he threatened me, saying he wanted to kill me, and I really thought that he might do it. Sometimes he would point his gun at me. He'd get so angry that his hand would shake, his finger would shake against the trigger, and I'd feel all flat through the middle, like roadkill."

She was shocked at this, so's I knew my white lies were working, that they were clearing my path to the one big truth.

"I gave him chances, too. You have to understand: if he had done just a single thing right, I would have left him alone."

"But what did you do?" Natalie asked.

It felt like the quick pace of my heart was shaking all my other organs. "Well, I took his gun away, and then I shot him with it." I waited patiently for peace, the way they told you to in church and at school and in the movies; for some dumb reason, I figured that now I had come clean, everything would get better.

Deep wrinkles appeared on Natalie's face in places I'd never seen them before – high up on her forehead, just before the hairline, and to either side of her nostrils.

"Sort of . . . in the foot?" she asked. "In self-defense?"

"No," I said. Inside I was jellied, as if the tension I'd been carrying around had melted and jiggled me up. "He's dead."

Abruptly she shoved her chair back from the table and stood. She pulled another bottle of wine from the case – I heard it clinking – and then took a long time with the uncorking.

"But you have to understand," I called to her over in the kitchen, "he wanted me to do it. He *asked* me to, practically."

When she finally came back, holding the bottle, she didn't sit again, but stood at one end of the table, looking down at me. She said, "Euthanasia? Was he sick? Cancer?"

I explained how he didn't like living anymore. "He wanted to kill himself, but he couldn't do it; he practically begged me to do it for him. For a long time, I resisted, but then it was all too much. There are so many ways to stop living before you're even dead."

"And you came here right after you finished your time in jail?"

"No one knows," I told her, sealing our bond. "Just like the secret you told me. Nobody in the whole world knows except you. And him, I guess."

She dropped back in her chair and poured the fresh wine into her glass, but she didn't offer me any. I didn't want it, anyhow; my head was already pounding.

"Thou shalt not kill," she said quietly. She tumbled the red wine in her glass; it sloshed to the lip, and then back. To the lip, and back. "You know that, don't you? A sacred rule has been broken. If you've taken . . . a *life*. And a life that you were supposed to cherish. Under God. Were you married in a church? Oh, it doesn't matter now, I guess, since you obviously are not God-fearing in the first place."

My headache began to dissolve into a fear that spilled steadily down my vertebrae; my extremities tingled and numbed, tingled and numbed.

"You have to turn yourself in," Natalie said. "Tomorrow. I'll go with you. I know you don't want to get in trouble; I know. It will be hard. But this is what you've been running from for all these years –

how long ago did this happen? – and you won't be at peace until you face the consequences of what you did. In fact, you might be damned forever. I could tell as soon as we stepped into church together that you were disquieted. And your luck – you don't have any; you never win. You must do the right thing to get yourself back, don't you see? Now it's all starting to make sense to me. You can't get a job or a condo. You needed someone like me, and God sent you to me. He wanted me to help you. We'll go tomorrow. You can make a confession, just like you did here. Everything will be alright." She spoke quickly and kept nodding her head.

"But he wanted me to; you were right before – it was like self-defense," I said, trying to reason with her, to explain why a crime you go to prison for was as far from what I'd done as a seed is from a tomato. "It was so long ago." My tongue had numbed with fear, and I hoped she could understand me.

"Those are the best sorts of confessions to make," Natalie said. "You'll heal old, festering wounds."

It hit me all at once how hefty of a mistake I'd made. My mind must've needed a moment to escape that room, that conversation with Natalie, because I began to daydream about my life in prison, the iron bars through which I'd stare out at the mocking blue sky while Natalie welcomed police officers into the condo so that they could raid my bedroom. They'd release these tapes to the public after my trial, and some reporter would make a podcast out of them; it would become wildly popular, everyone would latch onto the rawness of my life, I'd have a million fans and receive boxes of mail every day.

Natalie clearing the dishes broke me out of it: I couldn't go back to feeling jailed up. I'd been that way with Jim Dave for years, and I wasn't about to return now.

"I'm afraid," I said, but Natalie failed to look me in the eye. Maybe this was a good thing: my face was probably tortured with worry. Desperately I wished that I could move backwards just ten minutes in time. It wasn't that much: ten minutes, a blink.

"I'll be there to support you," Natalie said as she stacked plates, her eyes far away, shining like she could picture herself a hero, all glory and hallelujah. She would probably tweet about my demise and paint herself as my savior. She dumped the last of the wine into her glass – Natalie believed that wine went bad faster than mayo at a July picnic, she never let it languish overnight – and sipped thoughtfully. "Maybe this is why He brought us together." She lifted her glass towards the ceiling. "Mysterious ways, and all that."

I nodded stiffly, helped Natalie carry the dirty dishes into the kitchen, and locked myself in my room. My blood felt as if I'd had a transfusion of grasshoppers – the moment I tried to sit still and think, I had to jump up again.

Apparently I'd forgotten the lesson I'd learned from living with Jim Dave: never trust anyone. He'd shown me that the job of the people closest to us is to gloat, to throw a knowing *I-told-you-so* smile, to make sure you understood they were superior, to hold over your head any trauma you had stupidly revealed. And I had learned the importance of living a life of secrecy, relying only on yourself. Why had I been so weak as to share this part of me with Natalie? I felt even worse because this was not my first rodeo figuring that here was a person who cared about me, who would listen, who would not judge because I was more important to them than whatever had happened. But this was always a miscalculation – I was never more important.

The reason I had landed in this position now, with Natalie, was because I had let my memory of helplessness – of being at the mercy of another person – fade; I had forgotten that I could never count on anyone, even if they took me in and showed me small kindnesses, because whatever they knew of me they would use against me, to crush me. And I could not let that happen again.

In the middle of the night, I gave Natalie one chance, an easy one. I crouched at the edge of her bed, beside her pillow. The whole place smelled like potpourri, brittle and dry and sickly-sweet, and I thought about how Natalie and I were both getting old, slowly but surely. Maybe old age was leaving me dumb and forgetful. What had I been thinking, confessing to her.

I poked her arm and said her name a few times to wake her. Her eyelids looked sticky, but they opened, and so did her mouth, expelling a smell like overripe grapes bobbing in a sewer. Into this rot I said, "Natalie – I don't think I can do this. I can't talk to anybody else about what I've done. Just you. Don't you see? I can't tell anyone else, I'm too . . . it's just too awful."

Her hand snaked out from under the cover and grabbed my shoulder. "Be strong," she said. "God will guide you."

Carefully, I switched my tone from worried to angry. "I won't," I said. "I just can't. It's impossible."

She pulled herself up so that her back was against the headboard and she was looking down at me. "Don't say that," she said. "Come on, don't be that way. You can't put me in that spot."

"What spot?" I asked. My eyes were getting used to the dark, and her form flickered as my pupils made their adjustments.

"Well, if you won't turn yourself in, I'll have to do it for you. Now that I know, I can't just forget about everything. I would be complicit, don't you see? What you did could get me in trouble."

Steadily I breathed in through my nose, out through my mouth; I prayed that the night smells would calm me. "Of course," I said gently, as if I were the most fantastic actress in the world, "I'm so sorry. You're right." Slowly, I inhaled her dank sleep. "But we could both keep the secret. It could be ours, together. Just like the one I'll keep about your Las Vegas boyfriend – how did you know that he'd have drugs on him that night, anyhow?"

"That was completely different," Natalie said. The alarm clock numbers, glowing brightly as a blood moon, flipped to one in the morning. "I can't keep a secret like this. I'd never be able to set foot in church again."

Desperately I held onto the comforter where it cascaded over the edge of Natalie's bed. Truly, this was all for the best: even if she had promised her secrecy, I'd never be sure that I could trust her – she drank so much. Besides, she hadn't promised, and so I set my plan into motion. "I can't sleep," I said. "Will you have a nightcap with me? To calm me?" I held up the bottle of vodka that I'd brought with me into the room.

"You know I will," she said. "Everything will be okay. You'll see when we go to the police station tomorrow."

I'd brought in tumblers, too, and I handed her the one that had been dusted with sleeping pill powder. "To a better life," I said and downed my small shot.

Even in the dimness of the bedroom, I saw her eyes flash. She goes, "You are a cabbage woman, aren't you? You have layers upon layers, and peeling you back is such a surprise. Like with the hors d'oeuvres? I didn't eat all of them, did I? For days I felt confused over that: I'd stopped those antics years ago. But why did you say it?"

My stomach began to feel very hot, as if a balloon full of warm water had replaced the organ. I said, "Maybe I exaggerated a little what had happened . . . "

She goes, "I don't know why I didn't figure it out before." She giggled to herself as I poured her another shot. "I'm allergic to straw-berries. I would've blown up if I'd had that dessert."

I felt glad she'd told me this; it only fortified my resolve. Natalie wasn't about to forget my secret, accept that what I'd told her had been a dream; she remembered too much. I didn't like it; I'd figured that I was on top, that I'd been in control, but here she was, finding me out. "Why would you make a shortcake, then?" I asked.

"Precisely because I wouldn't eat it." She stuck her tongue into her empty glass.

I go, "Let's just have one last easy night together," and poured her another. "So's I have a nice memory to take with me tomorrow."

She agreed – she wasn't a monster – and she took a few more while we traded platitudes about how guilt was a thief in the night and I'd get back on track to walk with God, and then Natalie's eyelids started to droop, and I told her goodnight and carried out the empty bottle and shut the bedroom door.

I stood on the other side of it, my mind whirring, a tractor in a deep rut. Natalie had been a good friend, she'd helped me, but she'd also used me, and she considered herself so superior that what *she* thought I ought to do was more important than my life. I couldn't go to prison. They'd found the body. Besides, I'd given Natalie a chance, and she'd failed it. She believed in justice, or was it God?, more than she believed in me.

Never have I known a wild creature that wasn't bent on self-preservation: this was my instinct kicking in; anyone else in my place would labor for their life too. I quietly opened Natalie's bedroom door. She was passed out under a heavy sheet of alcohol, the way she slept most nights, but made more profound by the powdered sleeping pill, and she didn't stir when I dropped the plastic trash bag over her face. It moved like a little ghost, gently, up and down with her breath.

Over that I laid a pillow, atop which I draped my weight. It didn't take long, though the time moved slow. Her body jerked twice, but I don't think she really knew I was there or what was happening. I could tell when she let go; I felt a sort of *whoosh* that brushed the hair on my arms, and even before the body went slack, I knew my plan had worked.

I understand if this sounds strange, but in that moment my witchiness was returned to me – in full and stronger. The pulse of Natalie's powers, which I'd sensed when she'd told me about sending her boyfriend to prison, brushed through me, and some bits of it stuck. My flesh felt fuller, not heavier, but firmed up and strong. The blood wheeled easily through the miles of my veins. This was my start of becoming who I was meant to be.

There was so much to do that I didn't have time to feel horror, though the horror was there, hard and foreign and part of me, like a tumor I was afraid to prod. Quickly, first, I had to clean the bed of its mess before it soaked in. I kept the lights off so that the neighbors wouldn't notice anything out of the ordinary, but my eyes worked perfectly: I swear I could see everything, just as if it were day; my pupils must have been huge.

I couldn't drag the body out at that hour; any activity this late would look suspicious, and for some reason the neighbors seemed to watch for trash violations around the clock. Instead I decided I would pack it in a suitcase, and it did kind of represent for me a new journey. Before I hadn't been absolutely certain that I was the kind of person who would do anything and everything to save my own hide, but I was, I was that person, I was strong enough.

Of course Natalie owned suitcases of every size, so's I picked the one that would fit and folded up the remains, then wrapped them like a mummy in cling wrap, two boxes. The squashed face through the layers of plastic left me with an out-of-body feeling, a chilled premonition that I was wrapping up my own body, that it was my lungs shriveled beneath a slack chest. But no, I breathed deeply: I'm still here. Then I wrapped tape around the whole mess, and I twist-tied it inside a big trash bag. Only after all that did I zip it into the suitcase and stow it in the very back of the closet. The body would be like a big hunk of steak in an unplugged fridge, slowly going bad and turning green, but the putrefaction would go unnoticed because the plastic seal was really doing its job.

Next, I started my preparations to flee, and it was probably when

I was thinking where to go, my mind jumping immediately to Mexico, though I still had barely any money, seeing as there was only a hundred dollars or so in Natalie's purse, that I had, instead, a different idea.

My original plan was to steal Natalie's license and hightail it for the border, but the thought of taking over her identity in a more serious way sort of crept up on me. Once you got down to it, the circumstances made it so damn easy. First of all, we look just alike. We're the same age. She doesn't have any family or friends coming around to check up on her all the time – or ever, that I've seen. Her neighbors have learned to steer clear. Plus she left all her passwords on a notepad right there next to her computer. And in the end, I just figured it would be best if I stayed put, where I could hide in plain sight, where I had access to food and shelter and Natalie's checkbook.

The thing is, Natalie's internet boyfriend arrives day after tomorrow.

HOW TO PREVENT FREEZER BURN

Never before did I realize quite how much makeup can transform a face: Mary Ellen used to wear a light pink lip gloss, a touch of mascara, maybe some filler for her eyebrows; Deedee wore minimal beachy makeup; and Natalie used makeup like it was batter. Full foundation, then powder overtop, maroon or scarlet lipstick, eyeliner, eye shadow, something called Eye Magic that I found in the front of the drawer, blush, eyebrow pencil – the works. Once I had completed her routine, making sure to smear concealer into the deep lines under my eyes, because though I had finally snatched a few hours of sleep, it wasn't enough to undo the black trenches of worry and insomnia that have dug themselves in on either side of my nose, I stared into the mirror for a long time. I looked just like her. I really did.

I threw out all my old stuff and made up the guest room to be like a guest hadn't set foot in it for months. Then I took my car to be crushed, and it made me a little sad that they didn't question why I was junking it, but just smooshed it up like it had never been worth a thing in the first place. They were the kind of operation that knew not to check for the VIN, which I'd filed off months before, and of course I had switched out the license plates before leaving Chautauqua County. I took off those plates to keep, just in case. That was the car I'd bought when we were still working at the garage and had some money to our name, and it had carried me from place to place for years. It had a little window in its roof, which used to seem so fancy, and Sallie had loved to stick her fingers out of it when she was a kid. She'd called it "tickling the wind."

Anyhoo, I've transformed everything back to the way it had been before, back to just Natalie. This is the first time I've lived all on my own.

Now I have six credit cards – two specific to department stores – a library card, a grocery rewards card, a health insurance card (I have health insurance!), a business card from someone named Antar Haiji, a movie ticket stub, and, of course, my driver's license. *And* a passport.

The weird thing is, the documents show my new birthday as November sixteenth, and three years before I was born. It doesn't make any sense: Natalie said she was the same age as me, which is fifty-five, and that we were born in the same month: September. I guess that she had a few secrets herself. I've aged three years overnight.

Natalie Eloise Heap – that's me. Natalie, Natalie, Natalie.

Thu Dong sent Natalie a message: *aa flight 309 tomorrow 3.42p see you at passngr pickup my angel.*

I did not want a boyfriend, and now it seemed like I had no choice but to inherit this one. If I tried to cancel our plans at this point, say I was sick, it would look suspicious; plus, in my experience, men usually wouldn't listen to such a request anyway: they would just as likely board the plane in the name of chivalry and try to take care of you with a microwaved can of soup and a sexy movie on the TV. I wrote back: *kk look for me in neon yellow dress #godsplan.* It seemed like the reply that Natalie would give, and I was Natalie. By the by, her username for everything is *soopersponge_royaltie* – guess I'm stuck with it.

I started to look through the messages that the two of them had sent one another over the past few months so's I could get a feel for their relationship. Were they sweet? Snarky? Did they make inside jokes?

One of the first things I saw disturbed me thoroughly: it was a snap of Natalie's pudenda, which was fine, I have one myself, but the unsettling bit was that it was imprinted with a little tattoo: three green olives on a toothpick, her preferred garnish for a martini. Cute, but terrible for me.

When we got down to it, would Thu notice that I was missing this tattoo? Surely he would. He had replied to the snap with a drawing of Homer Simpson on the telephone screaming, "Hurry, operator, get me the number to 911!" As I scanned through their little bleeps and bloops back and forth to each other, he mentioned it time and again. He loved those olives. He wanted to suck them dry, suck the little pimentos right out of them, lick their salty . . . I stopped reading, because I had to go get a tattoo.

I didn't want to bring the picture of Natalie's olives in case the tattoo artist recognized the work or thought it was creepy that I had a picture of that part of a lady and started asking questions, so when I pulled into the first shop I saw, I explained to the artist what I wanted and gave him a little drawing of it I'd made myself.

"You got any others?" he asked, and I said other whats, and he said tattoos, and I said no.

"Wow, just going straight to the source then," he said and told me to take off my pants.

It hurt something awful, like stepping down hard on a rake, and then having that rake flip up and bonk you in the noggin – only, my pain was lower.

After he finished, he leaned back and handed me a mirror. The green of the olives was a little too kelly, and the tilt of the toothpick looked slightly off, but overall, I didn't think Thu would question it. The skin all around the tattoo was red, though, and I asked the man why. He said it would be red and puffy for a few days, and then he handed me an instruction sheet on how to care for it. He said, "Keep it covered so that it's not brushing against your clothes or . . . anything else."

"No," I said, "is there a way for it to go back to looking normal? I can't have it being all like a cherry jubilee."

But he just shrugged and sold me a pricey jar of ointment.

I paid for the tattoo with Natalie's credit card, and everything went through just fine. That was yesterday, and my skin is tender there and still red. Now it's the big day, and I only have two hours before Thu's plane shows up, so's I'd better put the finishing touches on the house and myself and maybe watch a few more of these little animated pictures they sent one another, things like cats clawing their way out of the bathtub over a caption that reads "Mondays!" or penguins barfing up fish next to "Learned it from my mom!" I don't understand their relationship, but then, that's kind of my deal with everyone. My own parents had this routine that always confused me: my ma would set a glass of ice in front of my pa, and he would take out the chips, one by one, and press them to the back of her hand until they melted. They'd do this summer, winter, whenever. They wouldn't talk or even look at each other, but they both had goose bumps up their forearms. I never did get it.

Natalie, you slick feather, you.

Turns out, Thu is more than a boyfriend – he's a business part-ner, to boot. In one hour I found out more about the bingo scheme than I had from Natalie in all our weeks of living together.

Wait, I'll start from the top – I want to remember this just how it went. While Thu was here, I couldn't record, of course – we were sharing a bedroom. So's I'll begin with meeting him at the airport.

When I picked him up, he handed me a bundle of flowers – he must have carried them all the way on the plane and guarded them from suitcases and rude passengers. I've never been on a plane, but I've seen in movies and such how they jostle you.

"Bian! Hello! You're stunning!" he said as soon as he saw me parked at the curb. So much for the anxiety that had turned my cuticles into ragged red scraps: there was no flash of doubt in his eyes, no passing thought that I wasn't the same woman he'd been talking to. I'd dressed in neon yellow; my makeup was impeccable. He called me by the nickname I'd seen in their messages to each other. I had no idea what it meant – maybe some kind of short for beautiful? – but it sounded nice, coming out of his mouth. He was about half an inch shorter than me, with wire-rimmed glasses a little too narrow for the shape of his face, and he turned bright red just before he said, "That plane must have landed me in heaven, because you are some kind of angel."

"Hi," I said and wrapped my arms around him, "it's so nice to . . . meet, darling." This was my nickname for him, but it felt awkward. I didn't like the shape of it at all on my tongue.

He held me stiffly, as if trying to keep our crotch areas at a safe distance, and then he tossed his tiny suitcase into the back seat and hopped in; I followed.

"It's like I've stepped into a video game," he said, "seeing you in real life – it's just so neat." I could not remember the last time someone had told me a thing like that. "Your voice sounds different in person, more rich or something; it's lovely, it really is."

"Well," I said, "you know how microphones and those electronic waves everything goes through distort sound. Makes it tinny."

He agreed and asked how he sounded to me, and I said, "Different."

We drove down the highway raised above the marshy ground as Thu exclaimed over the landscape. "Look at that leggy bird!" he said, and, "Are there really crocodiles here?" and, "There's the ocean! I caught a glimpse of it – look!" He kept pushing his glasses up the bridge of his nose, and his excited energy made him seem very young, though he was about my age.

At the condo, we carried Thu's things inside and then stood in the kitchen. "I'll mix martinis," I said, because I knew it was what Natalie would have done. I dropped the ice into the pitcher, the vodka, the olives and their juice, vermouth, and I used a long silver spoon to stir everything together. I started to feel like I was in a movie, what with Thu staring at me with adoring eyes. And maybe it was because my head felt sort of fuzzy from lack of sleep, or because I was wearing a pretty dress that I'd found in the closet with its tags still on, or because for the first time I actually liked the taste of a martini when I brought the cold spoon to my mouth, but I started right then to actually *feel* like Natalie.

With a nervous giggle, Thu asked me why I kept the shades drawn when I could be letting the light fall over my beautiful face, and of course I didn't tell him it was because I was paranoid and thought I'd seen a lanky figure creeping around my bougainvillea the previous day. Rather than answer Thu's question, I kissed him.

"Oh, good," he said, pulling away after just a second, "because the only thing wrong with your lips was that they were too far from mine."

"Do you want to go into the bedroom?" I asked him, not exactly because I had started to feel anything for him, but because I knew it was what internet couples did after meeting one another for the first time.

Worriedly he sipped at his drink and then folded his hands in his lap. He goes, "I have to tell you something."

Well, I took a big gulp of air and waited to hear what it was, which turned out to be that he hadn't had a bona fide girlfriend in twenty years.

"I know that I talked a big game in our chats and all. I wanted to impress you so very much that I decided to leave out the fact that I am actually kind of terrified of women." His fingers drummed against the tops of his thighs in a senseless beat.

With his revelation, I felt a surge of power: this man was ready to tell me everything true about himself, while he got nothing of truth from me. "Then you are a lucky man," I told him, "because I am not just some woman, but your girlfriend."

He liked this, I could tell. He let me take him by the hand and lead him into the bedroom, where he nuzzled his face against my new tattoo – he didn't seem to notice its redness, maybe because he was flushed all over too; he was one big blush – and it hurt like the needle was jackhammering me again. But he took my groan to mean something else.

After our little experience, I could certainly believe that Thu had not touched a woman in decades. He handled my boobs as if he were forming a snowball, and he lay melted beside me after only a couple of minutes. But I still remembered how to put a man at ease. It was strange, because Natalie had been waiting a long time to meet him, and here he was, with me, but also kind of with her, too – her powers, her most important parts, had been absorbed by me.

The next morning, Sunday, Thu asked me about church: he knew that it was an important part of my life, and he'd been promised that he would be shown off there a bit. He'd even packed a wrinkled suit topped by a dweeby little bow tie, but I told him that I wasn't quite ready to give up our precious alone time, and he seemed fine with us going out to a fancy brunch instead at a three-story restaurant where we sat on the rooftop terrace and stared out at the ocean waves crashing. I swear, I have never found myself in such a romantic setting in my life – and it wasn't even that much of a pity to be there with a dork like Thu. You would think that smooth jazz and mimosas were silly contrivances from the soaps, but I am here to tell you that they can actually mean quite a bit; they can be *inspiring*; plus, they can help you gloss over whoever you are with. When Thu took my hand across our bistro table, my spine felt like it was popping out pinfeathers, all prickly and itchy to fly.

We talked, too, and it was funny, because I was learning not just about Thu, but also about Natalie. He did say one thing that hurt me, though, at our uppity brunch; he said, "Did you have any trouble getting rid of that lady, the awkward one who set up shop in your spare bedroom?"

"*You* are the one calling *me* awkward?" I almost shouted, but I caught myself in time and took a gulp of my drink. I said, "No, not any trouble at all."

Inside, though, I was seething, and meanly I thought "serves her right" when I pictured Natalie as a plastic mummy in her suitcase, the way her flesh would dissolve into borscht, leaving her naked in the ultimate sense, without even a few lipids of fat to keep her warm. Her manicure would be grown out and her dark roots would be showing – didn't they say that the hair and nails kept sprouting after death? – which she would absolutely hate, she was forever trying to look good, though of course her largest grooming oversight would be the soup bone of her skull emerging from her ragged scalp.

Lost in this fantasy, I didn't pay much attention to Thu going on and on about some video game called Sims. He must have been able to tell because, like a real gentleman, he switched the subject to me. He goes, "Tell me about your mom, and why she made you bulimic, back when you were younger."

Well, Natalie had never mentioned anything of the sort to me, and here I thought we were close as two girlfriends could be – but obviously, I'd been mistaken: she'd talked about me behind my back. *Awkward.* I said, "Bulimic?"

He covered my hand with his sweaty one. "Of course I understand that you wanted to wait to talk about it in person, because it can be a weird topic over the computer."

I go, "Oh, right." Thu might end up thinking that Natalie is more forgetful than he'd realized, but that was just a penny to pay. The sun had reached the middle of the sky by this point. Trying to look placid while my mind scrambled for the story, I stared out over the diamond water. I said, "Well, my ma, she was in commercials, and she had to keep her figure to earn a living, and she expected me to do the same. But you can see" – I ran my hands down myself – "I'm not that way."

Turning bright red, he told me that I was the way he liked.

"So Ma would watch everything I ate, and she had these tongs, I think they were more like barbecue tongs for turning meat, and she would pinch me with them in the morning. My stomach, my thigh, under my arm. And if she thought the tongs weren't able to close enough, she would give me a little pile of green beans for supper. The frozen kind, too; not anything nice and fresh, no butter."

"That's awful," Thu said.

"And so I was hungry," I told him, "all those green beans only made me more hungry, so I would steal food from the corner store or my friends' houses and eat it all late at night in my room. Only then I would lie on my bed and pinch my stomach, and I could just tell that the tongs would be too far apart, and so I'd have to get rid of it."

Thu understood me; he kept nodding with concern.

"My ma, you know, she was two-bit famous, and she let that become more important than taking care of her daughter."

My story done, I bit happily into a fancy seeded roll slathered with butter. I'd never known anyone with bulimia, myself; what a strange disease, bringing your food back from the dead. Or I guess I had known someone: Natalie. And now I *was* that someone.

Thu said, "For some reason, I thought it had to do with your mom's cancer."

"Did I say that?" I asked.

He played with his tiny fork, a lemon wedge speared on its tip. "I thought so, but I'm not sure . . . I must have gotten it confused."

I go, "Sometimes when you're our age, you get your own life confused. There's just so much past to keep track of."

"Easy on that champagne," he told me. "We have business this evening."

"We do?" I asked, all flirty, because I thought he meant business in the bedroom.

But it wasn't – it was the bingo scheme. Thu and I set up shop in the condo with our computers and our smartphones. I was sweating like a pig on a spit, I felt so worried that I would give myself away; I knew nothing about this bingo scheme, or how to run it, none of that. I'd mostly just ignored that part of Natalie's life, assuming that it was no more than a housewifely pastime.

But Thu proved me wrong. He asked, "Did you sell all the cards?"

I told him yes, most of them.

"Great!" he said. "Then the pot must be pretty big. We've already bought the decoy prizes, the wine subscription and giant teddy bear and that crap, so how much is left over?"

Hoping that Thu wouldn't notice my distress, I mopped at my forehead with a tissue.

"I'll just check our Google spreadsheet," he said, tapping on his laptop. His demeanor was completely changed; his shyness was gone. I'd become a business partner, and so he didn't need to worry about the way he smelled or if there was anything on his face. He wasn't trying desperately to remember his cheesy come-on lines at every turn. He goes, "Wow! Almost seven grand."

"Yes," I said, "that's right." I grinned and nodded and acted like I knew what I was doing, and luckily Thu seemed ready to take charge.

The scheme was simple: we started with five real games, where the letter-number combinations were auto-generated by a computer program that Thu, who is a programmer for some hat company, had created, and they were sent to the group via a special website that anyone who'd bought a card, or hundreds of cards, could log into; once somebody pushed the "Bingo!" button, the website flashed into a moving image of balloons and confetti, and we asked the winner to send us the number in the bottom left corner of their card. We used that number to look up the card and confirm the win. Then, for the final prize, the big pot, the only actual cash, all we did was have one of Thu's fake accounts push the bingo button first. How it worked was we used his computer program to make sure that none of the cards we'd sold would reach a bingo. Then we called out a bunch of numbers, and Thu's creation of the month, a Ms. Amelia Pown, pushed "Bingo!" and sent in her fake card identification number, and I declared her the rightful winner, and that was that.

When we were finished, Thu said, "If you were as easy as this game, I would have made the trip out here a long time ago." Then he blanched at his own forwardness.

A wash of relief that it was all over, that Thu still believed in me, chilled the sweat under my arms, and without really thinking I said, "Oh Bubbles, we made so much money!"

"Bubbles?" he said, and my mind started to race for an excuse, but he goes, "Oh, I get it: because the bingo numbers usually come out on little balls, little bubbles, right? You can call me that, sure. Don't forget to transfer my half of the money, or would you rather write a check since I'm here?"

While I mixed us celebratory cocktails, Thu praised me, stuff I wasn't used to hearing, like: "You were just so smart to think up selling bingo cards: they are instantly renewable, unlike lotion or makeup or that kind of stuff ladies like to sell, and we're making people happy, giving them a fun game with real prizes . . . you are brilliant in business. I'm so glad I answered that Craigslist ad you posted for a 'computer whiz,' that was so cute." He raised the glass I handed him. "Here's to working together on many more games."

Already Thu was getting comfortable around me; when I took his hand, it was only slightly clammy. He stammered less, and even his blushing appeared muted.

We had a fun rest of the night, with me feeling rich and generous, and then I took him to the airport the following morning. He had to go back to his day job, but he'll return in a couple weeks; we already have plans. He wants to search for shells along the beach. Though he's from California, he never visits the ocean: he lives in Fresno, where the earth is dusty, the groundwater is gone, and just a quarter-inch of rain floods the place.

When we were almost at departures, he reverted to his nervous self. He stammered, "I probably shouldn't ask you this, I mean, we are a bit past this, age-wise, but I should know: you don't want kids, do you?"

"Oh, no," I said. "If it hasn't happened yet, it's not going to happen."

Immediately, he settled. "That's nice. It means our futures could mesh." And he smiled in what I figured was a relieved kind of way, and I had blocked out the fact that I did, in fact, have a kid, who herself had a kid; but in that moment, I felt free and unburdened, and right now I guess what I'm realizing, what I'm trying to say, is that it wasn't just a feeling, because if I'm Natalie, if I've become her, then when you get right down to it, I'm not really a ma or a gramma anymore. I'm a bingo businesswoman with the sort of boyfriend who calls women – or at least women who will sleep with him – goddesses.

THE LIFE CYCLE OF THE COCKROACH

I don't believe in ghosts, which must be why they only come to me in the dark, when I am dead asleep. For the couple of nights I had Thu in my bed, I tried to stay awake, but even with his uncomfortable heavy arm thrown across my chest, I drifted off. My ghost bothered me a bit, but Thu must not have noticed a thing – he always seemed rested and happy in the morning – and I would rise before him so that I could smear concealer beneath my eyes.

This time, during my night alone, despite the soothing martinis I'd put myself to sleep with, there was a new development: it was Natalie's ghost that visited me. She was a version of Natalie, but yellow, with larger nostrils than she'd had in life. In fact, her nose looked a touch more like mine.

It might seem strange to record my dream in so much detail, but I keep thinking about it and the more I do, the more real it feels. So's I will put it down here the way it went.

"Did you sleep with my boyfriend?" ghost Natalie asked. Her flesh was beyond jaundiced; it glowed yellow, a bit radioactive.

"Only because I was being you," I said. I wasn't exactly shocked that she'd shown up; it was just my subconscious being predictable. "He's a really great guy, real sweet, and you know what? I think he might love you. Or me. Us, maybe."

"I was saving myself until the second time we met," Natalie said. "Honestly. And I told him that. He knew. We needed to go to church together first."

"Well, then," I said, "I guess he also figures that women are fickle, seeing as he sure did not protest when I changed your mind."

There, next to my bed, which was her bed, Natalie grew larger than life. My skin felt chilled even under the covers on a warm Florida night, and I worried that she was doing something to me from the inside-out, maybe freezing my guts, somehow.

She said, "I can't believe what you told Thu about my mother; that wasn't accurate, not at all, not one bit. And you called her 'Ma.'" She shimmered with disgust.

I thought over the way Natalie said "accurate" and how I felt pretty sure I had never used that word. So if I wanted to sound like her, which I did, I'd better start.

"My mother never pinched me with tongs," Natalie said. "In fact, she never made me feel inadequate, not in my appearance or anything else."

I asked the ghost, "Then why did you tell Thu she was the reason you went all bulimic?"

I didn't think that a ghost could cry, but a few tears dripped down her cheeks. "The reason was because my mother grew very ill with cancer when I was seventeen years old, an impressionable age for a girl, and her being so sick and then dying a year later took a toll on me. During that time, everyone was always bringing comfort food. The neighbors baked cakes and casseroles, the ladies from church brought cookies and quiches, my mother's friends all knew how much she liked lasagna. But my mother, she could hardly eat, so we had all this food sitting in the kitchen, and I got into the habit of stuffing myself. I would eat it and eat it, and then my stomach hurt, and I felt guilty for eating my mother's food, even though she wasn't eating it herself, and I'd go into the bathroom and purge it. That's what I would do. And the habit stayed for three years. But you made my mother sound like a monster. It wasn't her fault that she was a celebrity, that being the child of a celebrity is hard."

I had almost started to feel sorry for her, but then she'd added that last stupid jab about celebrity. People always fixated on the dumbest little things. I said, "Being the star of a soap commercial is not accurately what I'd call celebrity."

She goes, "You absolutely don't understand – and it was *sponges.*" I'm telling you, she said *sponges* just like that, like she was saying *gold watches* or something, and here I am the one labeled as a hick for saying *Ma.*

Her tears were steady now; a ghost cries like a person, but uglier, as if their body were made of mist and then bits of it were condensing, leaving the cheeks ravaged.

I go, "You have to admit that you could have prevented this, but you refused to listen to me. Turning myself in would have ruined my life forever."

"You ruined someone else's life forever," Natalie said, "*two* someones, and having yours ruined, well, that is the consequence."

"You know what?" I told her. "We're both of us thinking about this wrong. Natalie's life wasn't ruined because I'm her: I'm Natalie; I get to rewrite her history. You – you're Mary Ellen. She's the one gone."

In this dream of mine, the ghost, who'd only known me as Dee-dee, already understood everything about everything: I didn't have to explain who Mary Ellen was.

"It was like you didn't care about my life," I told her, "not one bit. You didn't think much of me, did you? You told Thu I was awkward? You wanted me in prison – you want everyone in there! To get shanked. You decided what was moral because you forgot that I was your friend."

Her body blinked, a TV on the fritz. "You were never my friend," she said as she dissolved into wavy lines. "Look what you've done to me." The zigzags of the Mary Ellen ghost inched towards the closet, floating gracefully as an olive bobbing in a martini, and then I began to realize where she was going.

"No," I said, "no!" It felt like someone put a hand over my mouth, but I couldn't be sure. Maybe I was being suffocated, the way I'd done to her. She was floating back to her physical body, the mummified version of it inside my closet, and I knew that once those wisps of her reached it, she would be able to reanimate herself, to uncurl her broken fingers, inflate her collapsed diaphragm, and then she would come for me. With a physical body, her haunting would take on new meaning.

That was the last part of the dream that I remember. Sleep has become like a marathon, where even if I start strong, I am exhausted by the end. I'm starting to think I might feel more rested if I never slept at all.

When you think about it, everything had come so goddamned easy to Natalie, even in death. She didn't have time to agonize over a will or decide what sort of music she wanted at her funeral or do all the zillion chores that eat up your life at the end of it. Instead it was quick and easy, no suffering illness, no weeping mourners, probably if you thought about it the least painful departure from this earth that one could hope for.

I am more than ready to catch a little peace, myself. Now that I'm Natalie, I can only expect that a thing or two will come easy to me.

Of course I had to find a new church. Natalie was a churchgoing woman, and if she didn't show up for a few Sundays, I felt certain that her church friends would come around to check on her and bring her back into the flock. They were already sending little messages through the computer: *hey girl check out my new hat #godsplan* and *can't wait to see you on Sunday! #godsplan* and *Hey can u bring my big bingo teddy I'll pick him up at church parking lot? #winnerwinnerchickendinner #godsplan*

I worried about the bingo scheme and how it would fare if I abandoned the church most of my customers attended, but there was no way I could go back; the risk was too great. Natalie didn't have many friends, but the church ladies were long-standing mainstays, the kind who were kept at the comfortable sort of distance where you only saw them in their prescribed place, at the prescribed time: Sundays, eleven o'clock. If anyone was going to notice something off, it would be them – besides, they had seen me that one day when Natalie took me to church. They all knew Deedee.

In fact, one of them, a horrible petite person named Lottie, sent me a private message: *Hey Natalie what was with that woman you brought the other Sunday? She had crazy eyes! LOL I know everyone deserves an introduction to Him but you sure know how to pick them don't you?*

She was a rude little woman, and they all had the potential to ruin me, so's the best way to get rid of them was to join a new church, one they didn't like.

The computer makes everything so easy. I typed right in there to see if Natalie's church had a rival, and the place popped up, just like that: Bayou Angel's Nondenominational Christian Church, located in a strip mall off Balboa Avenue.

The church was nicer than you would expect for a storefront, with comfy pews covered in cushions and a pretty mural of God up in the sky with the sun and clouds on one side of Him and the moon and stars on the other, and a trio of angels in the center.

The pastor, who is named Maria and I think is Cuban, came up and greeted me right away, saying that it was so nice to see a new face. Everyone was sweet; they were all taking pictures of themselves in their Sunday best, and I joined in, knowing that I would need the photos for my plan later. I myself had dressed in a blue pantsuit, sky blue head to toe, with matching pumps. The church ladies posed in front of my phone as if they were used to the runway.

After the service, Pastor Maria found me on the sidewalk, where everyone had spilled out to socialize. She asked, in a polite kind of way, what brought me to her flock.

"I used to go somewhere else," I said, "you know that brick place over on Palm? But something about them grated my cheese on the wrong side."

She tried with all her might to keep her face neutral, but I could tell she wanted to grin: she'd stolen a member from those uppities on the snooty side of town.

To solidify her confidence in me, I go, "You, though – you're great. That stuff about treating everyone the way you want to be treated? But in a more deeper way? Very nice."

After that smidgen of flattery, she was more than glad to get one of the other congregants to snap our picture, and right when the phone made its fake camera click, a nostalgic soundbite for those of us who remembered film, she squeezed my shoulder.

"We'll see you next Sunday, I hope?" the pastor said. "We'll be having a special event, what we're known for, the communing with angels."

I told her that if I could help it, I wouldn't miss it.

Straightaway I drove to the condo and pulled up my new pictures on the computer. My makeup was impeccable, with those signature-Natalie little black wings on either side of my eyes and deep maroon lipstick. I only posted the pictures that had been taken from a fair amount of distance. I added the caption *had such a Sunday at Bayou Angel I could accurately say it was elevating #godsplan*.

Then I poured myself a glass of rosé and stood in the kitchen, sipping. Only after I finished the drink did I realize that it wasn't the sort of thing the old me would have ever thought to do, but the new me, of course; rosé in the early afternoon was exactly the new me.

I poured another. It was funny because, while I had started these habits to delve into the Natalie mindset, I was getting to the point where I didn't give them a second thought; they truly were habits now, which proved I'd become a new person. The smooth feel of the glass in my hand as I carried it from room to room, the heaviness of my tongue, and the way worrisome thoughts could slide down my throat with the next sip rather than peg themselves to my brain, all of that pleased me. Just the way I assume it had pleased me before I was me.

Back in front of the computer, I checked my results. Already I had seven comments from five different women at the prissy church. A couple of the comments were just little pictures of a shocked face and a confused face, but the others were things like *wait you didnt ditch us did you?* and *is this why you weren't around? wht happened!* and *they do some witchy stuff watch out* and *Come on they are crazy over there. They think anyone even unicorns can lead the church.* Mean-hearted Lottie sent *WTF this is a joke right? Return to your senses!*

It took me a few minutes to think up the best reply, and then I used my two pointer fingers to jab into the computer *Maybe I like unicorns better. Accurately getting tired of all the nonsense and noise from over your way.*

Then I sent it knowing full well that I was booting the hornet's nest, especially after I'd cancelled the hors d'oeuvre party with them the other week, so my plan was to keep off the comments and save myself the grief, but one more slipped in before I could close the window: *u get a hairline lift or what? maybe surgeon cut into her brain.*

In the mirror, I saw that my hairline was a smidge farther back on my forehead than it ought to be, and so I took scissors and cut long, wispy bangs like the ones Natalie had sported in a picture from some years before.

They look nice on me.

Now I've got to go rinse out this bottle of rosé. Very carefully I wash out my recyclables and unscrew the lids from the jars so as to avoid a run-in with one of the Cheryls who cock-struts her position in the HOA, which has an apparent passion for saving the planet one empty wine bottle at a time. Recently I found a handwritten note taped to my front door explaining that my filthy containers were unfit for the bin – that *I* was the reason a raccoon had infiltrated our development. The last thing I want is some angry Cheryl snatching an up-close peek at Natalie and saying, hm, you look a smidge different, did you fall on your nose or something?

Another article has appeared in the Chautauqua County paper and also a podcast. I figure that since I am Natalie Heap and she has no connection to Chautauqua County or the Washies, it's alright for me to check the relevant websites from the condo. Besides, Thu has taught me how to totally wipe the computer's history. Through the internet, he's a bunch more bold, more confident, and he decided that we should watch the same internet porn together from our opposite sides of the country, which really means that Thu watches it while I surf the web. Anyhoo, even if someone had reason to look on my browsing history, they wouldn't find a thing.

The article wasn't much, just a blip, really. *Local authorities are highly interested in speaking with Mary Ellen Washie. Anyone with knowledge of her whereabouts is asked to call this number immediately.* And then there were some facts and figures about me, along with a close-up picture of my face from my old work ID card, which, truth be told, I didn't much recognize. The person in the picture had basically nonexistent eyebrows, lips, eyelashes; her hair was lank and darkish and stringy. She looked angry with hangdog eyes, and I felt not the tiniest thread of connection to her.

The podcast was a jumble of stupidity, of course, and at first, it really boiled my eyeballs, but then I reminded myself it truly had nothing to do with me; it was about some forgotten, discarded person, who was nobody to no one anymore. I'll play the podcast here:

Thank you from the bottom of my heart for tuning in to my second episode of NEXT TO MY NECK OF THE WOODS: I TOLD YOU SO, which I'm dedicating to my husband, who thought this whole project was a waste of my time, that I should stick to what I do best, aka parenting and mommy blogging, but look now! I knew it wasn't just some simple missing-persons case. I knew that something sinister had happened, and my intuition is virtually always right.

On a sunny afternoon, with the birds tweeting from every tree branch and the clouds floating happily by, the body of Jim Dave Washie was pulled from a sludge pond. What happened to this man to turn him into no more than a DB? My aim is to find out.

Your host has become an infrequent patron of the roadhouse where Jim Dave Washie was last seen alive, and as a sort of undercover agent at such establishment, she has unearthed interesting tidbits.

Franklin Dodds, the roadhouse owner, insinuated within your host's hearing that Jim Dave Washie was carrying on an extramarital affair at the time of his death.

Jim Dave with a sidepiece is an absolute fabrication; I know for a fact it's as false as a happy second son. Every time I saw Jim Dave, which was far too often, seeing as we lived together, he had his butt planted in his armchair in front of the TV. No way, no how did he have the energy to put on deodorant, much less go out and find himself a mistress.

In reference to this alleged mistress, Dodds said, "She was a sweet pea," to another patron down the bar, though seemingly loud enough that he wanted your host to hear, "and I don't expect she could be a murderess, but what about maybe her husband? I don't know the guy, only heard he might light a firecracker. Besides, what kind of man is he if he's never been in here to drink?"

Unless he was doing it while I was at work. He did make me work ten, eleven hours each day just so's we could get by – could he have been using that time to step out on me?

At a later date, your host broached this topic with local drinkers who declined to provide their names. "I don't know either way," said one, "but Frankie Dodds knew Jim Dave better than just about anyone, I expect."

Your host attempted to get in contact with the Washies' daughter, Sallie Blackburn, about this matter, but she could not be reached.

Only – I don't know why I give a damn in the first place. They think Jim Dave had some slut whose husband offed him in a fit of rage, well, that can only be a benefit to me.

The roadhouse is a place where rumors fly in and out with the opening and closing of the door, but more often than not, your host has discovered that these rumors are based in fact. If Jim Dave Washie's mysterious death could be solved by a phone call to his alleged mistress, your host will attempt just that. How hard could it be to locate this mystery woman? The investigation into Mr. Washie's murder and his wife's FTA, excuse me, failure to appear, has been dragging on for months. Perhaps your host is just the person to break this case wide open.

It's so easy for a marriage to look happy from the outside. But once you start digging, once you just scratch the surface, you will find out fast enough how strong the foundation really is. More often than not, rumors have some truth to them. Just think, if we had paid attention, then rumors about the Washies might have foreshadowed the tragedy to come: Jim Dave Washie's cold body laid out on a stainless steel table in the county morgue. The nature of Chautauqua County is that people are few and far between, and they invite a solitude and isolation that makes their everyday existence a mystery. If only my arms were big enough to wrap the whole place up in a hug. BOLO for Mary Ellen Washie and don't forget to subscribe!

I can barely believe that even a thing as dumb as a podcast has gone this corn mush, but the episode has over twenty listeners, my stars. The faintest hint of an audience can leave you wild to do something clever; no wonder our little host is adding in all manner of idiotic flourishes. She wants them to love her. I know; I understand the feeling. The difference between us is, I can't ever have an audience, but if I could, watch out, world. My loyal listeners would blow off the barn roof. Well, it's five o'clock, time for a drink.

After the affront of *BakinMama4C*'s speculations, it was clear as creek water that I needed to rest, relax, and recoup, so I decided to try a routine that Natalie did pretty often: bottle of wine in the bathtub. My new bathtub was a big deep oval, and I filled it with warm water and lavender bubbles, so's finally the house's usual smell of potpourri was overwhelmed. I sank in with my glass of merlot and listened to the off-beats of jazz – music I never took a liking to before, but that suited me, in that mood, just fine.

All the wine and warm water must have lulled me into sleep, because just when I was starting to feel really good and relaxed, the ghosts came to me.

That's right, ghosts, as in two: both Jim Dave and Mary Ellen. Together.

Jim Dave's blue ethereal body dripped slowly from the faucet, the drops forming into his shape. It was like my limbs were stuck fast, as if my bathwater had turned to gelatin, so's all I could do was watch him come on. And then when he was finally made, he stepped out to the side, over on the bath mat, where ghost Mary Ellen, all yellow like old urine, zipped in beside him.

"Oh geez," I said. "What now?"

Ghost Mary Ellen sniffed, her nostrils moving like a woodchuck's, and then she said, "I see you've effectively covered up the stench of my body." She reached out and touched one of the countless bowls of potpourri that I'd set out all over the condo, and I wondered if she could feel the prickly dried spices, or if they passed through her fingertips like a cloud.

"I wrapped you up too good," I said. "Even without this stuff, your smell wouldn't get out."

She asked, "Then why is it everywhere? You never liked pot-pourri."

"But you did," I said, "and now I'm you."

Jim Dave addressed me. "You don't feel guilty? Not even one tiny bit of guilt? Not for a single thing that you've done?"

I said no, then cast around inside myself to make sure that it was true, and it was. I don't think that I could be who I am if I were a shamefaced sort of person.

The Mary Ellen ghost said, "I've noticed that the guiltiest people up here are the children of celebrities. And we number so many! It's difficult to be at peace in the physical world when your parents are famous and the paparazzi are snapping photos of you and men want to impregnate you so that they'd be related to a star. No one understands who you really are. They want to put you in these tiny boxes, and then if you don't fit, they shove you into their preconceived notions anyway."

"Uh-huh," Jim Dave said. "That kind of thing chokes my goat. It's right there the reason no one first thinks you and me are together." He took ghost Mary Ellen's hand.

"What?" I said. "What do you mean, you two are together?"

"I'm happier with her than I ever was with you," Jim Dave said. He turned to ghost Mary Ellen. "Did you know that even on our wedding night she didn't want to take off all her clothes? I faked sleep so I wouldn't have to beg anymore."

"Don't lie," I said, "we did plenty of stuff. I was two months along!"

"He and I have found passion and peace both, in each other," ghost Mary Ellen said. "Even in this place where we're not supposed to feel easeful, ever."

I tried to shake my head, but it wouldn't barely move. "You two are messing with me. Ghosts don't have *romances*. And even if they could, there's no way you could actually *do* it."

"You're wrong," Jim Dave said. He started to unzip his pants, and I wanted to look away, but I couldn't. When he pulled them down, I saw that his private parts were green.

"Yellow and blue." Ghost Mary Ellen pointed to their different colored bodies. "Together makes green." She lifted her dress and there, too, between her legs, it was all green, so close to the shade of my olive tattoo that I couldn't tell if she still had her tattoo.

"And bonus," Jim Dave said, "it's our new way of haunting you, seeing as the putrid body stuff wasn't getting much of a rise."

It was true that I preferred an eyeball metronoming at the end of its nerve to these throbbing green sexual organs, but I made sure to hide the fact that I felt chilled and sick, just sick with the thought that Jim Dave had made love to *her*, when he hadn't touched me in years. My husband and my best friend, just disgusting.

Jim Dave opened his mouth, and ghost Mary Ellen floated up high enough to drip her yellowed saliva into it. He stuck out his tongue and let the spit polka dot it green, and then he smacked his lips around the nasty mix.

My guts felt like they'd been replaced with offal, all sloppy and blood-full. I tried to shout, to yell at them to git, but my mouth froze, and gasping only clogged my throat. Suddenly I was thrown into wakefulness; my nose had tipped below the line of the bathwater and my body was flooding. I sat up, coughing and retching on the old water gone cold. Chunks of my supper came up with the filmy water, and my middle contracted in pain. Once my lungs had calmed enough to breath, I wondered if I could have died in there, drowned.

SETTING THE STAGE FOR GODPARENTING SUCCESS

Well, look at who is full of surprises: it's me, Natalie.

I just received a very official-looking letter in the mail and opened it to find a summons to court for my DUI. The court date is next month. Then I went through the stuffed mail drawer to see if I could find out anything else, and apparently, my driver's license is suspended too and might stay that way for a while.

No wonder Natalie had been on the lookout for a live-in chauffeur — and here I'd thought it had all been my charms that had garnered me the invitation to move in. If I'm caught driving on this license, I could get time in jail. I read something about how whenever they take you to the police station, they can swab you for DNA and search their database to see if they can match you to anything. Guess I'll be taking more taxis from now on, though I wonder if the neighbors would find that suspicious. I can always say my car battery died, or I have a flat, or something like that.

What a thrill to be finding myself at this age; it is truly like I've been reborn. I'm a whole new woman, the good and the bad, the magic of discovering myself, or maybe it's the power of a woman compounded . . . look at me, talking all this big nonsense. You tapes are enough to puff up anyone's head.

Sunday again, and I went back to Bayou Angel's. It wasn't that I needed more photos to keep the church ladies away, it was more like I actually *wanted* to go. It had been exciting last time, with everyone so nice to me, and this Sunday was a special show with the angels and all.

I'd heard tell of talking with angels in church, though I had never myself seen it done, and I was interested to, and also to see what was the point of chatting with them in the first place. Could they grant us wishes, like a genie? Or would they tell us the right path to getting up where they were? Or if it was all a hoax, would I be able to see the strings?

When I reached the storefront, Pastor Maria came over to greet me straightaway.

"Natalie, hello, how are you doing?" she said.

I was flattered that she'd remembered my name. "Okay, I guess," I told her. "I've been a little tired lately, but I'm looking forward to the angel show."

She nodded, smiling. "It's not so much a show as we want to commune with them. See what they can teach us."

I agreed with her out loud, even though I knew she was just saying that to lend importance to her pet project.

Inside the church the air felt muggy, even though they had the dehumidifier humming. Up near the pulpit, a fan rustled a purple tablecloth; on top of the table sat a fancy bowl full of a thick and slightly yellow liquid that reminded me of the sugar water we used to set out back when I was a kid to attract hummingbirds. Maybe angels were like hummingbirds, frantic-fast and subsisting on sugar to keep up.

"Ladies and gentlemen," said Maria, placing herself behind the pulpit, "we have a special service planned for you today." She started to explain the history of the angels, and my mind drifted. I looked up towards the ceiling for any sign of wings gently moving the air.

If you had asked me a few months ago whether or not I believed in angels, I would have laughed in your face. But acquiring my ghosts, even if they were confined to dreams, had made me more interested in seeing what angels were all about. I mean, who was I to say that just because I couldn't see them – or hadn't seen them yet –

they weren't around here, somewhere?

Before the angel ceremony began, Pastor Maria had us line up before her, and when I reached the front of the line, she parted my new bangs and dotted my forehead with a speck of liquid from the fancy bowl. It smelled like Lemon Pledge – the stuff my mother used to spray on the furniture – and I felt it drip slowly down between my eyebrows.

"This will let the angels know we're ready for them," said the pastor, and everyone around me in the pews murmured, kind of excited, like, and I was excited too. The ladies wearing them took off their pastel hats so that they'd be better able to look up, over our heads, where the angels would appear.

Watching for the angels made my eyeballs throb; my eyes felt like two tiny frantic hearts stuck there in the front of my skull.

A couple of minutes later, Pastor Maria was explaining why the angels were real through a tangled analogy that went like this: "No one counterfeits three-dollar bills, because there is no such thing. Only things that are real can be counterfeited. This is why we know that angels are real, because plenty of nonbelievers counterfeit seeing angels since they want their own story about the amazing experience that we get to have as true believers here today." Suddenly, everyone in the room gasped.

I looked around frantically – all of their eyes were focused on the air above the pulpit. I stared and stared, but I didn't sense anything, not even the slightest movement of air.

"The angels," the woman beside me murmured.

"Are you sure?" I said. "How do you know?"

"Only angels would look like that, with wings and all. Clear as day. And can't you hear them? That little whistling?"

I concentrated, but nothing happened. Everyone around me was restless with joy, and I felt completely left out, as if I had no place in the world. One woman wearing a sequined blouse stood up, clutched at her heart, and then slumped sideways into the waiting arms of her husband. Another congregant rocked back and forth, sobbing. Surrounded by all those people, all of us lemon scented, I felt like an unwanted outsider.

After the service, the congregation buzzed around happily, a busy swarm of bees delighted after a day's honey-making. That's the thing about people, they can rationalize away anything, even the complete and utter terror that we ought to feel when encountering beings from another realm, from death. It's truly amazing, what all the brain can do.

The exit was blocked by these lively chatting groups, and I was sucked into one of them when I just wanted to leave.

"I feel such a great sense of peace," said the woman who had sat next to me during the service. "It's too bad that they didn't actually speak with us today, but just seeing them, that was all I needed to know I could keep going, that everything would be alright."

"*Hearing* them was all I needed," said an old woman gripping her son's arm. "My eyesight isn't what it used to be, but my goodness I think the pitch of their wings fluttering healed me. I'd been feeling near death, I tell you, but the vibration they laid down on us has made me" – her son rolled his eyes at this – "reborn!"

"That is a really accurate observation," I said, but inside, I was roiling with hurt and anger. Why did everyone else get angels, and I got ghosts? Why had my whole life become a series of bad and worse choices? As the group tried to one-up each other with their blessedness, I pushed my way towards the door. Just when I had made it outside, where the smelly parking lot with its greasy oil slicks and humid heat started to remind me that the real world was not all angels, that in fact, the real world was a sort of hell with just enough sunshine to trick us into thinking otherwise, the pastor, Maria, ran after me.

"Where are you going so fast?" she said. "Aren't you coming to the brunch reception? We'd love to have you. It's a fundraiser; keeps us running, you know."

"I can't," I said, trying to think up some excuse, but I just kind of stuttered.

"Oh, no," Maria said, "what's wrong?"

I couldn't hide from her anymore because I was crying out of sheer tiredness.

"Did the angels frighten you?" she asked. "They can do that to some people. Maybe because they aren't quite ready to accept so much beauty and goodness in the world. But next time, you'll have the tolerance to process what you've seen today; next time, *gracias a Dios*, you'll be ready to let the joy inside."

"I didn't see them," I said. "I didn't see them at all."

She was surprised, you could tell how surprised she was. She goes, "But they were *there*, you know that, right? Everyone else saw them. Maybe your eyes weren't soft-focused enough."

Because she was a woman who believed in angels, who conjured up things living in the sky, I decided to try out my dilemma on her: "I'm not blaming your ceremony; it wasn't you, it's me. I mean, I keep having these dreams, I don't sleep much, but these dreams about ghosts."

She goes, "What do you mean – *ghosts*? Maybe you got the angels confused?"

I told her, "Not in church – in my sleep. The ghosts are in my dreams."

People were starting to leave, probably on their way to the celebration brunch, and so Maria pulled me aside, around the corner, where we wouldn't be disturbed.

"Ghosts," Maria said. "They must have blocked you, somehow, from seeing the angels."

"You believe me?" I asked.

She goes, "I haven't completed a professional evaluation, but it's certainly possible. I have met dozens of the possessed, and I understand how such a thing can affect almost anyone."

Immediately I felt a cautious relief. After all, Pastor Maria had set up this whole angel ceremony and was a religious woman and plenty of people considered her an authority and probably, as a pastor, she knew a thing or two about death and how it can linger. "The ghosts keep me from a good sleep," I told her, "that's all."

She goes, "But sleep is a necessary function. You do look peaked. Probably you need help to eradicate these demons. If you let them stay around, they can ruin you; they can turn you into a sort of ghost, yourself. I've seen it happen. Another one in our congregation, a young man, when his fiancée died, she haunted him for months. She would send him emails and he would delete them without opening them, but they would just appear again in his inbox."

"What color was she?" I go, and she asked me to repeat it. "As a ghost – what color was she?"

Pastor Maria said, "I'm not sure, but the point is, we helped her move along so that she didn't have to haunt her fiancé anymore. You see, that's an interesting misconception about ghosts, that they want to haunt you. They don't, really: they want to move on, and you have to give them a way out."

"How did the church do that?" I asked. "I mean, help this ghost woman move along."

Maria waved at a couple members of the congregation who walked past us to reach their car. It fascinated me, how fast her face changed from serious to carefree and back again. She said, "The best way to describe it, though I don't really like to, because of all the silly Hollywood connotations that go along with it, but if that were your only reference point then I guess it could be what you might call an exorcism."

I pictured my head twisting all the way around on my neck and coolant-colored vomit spewing from my lips. "Oh, no," I said.

She pointed at me and laughed. "See! That is why I don't like to use the word. I'm sure it's nothing like what you're imagining. It's a ritual, is all; it is a series of concentrated actions that allow release."

I wished I hadn't said anything; I wished I'd pretended to see the angels so that I would fit in. I could have done it, too, said something like, "Oh, their beautiful wings." Then I would be heading off to a nice brunch instead of spilling secrets and worrying about my tongue turning into a snake.

"Think about it," Maria said. "I'm not asking you to make a decision now. We only want to ensure that your soul is full of light – of lightness – so that you can be your greatest self." She squeezed me on the arm and then left to join the group driving off to brunch.

Well, all this talk into my little machine has worn me right out. This morning I awoke with a rough throat, and then I found a pile of spent cigarettes in the kitchen sink. I quit smoking years ago, but unless my ghosts have lungs, it must've been me. Keeping level with Natalie's favorite pastime – drinking – does come with certain surprises like this.

Anyhoo, the bottom line is, I don't have time for an exorcism: Thu is coming day after next. I won't be recording while he's here, of course – in fact, I'd better hide my paraphernalia. There's so much to do to prepare yourself for living with another person, so much to smooth over and tuck away. The true con artists are the people who live every day right there next to someone else.

With a fair amount of apprehension, I've been checking the podcast website, and a new episode has just popped up. I haven't listened to it yet; I'll go ahead and play it here. I'm curious to see what special sausage our little host is frying up this time.

After your host received the shocking news that Jim Dave Washie, whose body was recently fished from a muddy pond, was allegedly having an extramarital affair, she decided to take matters into her own hands and delve deeper into the world of investigative journalism, which is a much more interesting occupation for these mitts than their usual scrubbing of dishes.

It took not but four days for your host to locate the deceased's mistress, who wishes to remain UNK and will therefore be referred to, by request, as "Sweet Pea" in this and forthcoming podcasts.

This is really stealing not just the eggs, but also the hen, for most ridiculous. What a travesty.

Sweet Pea admitted to me that, "We'd had relations a time or two. Just small bits, really. Nothing I would call fixing to tie up."

She is a woman who knows what she wants: when she met your host, she ordered a Diet Coke, no ice, and then stirred in two packets of Splenda. When you —

Hold on, I have got to pause right here, because my belly is about to shoot through the floor. I know this woman. I *know* her. It's Minnie Pearson, who had worked with me cleaning houses, and who had pretended for a time to be my friend. I wonder if she decided to diddle my husband because she hated me for seeing that she swiped half-empty perfume bottles and lipsticks from our clients. How could Jim Dave have gone for her – though honestly it is more than likely that it's all a lie. At the cleaning company, every time we got a break, driving in the van from one house to another, Minnie would take out her Diet Coke and dump in the Splendas. I think she pretty much survived on that junk; her fingers were always trembling. Oh my God. Alright, I've calmed down enough; I'll start it up again.

— r host asked Sweet Pea if she was surprised to hear of Jim Dave's murder, she said, "I'm not surprised for much of anything, around here. Everyone claims it's all small-town nice, but I've realized things that would shock and appall. And Jim Dave, he wasn't what you might call the brightest blade of grass. He went along with what-ever, if he thought it might bring him a touch of happiness."

Your host then asked Sweet Pea if she had any idea who had wanted to kill Jim Dave Washie.

"Why haven't they looked to his wife Mary Ellen? She was a strange one, let me tell you. Have they even found her yet? She had this crazy attraction for playing house. Anyplace she goes, she settles right in, pretends it's hers. She loves to do that; it's creepy. And I know that people are saying to look to my husband. I've heard the rumors. But to this day I don't believe he knows I stepped out on him. Men here are wrapped up in their own lives, and unless they are much prone to jealousy, I just don't think they would notice a thing about you if it weren't in front of their face."

This was maybe the truest tidbit I had ever heard Minnie say. I must admit that I felt the smallest twinge of sympathy for her, a woman who'd lost even the crap job of cleaning the Institute people's houses for shit pay, who looked forward to nothing more than a warm Diet Coke and a cranky husband. But then I reminded myself: I couldn't feel sorry for her, because I was starting to actually believe that she and Jim Dave had snuck behind my back and he'd put it in her skinny tremulous body and they'd kept this from me as if I were no more than a stupid child. After all, Jim Dave had found him a hookup even as a ghost in my dreams, so's my subconscious had to be telling me something, and if the alive Jim Dave could have done such a thing with anyone, it would be Minnie, whose self-esteem went lower than a gopher hole.

Listening to that garbage has piled me up with hate, the sort that becomes physical, a tingling at the back of the eyeballs that disintegrates the outer edges of my vision.

It's a strange feeling, to listen to a podcast about your own person; or rather, a person you were. It's almost funny that when people finally start wondering about Mary Ellen Washie, it's too late; she no longer exists. She's not anywhere, and for all their pondering, she'll never again materialize.

Thu will arrive in just a few hours. I've had a big think over how to explain to him that we'll be ferried from place to place in a taxi, but every reason I come up with would only lead to more questions. Ultimately I've decided that I'll be fine driving my own car. Of course I'll steer carefully, obey the speed limit, and never try to make it through a yellow light. Plus, I have to admit that I have started to fear even the brief jaunt outside to get from my front door to a cab waiting at the curb. It seems to me that the yellow car acts as a beacon for all my nosy neighbors.

I know! I'll ask Thu to drive us; that will make him feel important, to boot.

Well, let me tell you about Thu. Our second visit went fine, all things considered. Again I picked him up at the airport, where, blushing, he greeted me with a cheesy line – "Are you a beaver? Because damn!" – and again he handed me a bouquet – but this time, I think I figured out his trick. He doesn't bring the flowers all the way from California, holding them careful so they aren't crushed; instead he buys them inside the airport terminal when he lands. Another man came out of the terminal with the exact same bouquet that Thu gave me. I'm not sure why this makes any kind of difference, but I felt a twinge of irritation when I saw the duplicate.

Everything ran along fine for the first day. Thu drove us to the beach, though it turns out he doesn't much care for sand and so we didn't stay long enough to find any good shells, and then we thought up the decoy prizes for the next round of bingo: membership to a book club hosted by a handsome author, a Merry Maids housecleaning, and another giant teddy bear, which for some reason everyone covets.

It was on the second night of his visit when we were sitting around the condo that he asked me, "Have you ever played the Sims?"

I go, "The whats?"

He pushed his glasses up his nose and patted the couch cushion next to him. A computer sat cradled in his lap like a baby, and once I settled, he showed me his little Sims.

They were computer people who moved rather stiffly around a marble-floored mansion, and the oddest thing about them was how he had made them to be like us. The woman was big-chested and blond and brightly colored, with a hunky ring on her marriage finger, and the man was a buff version of Thu, without glasses, who kissed his wife before he went off to his job at the marshmallow factory. I suppose the game would feel too close to life if it didn't include these nonsensical details. When buff Thu came home, the pair got into their luxury bathtub naked, and then they snuck around their darkened neighborhood, peeking into windows at other couples feeding their pet alligators or having sex on a bearskin rug or teaching their children to set fires. When Thu's Sims returned to their own house, the tub had flooded the second story, and they went to sleep atop a floating bed.

Thu goes, "Fun, huh?"

Well, I didn't know what to say. The thing that had struck me most was how, in a little video game where he could have done anything, he'd created me and him together, married, with a big house all our own. Why was it that the only men who had these sorts of fantasies didn't have much experience with women?

Anyhoo, for me this was an excellent sign: it meant Thu was more wrapped around my finger than I'd figured. I must admit that I had been worrying about him a little, since he knew about the bingo scheme, and it was direly important that the law have no reason to look at me. If he were stupid enough, or mad enough, he could point them my way, so's I needed him entirely on my side, and his little video game made me feel more secure that he was.

Later, when we were snuggling on the couch with a cocktail, he goes, "Bian, what did you think about my Sims' walk around the neighborhood?" His heel nervously jiggered up and down against the floor.

"It's a cute game, Bubbles," I said.

He scooted closer and wrapped his arm around me. He goes, "It seems like you enjoy the videos we've been watching together – didn't you like the one about the guy who owned that motel?"

"Oh, right," I said. The truth was I hadn't paid much attention when Thu had used our computer chats to show me porn – I'd mostly placed online orders for cases of Argentinean wine and satchels of potpourri.

He goes, "And I was saying how your condo complex, here, kind of reminds me of a motel?"

I drank my cocktail to buy time as my concern grew: I took great precautions to avoid my neighbors. "These units are more like town houses," I said. "I can't really see anybody's front door from mine, and I only share the garage wall with a neighbor." A neighbor I had never spoken with, and I intended to keep it that way. I certainly didn't want him busting out of his house, asking why I'd been staring through his window with a hand down my pants.

As if I'd asked, Thu said, blushing fiercely, "I'm not sure how I first got into this. Voyeurism. I've always been this way, really."

So far, Thu's and my sex had been what I would call regular, as in, it was fast and clumsy, and he seemed to enjoy it while I just lay there. I'd been hoping that we could continue on in a manner similar.

Thu kept talking, quick and nervous, as if he'd been thinking about how he would tell me this for a long time, and if he didn't hurry it out, it would get stuck. "Maybe it started when I was a kid, and I was reading in the closet in the room I shared with my older brother – if I was in there, nobody ever asked me to wash vegetables for dinner or clean the litter box. Anyway, I was hiding there when my brother brought in a girl. They started doing things, and I could see; I could see almost everything. I guess it was my first sexual experience. I wonder what it means, if I have never progressed past that moment. Or maybe it's because my brother died in a car crash a couple of years after, and this moment is the most vivid memory I have of him, and I never did get to ask him if he'd known I was in that closet or not."

My first impulse was to blurt out that my sister had died, too, when we'd been young; for a few seconds, before I remembered that I was an only child, I felt closer to Thu because of this similarity. But luckily who I am – Natalie, Natalie, Natalie – won out and I said, "You had a cat?"

He looked at me funny for a moment, and then he shook his head as if clearing it. "That is what I really appreciate about you," Thu said. "You say what you want to say, instead of some fluff that you think people should hear."

I said, "And now you want to hide in other people's closets, or their gardens maybe, and try to catch them at it?"

He looked truly disappointed in me. "No, Bian – we're the ones doing things. We're the ones who are – maybe – being watched."

Well, this unsettled me even more. My entire goal at the moment is to be completely unnoticed, to fly under the radar.

Thu removed his glasses and polished them with his shirt. "We could start small," Thu said, blinking at me with his naked eyes, "by keeping the curtains open. That's easy enough, right?"

When I didn't cave right away, he said, "I envisioned this being an integral part of our relationship. I've never been able to share this side of myself with anyone before, and things between us have been going so well, I finally felt comfortable . . . "

I thought about the little Sim people and the importance of Thu staying totally on my side: I would have to give him this. So's I accepted – it seemed easy enough, after all, to just open the blinds. This voyeur stuff was *his* pet pig – might as well let him slaughter it the way he liked. "You're right," I said. "We'll try it. Let's go." I was on a time crunch – it was still light outside, the sun reflecting off the window, and so anybody who noticed us would need to be a real creeper, trying to see in.

"This is excellent!" Thu said, extra-pleased that I'd jumped the stick for his little game.

"Yeah, it'll be a real sense of exhilpation."

He looked at me funny, so I explained it like this: "You know, exhilaration and anticipation. It's a word I made up. It's an interesting feeling." And I willed the feeling to start there in the pit of my stomach, but it was weird, doing it with the daylight falling across my ass.

"I'll get you a white picket fence," he said loud into my ear. Before, he had never really spoken during the act, but I suppose he needed to ham it up a bit for all the potential peepers. "You want a white picket fence, right?"

"Okay," I said, but he pushed a hand against my mouth; these were rhetorical questions.

"You love that fence, don't you? I'll pound those pickets into the ground." He was near to what I would describe as *vigorous*, and he even flexed his arms in the direction of the window.

He goes, "You want to sit on that fence, on a nice hard picket." He turned me so that I was on top, and all the while I could not stop thinking of splinters.

Afterwards, I must have nodded off for a second, I'm so tired lately, and when I woke, Thu was in the closet. "What are you doing in there?" I said from the doorway, my voice much meaner than I'd intended. I glanced at the large suitcase just a foot to his left.

"This is kind of part of it, for me," he said. "Going into the closet after."

"No, Bubbles, it's too weird, too morbid and kid-like, to be in here." I grabbed his hand and pulled him out, then shut the door with my foot. For some reason, I had the feeling like a heart was in there, inside the suitcase, beating fast and loud.

"Thank you," Thu said to me. "You're right. Something in there did feel . . . wrong. It's too strange of a habit, for me to escape into a closet after."

The thing is, every relationship is a balance; every relationship is a risk. But you also have to think about what you can get out of them – it's tough to do every single thing on your own.

CLASSICAL MUSIC FOR THE HOLIDAYS

I found Sallie's profile on Facebook, so I changed all my pictures to flowers and bridges and me at quite a distance wearing sunglasses – people do that sort of thing, maybe they're getting a face-lift, maybe they have a stalker or are fattening up, it's not too strange – and tried to befriend her through the site so I could see what she'd been posting. I didn't think it would work, since I made no explanation for why I wanted to be her friend or how I knew her, but I've heard that some people just click away with abandon, and that must be what she did, because just a pair of hours later there we were, Natalie Heap and Sallie Blackburn, friends.

Her page was stuffed full of pictures. She'd changed her last name and dyed her hair and my little grandkid Mae was so big I really couldn't recognize her. In fact, seeing all these pictures, being closer to Sallie than I had been in maybe a year, only made her feel all the more distant. Which I guess passed snuff when I took into account the fact that I wasn't really a mother or a grandmother; I didn't feel like one inside, because of course Natalie Heap had never birthed a child.

Sallie had about a million pictures of just her face, wearing sunglasses and not wearing sunglasses, smeared with lipstick or weird-colored eye shadow, just close-ups of her pursing her lips or winking and whatnot. I tell you, I couldn't understand it. The girl I'd known had been so far from vain it made you wonder if she was a real teenager. I could have draped sheets over all the mirrors in the house and she wouldn't have noticed.

While I was skimming through a photo album that seemed to be about a thousand pictures of Sallie before and after a haircut that had sheared no more than two inches of split ends, a little bubble with Sallie's name next to it appeared in the bottom corner of the screen. *Available to chat*, it said.

And so I considered my options: reach out to her and try to see, ever so subtly, if she had any useful information about the search for Mary Ellen, or leave well enough alone.

I clicked on her name and typed in a hello, and then I sat there, clutching the mouse.

whuddup, she wrote back.

With my two-fingered typing, which Thu had commented on, because apparently he thought that I was a swift typist, the ten-fingered kind – truthfully, it was a relief to have him gone and no longer bothering me, checking whether or not I still liked orange juice, staring at my tattoo – I chicken-pecked back to her, *Your new haircut looks great.*

She typed, *thx . . . have we met?*

All the lies I would tell her flowed through my mind as easily as the syrup from a fresh-tapped maple tree. *Don't you work in that hair salon?*

not me but it is funny you say that

Oh well. You look like this cool girl I once knew who did.

I waited for a long time, but she never typed anything back, and I didn't want to appear too needy or too curious. The rest of my lies will have to wait.

I loathe leaving my condo by foot, but tonight I just had to take out these damn recyclables. I'd collected quite a few empty bottles, and I added to the pile this evening, so I carefully rinsed them and was carrying them to the bin when a strange thing happened: my body began to shake with fear. I couldn't understand why my chest was constricting; it felt like my own nerves were strangling me.

Then, my knees lost all their strength and I knew that I would die if I had to stay upright. But even when people are packed to the brim with fear, they still feel the pressures of society. I looked up and down the darkened street, and only because it was empty did I allow myself to sink to the ground. The plastic bag full of bottles clanked down beside me.

I tried to force air in and out of my lungs, the way Thu had encouraged me to do one night when I'd woken him up with my gasping. He'd told me that I must have a lot of anxiety since I always had trouble sleeping, which, once I'd been able to breathe again, I'd laughed off. Anxiety was for young people, or for rich people. But maybe the problem was that I was a rich person now.

The same pancake-lunged feeling that bothered me most nights was assaulting me again, and I was gasping, my eyes tight shut, when I felt a hand on my shoulder – a clammy hand – and I snapped my eyes back. For a panicked moment, I thought that it was the police, but it was Lottie, that horrible woman from the boring church that I had quit, the one who had said such mean things, and I knew that I was doomed, that she'd found me out, that she was just as bad as a cop in her capacity to ruin me.

"Deedee" – confusion layered itself overtop of my trembling nerves, but then I remembered that she'd met me as Deedee, that I had on no makeup, that my hair was pulled back and I was wearing slippers – she goes, "Deedee, are you okay?" She helped me to my feet. "What's wrong – a panic attack? My daughter has them."

"Are you following me?" I asked. I snatched the bag of recyclables and held it as a shield between us.

"I live one development over; I'm just taking a walk, getting my exercise. There are some relaxation techniques that would help you with the attacks, you know."

"I'm *fine*," I said, reminding myself that this woman would have no reason to suspect me of anything, much less playing dress-up as her ex-church friend.

"Mary Ellen," I thought she said, and I must have looked so confused that she said it again, "Merry Christmas – I know that the holiday season can be hard. Chin up, okay? And you're always welcome at the church. You haven't started going to that other place with Natalie, have you? I hope you aren't the one who took her there. It'll do nothing for your souls." Then she walked briskly away, pumping her fists up and down beneath her chin.

Thanks be I must've had a spell protecting me. After she left, I stood there, adrift, trying like hell to remember my name: Natalie, Natalie, Natalie. But it's all here in these tapes; they are more solid than memory.

It was my own fault that I was outside. From now on, my plan is to keep all the recyclables in the guest bedroom. It's safer that way. I never have guests, anyhow.

Today a fender bender near to ruined my life, and it has convinced me that I need to take some action against my ghosts. Again last night they entered my dreams like a warm fat noodle sliding into my ear. They disquieted my brain so that I awoke befuddled, as if I hadn't slept at all.

Then this afternoon I drove to the grocery store; I needed everything. After I'd made my purchases and tucked my shopping bags into the trunk, I started the car and prepared to back out of my parking spot. But a wave of tiredness hit me with such force that I just had to close my eyes. The next thing you know, a jolt and the crunch of metal woke me, and I felt certain that I'd ruined everything, my whole life. All I wanted to do was curl up and go back to sleep forever, but instead I jammed my hand into my purse and pulled out all the cash I had, a hundred and twenty-six dollars, and stepped out of the car to see what I'd done.

The vehicle I'd hit was a rusty two-door pickup, and a very worried-looking man jumped from the cab with his hands open in front of him, as if ready to confront a rabid dog.

"I'm so sorry," I said, "but let's not get the insurance involved here, I mean, there's no need to call anyone, I'll take care of the damage; it can't be much."

He was practically crying, even though the new dent I'd made in his passenger door was one among many.

"Here," I said and held out the cash.

But he seemed too frightened to take it. He said something in Spanish, which I won't attempt here, then said that he was sorry, then jumped into his truck and sped off.

I've been thinking over what happened, and the best I can figure is that he's here without papers, and he was worried he'd be deported even though the accident was my fault. For a second, I kicked myself for not asking him how a body went about getting an under-the-table job before I remembered that I was Natalie, that I didn't need such a thing anymore.

This whole incident has shaken me. Now I have the numbers of five cab companies programmed into my cell phone, and I am thinking seriously that I ought to seek outside help, that I might need this so-called exorcism offered up by Pastor Maria. If I don't get some real sleep soon, I'll be no better than a fish in a frozen pond.

Another restless night. The problem is, I have a meat body, and the ghosts have dream bodies, which means I can be cooked up, I can decay from lack of sleep, I can be sliced open with my bloody guts made into a boa around my neck, I can be strapped to a chair and electrocuted and poisoned and shot, and they can't.

The bottom barrel is that I have to submit to an exorcism, I truly do, because all this not sleeping is killing me. I had figured the ghosts would go away on their own, that I would ignore them and get back to sleeping normal and then time would scab them over and they'd fall off and finally the scar would disappear completely, but instead, my dealings with them have gotten worse. So's you see why I have no choice but to get the exorcism my own pastor recommended. If ever I am to be left in peace again, I need a force greater than myself to wash these phantoms from my mind.

Oh fuck fulls, oh shit bits, what have I done . . . .What have I done! It's a mindfuck to become a new person, and so quick . . . I didn't have but a moment to catch my breath and now I am sort of confused or not sure who exactly I ought to be at this point in time and all the reasons I had to get here are muddling together in my mind, or more like the mud is all over, squished into every crevice of me . . . If only life were clean and simple the way they pretended to you it would be when you were a dopey kid . . . Come to think of it, most all my life has been one big game of pretend . . . but that's just the way the cards are stacked. The most interesting is when we pretend to ourselves, isn't that right? I have lots of experience . . . Sometimes we don't even know it. For instance, with Minnie . . . Is there a chance I suspected what was going on between her and my dear departed? There is a chance . . . but I hid it so well from myself I did not even know it . . . It's in the Mormon Jell-O, though, all those bits floating suspended in their cow hoof goo, and I have an incredible intuition . . . I can see the pineapple chunks and mandarin slices and marshmallow poufs so clearly . . . maybe this helped me hurry up and give Jim Dave what he wanted . . . I'm hungry, starving . . . Because sometimes we know even if we don't *know* . . . That fucking body in the closet. The problem with evidence is how it weighs on you, and all you can do is think about the best way to get rid of it so that it can never bother you again . . .

When I went to make my next recording, I noticed that the tape was further along than it should have been, and so I rewound a bit and found the travesty that I had recorded last night, when I was more than a little blitzed. Listening to my slurry words with the long pauses between thoughts was a revelation, and I considered recording over the mess, but I decided not to just so that anyone who might ever take a listen would be reassured of the absolute truth in my words, the complete authenticity of my project here. I am not trying to hide a thing about myself; it is like I am pouring my brain out my mouth and straight onto these tapes.

Also I checked the closet, and the suitcase is still there.

Today being Sunday, I went to the angel church to up my clout with the pastor and check in about how, exactly, an exorcism might work. There weren't angels this time – those were for special occasions – but we did make a strange, humming sort of prayer to them.

Afterwards, Pastor Maria took me aside.

"You look awful," she said, which no woman wants to hear, especially not after she's spent two and a half hours dressing up in pastel yellow everything and redoing her eyeliner three times.

I told her that I supposed I was still being haunted, an issue that I expected we could discuss.

"Well," she said, "I can see that they have a physical effect on you. I'm not sure that you'll be able to stand them much longer, the way you can't stop fidgeting."

This was news to me: I'd always thought that I made a calm, collected presence out in the congregation.

"Are you ready to schedule that thing we talked about?" she asked. "You wouldn't believe how popular it has become in the last decade or so. You'll be among good company."

I crossed my arms. "The exorcism?"

She goes, "If we have to call it that."

I don't know why, but even though I myself had come to more

or less the same conclusion, I felt averse to the idea; honestly I kept flip-flopping about whether or not I could take care of this problem on my own, the way I'd done with all the other problems in my life – *big* problems, when this was no more than a bit of insomnia. Pastor Maria saw the doubt in my eyes.

"You want to move on, don't you?" she asked me. "You want to be able to experience the angels?"

"I guess so," I said.

"Well, let's make that happen. Let's get you back to yourself."

I told her that would be fine.

We walked to the coffee shop in the same strip mall as the church so that we could talk details over strong Cuban espresso. Once we had settled at a tiny bistro table in the corner, she said, "The first step is that you must learn to think of these demons as external to yourself."

"Alright," I said, even though I didn't quite know what she meant, but I was Natalie, a smart woman who could converse on basically any topic, or who bullshitted her way through. "Even though they are inside of *my* dreams?"

"They are not fantasies of your mind," Pastor Maria said in her voice that seemed too big for her body, "but actual spirits from the devil who must be cast out."

"My dreams with the ghosts are so strange," I told her, "almost like I'm in the world, but it's warped – I mean, I can make decisions, say what I want to say, I can even influence the ghosts a little bit. It's not like sleep at all; I'm not resting."

Pastor Maria goes, "That's lucid dreaming. Buildups of stress and anxiety can bring it on, and those feelings are feeding the haunting."

I asked her if maybe they were just nightmares, but I didn't add the fact that sleeping pills only seemed to worsen their effects.

She shook her head vehemently. "From all that you've told me about them, I'm sure that they are demons. I have a lot of experience

138

with this. You would be a fool to dismiss them as dreams; if you do that, you'll be ruined when they cause you real-world problems. You'll blame it on something else because you're too afraid to believe that what happens while you are asleep can derail your life."

I thought about my fender bender, my panic attack out on the street. In a near-whisper, I asked her, "You don't think I'm crazy?" This was a fear that I had not wanted to voice, because I worried that if I thought that way too much, it might become true. And if I were crazy, I felt certain that I wouldn't be able to handle my new life, that I wouldn't have the cunning to protect myself.

"Absolutely not," Pastor Maria said, and relief warmed me. This was why I'd had to say my fear out loud: for the reassurance that it was wrong.

She goes, "I have met plenty of the possessed, and they all ask the same thing. People are disinclined to believe in ghosts, or in angels, because we worry deep down that they won't turn out to be real, which means heaven and hell might not be real, and we are not strong enough to find ourselves disappointed. You are certainly not crazy – if anything, you're less afraid, you have a stronger conviction of who you are, and so these spirits have had an easier time attaching to you." She picked up her coffee cup, but then set it down without drinking. "And because your ghosts are not simply dreams, did not come *from* you, it would be nearly impossible for you to get rid of them on your own – which is why you need the service of an" – she put air quotes around the word – "'exorcist,' my service. And I hope you also understand that they are not really your parents, not any-more, and that what we will do cannot harm your parents in the least."

Right here I might mention that I hadn't been entirely what you might call truthful about who the ghosts were. I couldn't go around telling my pastor that my ghosts were the two people whose lives I'd abruptly interrupted. Instead, I'd explained that they were my parents who had treated me terribly, and soon after they'd died, they'd come to haunt me. All my other details were truthful, though: I did say how the male ghost was blue and the female ghost was yellow and they performed noiseful lewd acts that turned them green.

Pastor Maria twirled her hand, and the barista quickly brought her another tiny coffee. She told me, "It is very common for parent spirits to shock their children with sexual acts. That is because it's immediately and viscerally horrifying, to be presented with a parent's sex, and for certain spirits, certainly for your spirits, their purpose is to horrify."

I agreed with her and asked her if we really had to perform the whole thing at my house; I didn't want the neighbors to notice anything funny.

She said, "It must happen at your house because that is where they are the most anchored." She breathed heavily into her tiny cup so that steam fogged her glasses. She goes, "And I will need you following a couple of rules. First of all, stop dressing in *their* colors; it's like you are calling to them through your clothes. Many spirits present themselves without any color at all, so I know that yours are strongly invested in their chromatic identities."

I plucked at my yellow sleeve. "I'd never thought of that," I told her.

She goes, "It's important; even underwear."

"Sure," I said, "I can do it." I dumped a spoonful of white sugar into the black thimbleful of coffee left in my cup.

She goes, "I've been trying to figure out why your ghosts are so powerfully colored, and I have a theory." She peered at me over the top of her glasses, and I wondered if I was supposed to be taking notes. "They are trying to mimic you. Your yellow hair, your blue eyes. They think that they can intimidate you through familiarity."

"Maybe," I said, unconvinced.

Then she told me the other rule: to switch my sleep pattern. She said, "Sleep only during the day, when the sun is in full force. Say, from eight in the morning until four in the afternoon. Then make sure you're up the rest of the time. This will confuse them. They only visit you at night, yes? When you're sleeping? We want to throw them off. It will weaken their hold over you, weaken their powers." She scribbled something on a piece of paper and slid it over to me. "If you have trouble staying awake, I want you working through exercises on my website." She tapped the folded paper. "Watch the videos. Do the work. It will help prepare you."

And when I asked her at what point I ought to start my new routine, she said, "Right away. Immediately. Stay up tonight, watch some of my videos, then go to bed with the sun. Maybe buy blackout curtains, if that will help."

I didn't know about that; I wondered out loud if the curtains would help the ghosts by tricking them into thinking it was nighttime.

Pastor Maria goes, "Natalie, they're not inside your brain. The spirits might be haunting you, but they aren't *you*. Understand? I know these mandates might sound strange, but I hope with all my heart that you will follow them. They'll make my job so much simpler and ease the transition into the next world for your spirits."

"I'll do it," I said, and like a friend, she covered my hand with hers.

She goes, "Now, if you will please e-pay over half the funds before Monday so that I can buy all the supplies I need and also cover my expenses. Follow what we've talked about very closely, alright? I'll be seeing you soon."

As soon as I got home, first thing I did was I threw out all my blue and yellow clothes. I hesitated over the green ones, but in the end I decided to add those to the pile. Better safe than sorry.

Now it's nearly ten o'clock, growing close to my regular bedtime, and I don't feel tired; I'm determined to stay up all night, until the full body of the sun has risen in the sky.

NINE WAYS TO COOK AN EGG

Now it's well past midnight, the first night of my wakefulness, and I decided I'd better start another tape to keep my eyelids from drooping. I stayed alert by straightening up the house, and then I attempted to watch television, but it has never much interested me. I can't take the artificiality of it, how everything is reduced to flatness. For a while I sat there, staring out a slit in the curtains at the fat moon and trying to place the strange feeling in my gut, which finally I did: déjà vu. It took me a long time to remember, but it was night, and time was what I had plenty of, so eventually I dug up the moment when I had felt this way before. It had been back when I was a little girl and the plane had crashed into my house at the same moment I'd crashed my stick plane into my dollhouse. The power that I'd felt back then was, for some reason, niggling again inside my guts.

When you got right down to the bottom of things, it was my witchiness, awakened, the same way it had been in the moment that I'd become Natalie. The idea of an exorcism frightened me, but it also enthralled me, because it would be like a spell, one cast especially for me. The pilot hadn't died that day the plane blasted into my childhood home, but he'd been covered in the chemicals that he'd been spraying over the soybean fields, and his brain had been addled. After that, everyone said, he was like a monster, a man possessed. I had sometimes imagined him as a giant marionette, me holding the strings, as if the incident had put him permanently under my spell.

Overall, I rather liked the feeling, a knot of excitement tightening there in my stomach.

I decided to surf around on the computer, and the first thing I noticed was that, even though it was one o'clock in the morning, Sallie's little icon floated there, ready to chat. I waited five minutes, so's I wouldn't seem desperate, and then I typed, *Hi.*

While I hoped for her to respond, I scrolled through the posts from my electronic friends, things like casseroles and ice cream sundaes and wet cats and grandbabies dressed like cabbages. By now, the church ladies no longer wanted to meet for coffee. I was never tagged in their posts, the way I had been before. A few of them had blocked me entirely, and they had stopped sending me messages asking when I was coming back to church, except for one, that small-hearted Lottie, who wrote, *Could it be possible that you are still letting that Deedee woman stay with you? I saw her hanging around in your complex. She looks like a charity case if ever there was one. But you have to know that the best thing for you both is that you bring her back on Sunday. We have the Christmas decorations up. God is watching, especially when you make wrong choices. Come back, okay?*

Of course all this was a necessary change. I was a new woman, and I needed my church to reflect that.

Sallie still had not replied to my greeting, so I decided to try a little experiment. I concentrated on my witchiness, on my powers, drawing Sallie to me, and finally, it worked: my computer dinged with Sallie's message. *ur up late*, it said.

So are you.

well its hard, w/a little kid. i havnt been sleeping much lately.

Right. How is your baby?

almost five now.

I waited, but she didn't answer my question, so I tried, *I love the new haircut. Anything else new with you? I know I always like to change my hair to mark other kinds of changes.*

Her reply was such a battery of words that I sat there, gobsmacked, unable to type anything to stop it. Her messages hit one after another:

who are you anyway?

why are you messaging to me in the middle of the night?

are you a reporter?

seriously stop bothering me

i have a family my own family im doing my own thing you have

*no idea what my childhood was like i cant stand you. quit fishing i am
not telling you shit!!!!!*

Finally the words stopped coming. At least Sallie had learned her
lesson and wasn't going to speak with the scavenging reporters any
longer, but she was obviously in a fragile emotional state. *I'm not a
reporter*, I typed carefully. *I thought you were this hairstylist I knew, and
I just wanted to chat with you.*

A minute and then two vanished in the digital clock at the bottom of my computer screen.

really? Sallie typed. *my dream job lol*

*Yeah. Sorry to make you so upset. I didn't know you had the wrong
impression about me.*

She goes, *there's nothing else going on with you?*

I wrote, *Haha I hope not. I just get lonely living so far away from the
place I know.*

ok sorry i had a really bad day. i shouldnt have taken it out on you.

What's wrong? I wrote. *Why are reporters bugging you? Are you on tv
or something?*

if you really dont know, i dont want to tell you. She followed this with
a series of little yellow faces: shocked and confused and then smiling.
So strange that we can sense emotion from a teensy three-stroke
picture.

That's fair, I typed, but really I felt miffed that she'd cut off this
arm of the conversation. If I pressed her on what I wanted to know
now, she'd get suspicious and stop chatting with me entirely. *How is
the weather where you live? It's warm here, kind of weirdly warm.*

where do u live

At first I typed *Mexico*, but then I deleted that and tried again. I might actually want to skip down to Mexico someday. *Morocco*, I sent.

wow! morocco! i am hella jealous i've never been out of the country dont even have my passport but it would be thriller to actually do something someday. think of all the places there are to go.

I wrote, *Too many.*

so are you american though? i guess youre not up late, just early haha

I used to live in Beamus Point. That was where Sallie lived now. *Sometimes I get a little nostalgic and go reminiscing on the internet. That's how I found your profile.*

thats so cool, Sallie wrote. *you escaped.*

After that, she didn't respond anymore, not when I asked her again about the weather or if she knew the best shampoo to get your hair dye to last longer. Now I know that this might be confusing, mostly because of the way people think about motherhood and all that, the pedestal we prop women atop because this one time their uterus expanded and contracted and expelled out a person, but don't go thinking that these messages meant I wanted to take back my role of ma or gramma; I was no longer Mary Ellen, who hadn't been given the chance to be an exceptional gramma to begin with; that woman was a ghost. The truth is I had been on a fact-finding mission when I'd decided to message Sallie, and it had turned out an utter failure.

Feeling like a farmer trying to sleep in, all out of sorts from the change in my routine, I shut down the computer, shut down Sallie, and then I reached for these tapes. I believe they must be my favorite pastime.

When the morning after my first intentionally sleepless night arrived, exhaustion had seeped into my bones. I'd kept awake by eating lots of popcorn and refilling the potpourri. Sometimes a phantom smell of rotting flesh would curl through my nostrils, but I felt pretty sure it wasn't really there.

When I finally fell into bed around eight this morning, I let the sun wash through the curtains and lap against my toes. I put a pillow over my head and went straight to sleep, the black weightless kind where you get done your best rest.

I stayed that way for some time before the ghosts came.

"Oh geez," I said, sitting up, the pillow falling from my face. Only I don't think I was actually doing this; I think I was pretty much sleeping, having one of those too vivid dreams that keeps me hovering on the edge of waking until I bolt upright into hours of sleeplessness. "How are you around every morning, noon, and night? Don't you hate the sun?"

"It's okay," Jim Dave said. "We're not totally nocturnal."

I pressed him. "But it makes you a little uncomfortable. Right? The sun."

"Not much more than you. Look – your toes are getting burned." He pointed one thick blue finger, and it was true: my toes were turning pinkish.

The yellow ghost said, "We're here to tell you to not go through with this exorcism business."

"If you're afraid of it, then it's definitely what I ought to do," I said.

"We'll be unharmed," the Mary Ellen ghost said, "but you – it would be easy for you to get damaged. Most exorcists don't know what they're doing. I've heard horror stories, let me tell you. The patient bites off her own tongue. Or wakes up deranged."

"Aren't we deranged anyhow?" I said. "If we need an exorcist?"

"Not any more than the rest," the ghosts said. "If people don't have ghosts yet, they will soon, and then they'll be just like you."

"Pastor Maria was right," I said, trying to convince myself of this. After all, I'd followed her strange directives, but still the ghosts had come to me. "I need to get rid of you."

The yellow ghost sidled up to Jim Dave and wrapped a hand through his. "If you go through with it," she said, "you'll wind up with us forever. You'll cleave us to yourself, and we won't ever be allowed to go free."

"It's a political move or something here in the ghost state." Jim Dave shrugged. "To try and get the exorcisms to stop. Like a zero-tolerance policy, what we were told. Exorcism equals hauntings forever."

The other ghost said, "But maybe you want us to be with you all the time? You like us? Secretly? Because we make you less lonely."

When she said this, my toes felt like they were on fire, like the sun had snuck in and tickled them. I worried that the yellow ghost might be a kind of sideways right: maybe the ghosts had come to me in the first place because I didn't fit into everyone else's world, because maybe the space for witches and ghosts was different than the space for everyone else.

"We think you better stop it," Jim Dave said, "the exorcism, 'cause we don't want to be stuck staring at you for eternity. We want to go off and have ourselves a good time, Natalie and me."

"Who's Natalie?" I said, staring at the yellow ghost as she licked a green line up the arm of the blue ghost.

She put her tongue back in her mouth, looking confused.

I told them, "Seems to me Mary Ellen is the one that died. I mean, I'm Natalie; I'm here, alive. That yellow thing – that's Mary Ellen. You're just back to fucking your wife, Jim Dave." Then I awoke with a gasp, my heart hammering, and though I lay there till evening, spent as a mouse's corncob, I couldn't fall back asleep.

I admit that at first I'd thought Pastor Maria's rules were silly, but obviously my ghosts were scared. They wanted to avoid that exorcism like a drink from a poisoned well, but I wouldn't let them run me off it.

It was strange, having only a few hours between waking and night. I took my time putting myself together, redid my lipstick twice, then stood at the window, watching the middling sun sink lower until it changed color to the pink and orange of its setting. I might have bought a place closer to the beach, where the sound of the ocean would help me fall to sleep and the sunsets would be more brilliant – but of course I'd made a lot of dumb mistakes in the past.

Full night left me feeling more comfortable. And even though I had only been awake for a couple of hours, the evening darkness made it seem like I ought to have a drink, and so I poured the golden chardonnay into a fancy glass and admired its color: the yellow of my essential self, the exact same color as it would be when I peed it out.

It was about then I started to feel quite different. Like my hand, for instance, holding the glass: it looked like an alien hand. Skinnier than I remembered, and sinewy, and just sort of wizened-up *old*. I became aware of a steady grinding from my insides, like bits of my bones had broken off and were rubbing together within my soft stomach. All this to say, I didn't much feel like *me*, and this got me off to wondering who I really was. I'd changed greatly; I mean, I am a bona fide new person. Such a transformation takes time to adjust to, I suppose.

I dug out the scrap of paper Pastor Maria had given me with her website address and prepared to spend some hours working through her videos and exercises; I figured that maybe if I did enough of them, the ghosts wouldn't ruin my next sleep. But as soon as I logged on, I found that I had to pay for everything, as if her website were some sort of slot machine, needing to be constantly fed. Short videos, a dollar plus tax, plus a "service fee." Longer videos, five dollars. Five dollars! She'd told me that working through her website would prepare me for the exorcism, which I was already paying for; what a way to cash in. Maybe I could incorporate some of her techniques into my bingo scheme. Sell lucky daubers, five dollars each, or You-Tube classes on how to manage six bingo cards at once.

I paid a dollar plus tax plus fees; I watched Maria's video on breathing tips in preparation for an exorcism, which did not mention ghosts until the very end, when her voice-over accompanied a shad-owy image of what she said was a ghost, though it looked much more blob-ish than mine, and she explained how demons, like angels, do not have lungs, although because they do have the impulse to breathe, they may want to mimic our breath, and so it was possible, if you were skilled enough, to control them with the way you took in air.

Then the video ended. If I wanted to learn a new set of breathing exercises that would allow me to exert control over spirits, I had to pay for a five-dollar video.

I paid.

Carefully I watched to try and learn these new skills, but then I had an angry thought: how could I control my breathing while I was asleep? When sleeping, breathing became automatic; it couldn't be any other way.

Frustrated, I clicked off her website, and in the rabbit-hole way of the internet, I stumbled upon clip after clip of people claiming to film their ghosts. None of them looked right, though; none of them had colors or held conversations with the haunted. Probably the people making those videos were plain crazy – they accompanied the clips with theories about God, such as he was a bowl of pasta, or the final step in a giant assembly line; or pictures of their babies' birthmarks, which looked like regular birthmarks to me, but had been labeled as brands from Satan.

None of this struck me as useful, but at least the web held my attention – it keeps me nearly as wakeful as making these recordings does. I checked Facebook: Sallie wasn't on to chat, but she had posted a flurry of new photos of her face, this time done up in dark lipstick with black lines around her eyes. I wondered if she did Mae's face up too, or if she knew it was off for a little girl like that to look like a raccoon.

I've started checking mepodcast.net every day, sometimes twice a day, to see if anything new has been posted; I don't know why my fingertips tingle with anxiety every time I peck in the website address, but I was feeling like if there wasn't a new episode soon, then something terrible must have happened, something that could break open the case, and here I am, the last to know.

Only just now, I finally found what I'd been searching for, a new entry. Let's go ahead and see what sort of doozy is in store for me this time.

Your host here with my latest episode of NEXT TO MY NECK OF THE WOODS. I'm so glad you're joining me because this new evidence is truly wild, a real Code Three. Welcome to our fourth episode, IS THERE A BLACK WIDOW IN OUR MIDST?

I don't recommend starting in the middle, so if you don't already know about Mary Ellen Washie, the fifty-five-year-old Chautauqua County resident who disappeared after her own husband turned up murdered, then I recommend you go back to the beginning. Because now it seems that this potential black widow has also caused the death of her rival, her late husband's mistress, Minnie Pearson, by sending an anonymous note to Mrs. Pearson's own apparently volatile hus —

What is this? I feel just about mashed, I'm peeled and boiled and steaming in the pot. I've got to rewind, make sure my ears are on straight.

-five-year-old Chautauqua County resident who disappeared after her own husband turned up murdered, then I recommend you go back to the beginning. Because now it seems that this potential

black widow has also caused the death of her rival, her late husband's mistress, Minnie Pearson, by sending an anonymous note to Mrs. Pearson's own apparently volatile husband.

What had old Don Pearson done to her? I'd once seen him skin a live rabbit, the creature squealing like a newborn. The thing was, I'd only ever seen this man twice in my life.

Your host is deeply saddened that another DB has shown up in this case, especially since Mrs. Pearson was a recent new acquaintance. As outlined in a previous pod, your host had promised Mrs. Pearson to hold UNK her identity as Sweet Pea, the former mistress of Jim Dave Washie, but this confidentiality does not carry over into post-life.

What do we know about the anonymous letter? It was seized by our boys in blue soon after they discovered the body of Mrs. Pearson. The letter, addressed to Mr. Pearson, contained inflammatory remarks about the alleged affair between Mr. Washie and Mrs. Pearson. The letter was detailed, with descriptions of the two married individuals "going at it every morning, noon, and night." It also insulted Mr. Pearson for being a cuckold and mocked the fact that he could not take his revenge on Mr. Washie, since the man was already deceased. The letter was printed on white copy paper from a computer printer — in fact, thanks to advances in technology, we know it was printed on an HP LaserJet Pro. While there was no return address, your host assumes that the authorities are tracing the origin of the canceled stamp.

Oh shit, I am looking now at the printer beside my computer setup and mine matches this description . . .

Your host is not alone in the thought that this letter was likely scribed by Mary Ellen Washie. Her own daughter, Sallie Blackburn, has said on the record, "Unfortunately I can't think of anyone else who would have much of a motive."

How could Sallie keep talking? I got to admit, it rankled me.

Maybe I could bring it up, sly-like, next time we chatted.

At this point, it seems extremely unlikely that Mr. Pearson was Mr. Washie's murderer, and Mary Ellen Washie has long been suspected in her husband's demise — this letter increases that suspicion. She was a woman with motive to write the letter. Of course doing so when she is obviously in hiding is far from the smartest criminal move — though not one that your host finds unfathomable. In fact, your host has discussed the possibilities with the CC-Squareds, excuse me, my group of friends, and all fingers point to the missing woman. It was an exciting conversation, a real departure from the usual chitchat about recipes and whose kid can draw the best stick figure. Who would have thought we'd have a black widow right next to our neck of the woods. Your host can only assume that this new evidence is sufficient enough that the case will be TOT a federal agency.

Thanks be I'm sitting because I have keeled over. At least our little host has finally given herself away. The CC-Squareds, or rather the Chautauqua County C-Cups, are what a particular gaggle of women, most of them married to county police officers and all allegedly natural C-cups, call themselves. They pretend their group name is a big secret, but every one of them blabs any chance she gets. I just know that our little host let that one slip because it makes her feel sexy and popular, like high school didn't end for her two decades before. Minnie was forever trying to get in with them, even though she was flat as a plank. At least she got one small wish fulfilled before passing over, she'd gotten herself interesting to a CC-Squared. I don't know these women by anything more than sight, as they studiously ignored my D-cup existence unless I mispacked their groceries, but look at them now, obsessed with me, the old me. Well, a CC-Squared . . . I see why the podcast's police tips have been pouring in so easily.

Beneath the podcast there's a new section, or at least one that

I've never noticed before, where listeners leave their comments. I might as well check through it; I have all night. Here goes.

XTINAXOXO: *How dare she kill her own husband when they promised to love and cherish one another?*
DARKELVIRA: *maybe HE killed HER you dipshit xoxo*
XTINAXOXO: *How would he kill her he's already dead?*
mumstheword5: *what does she mean TOT something about toddlers?*
DARKELVIRA: *he killed hher BEFORE he shot himself*
eyehartdisney: *@mumstheword5 its cop jargon Turned Over To dont you know how to use google*
DR_WHOEVER: *This must be some backwater place everyone killing each other*
JACK67: *so this man finds out his wife is having an affair with a dead man and he kills her? the wife?*
DR_WHOEVER: *necrophilia is legal*
CROSS2BARE: *This washie woman must be pure evil. I would like to string her up on a flagpole by her stupid hair.*
SKYNNYMARGE: *The husband is the one who killed this lady! All the other one did was write a letter. Why don't you people ever blame the man?*
HPPYMAMA: *this had nothing to do with parenting please i thnk the link is broke*
DARWIN11: *men might be superior beings but they are also prone to voilance and anger, that is just nature*
DOUGSMOM: *son wont stop biting my behind very strange any advice thanks*
SOLESIGH: *We should witchunt this Washy and sew her vagina shut so no man ever wants her again*

Well, the comments go on. All these threats against Mary Ellen don't concern me as much as maybe you would think; I'm distant enough from that person to feel not bothered in the least.

I had turned off the tape recorder as I skimmed the rest of the comments, and while reading through laymen's ideas on the wiliness of women and toddler sexual awakening, I had a thought, or more like a distant, submerged memory. With a strange and heavy feeling in my gut, I searched through my files on the computer – receipts, old tax stuff, something labeled "MC" – and then I found it. A document saved with a jumble of letters, "owiuarnw." It was a note addressed to Don Pearson about his wife's affair. I looked at the date – just a pair of weeks after I had become my current self, Natalie, when I was still working on building up my tolerance, being as much of Natalie as I could, which meant martinis at brunch. There were some hours from those days that had blinked out of my memory, so's it was possible that I'd written this, I mean, there it was on my computer, but the question was *why*. Had I expected Don Pearson to go off on Minnie, or to kill her, even? But a letter couldn't do that, of course.

A letter from a witch, though; that was something else entirely. Maybe I'd cast a spell on the letter, or dropped a fallen eyelash into the envelope.

I hope I didn't lick the stamp. They could do strange things with DNA nowadays.

It surprises me how talking into this thing and making the recording here allows me to tease out my own thoughts. How much would I be thinking over anything if I didn't have to figure out how to get the words out of my mouth? Also, I just checked the stamp drawer – they're stick-on, thanks be.

DIGESTIVE PROPERTIES OF ROUGHAGE

So's the strangest thing has happened to me: in the middle of the day, when I was dead asleep, this loud knocking wakes me. I throw myself together and tiptoe to the peephole and there's this lanky young man standing there glaring at the door as if he could see straight through it. I checked the dead bolt even though I knew for certain it was locked and then hightailed it back to bed.

Well, about three hours later, evening coming on, me with my first pitcher mixed, there he is at the door again, banging away! Says he can tell I'm in there and he's not leaving until I let him in.

At first I ignored him, but he started making the kind of racket that might incite the neighbors to call the cops, and since the last thing I needed in here were pigs wandering around, peeking in closets, I made the better of worse decisions and let him in.

He said hello and shut the door carefully behind him. He looked like maybe he wanted to kill me, his eyes narrowed and red-rimmed, his hands shoved into the pockets of his rayon jacket, even though the evening was warm. I had the wild thought that my ghosts had infected him, that they'd wormed into his brain and put there the idea to murder me before I could complete my exorcism.

"Can I help you?" I said, trying to make my voice big.

He fidgeted a little more, standing against the door so's I couldn't escape. Finally he said, "I'm Natalie's son, Natalie Heap's. Son."

I swear to you it seemed as if the lights went out a little bit. It must've been my vision flickering. I'd fallen into some huge miscalculation, some trickster lie. For certain I'd been found out: here I was, monochrome matching with my makeup perfect, but no son would be able to see his mother in another woman. That was why he was looking at me so funny.

Only then he said, "You're her, aren't you? Natalie. My mother."

"Well," I said, my voice growing stronger, "I *am* Natalie Heap."

"I'm certain it's you. I've been looking for you for ages." His narrowed eyes opened wide with hope. A twitch bothered his left cheek. "You gave up a baby boy thirty-four years ago, right?"

I let my mouth hang open. Catching flies, my mother would've said. She'd been obsessed with appearances, with slimness and beauty, with pinching fatty bits between tongs.

"This was back in California." He seemed inclined to recite facts until I agreed with him. "You would've been twenty-four. I had red hair at first." He touched the top of his balding head, his fine and wispy hair. "I was born a little early."

"Huh," I said. Natalie had hated children, I mean, *I* had hated children, never had one, thanks be, but maybe that could have been a lie? Or maybe the birth had been blocked from memory, like a trauma? Or maybe having a baby and giving it up hadn't really counted.

He goes, in a voice quite trembly for a man, just like this: "I mean, of course it's you. I did my research. I did it thoroughly." He pulled his hands out of his pockets, and I realized he wanted a hug.

And I was feeling relieved enough that I figured I ought to give it to him. He hadn't found me out; I was safe. In fact, I was more than safe: "Yes," I said, "of course it's me." I squeezed him and felt the air that had been in his lungs whoosh out into my ear.

"Mom," he said, and I let go. "Or maybe I should call you Natalie?"

I told him yes, Natalie was better.

He stood there, kind of squinting, and it shocked me to notice the resemblance between us, the way our nose and mouth fit together the same. I squirmed, somehow feeling again that deep ache between my legs. I had a son; I'd always wondered about having a son, about how strange it would be to make a little man inside a woman's body.

To rid us of the awkward silence, I said, "Would you care to join me for a drink? I just mixed some; there's plenty."

We sat in the living room and took sips of our martinis to make it look as if we had a purpose. I felt determined not to say the wrong thing, which meant I didn't much open my mouth.

"I grew up in California," he chattered. "In Oakland, back before people actually wanted to live there. I'm a Czakowitz, now. Marcus Czakowitz. When I found out your last name was Heap, well, I was so jealous. My last name has always been the bane of my existence. Heap seems so much easier."

"Kids still find ways to make fun of it," I said, remembering a story. "They would push you in the dirt and yell, 'You're a heap of dust!' or 'Your butt is a heap!' or things like that."

He laughed into his hand; I laugh this way too. Any lingering doubts that he wasn't who he said he was began to melt away. "Yeah," he said, "kids." Then he went all still and serious. "I don't have any. I've always wanted them. I guess I haven't . . . found the right girl. Or sometimes I worry that what happened to me – not that I'm blaming you at all, Mom, of course not – but that what happened to me has made me unfit. You know, as a parent. Like I couldn't handle it, somehow."

The way he spoke sent a chill up my arm, not unlike the feeling I got when the ghosts entered my dreams. Then I remembered something: "Didn't I see you around near here before?" I asked.

After a bit more prodding, I got him to admit that yes, he had been trampling my perennials.

"Well, I'm glad that was you," I said, and I truly was: the lanky creeper outside my window had meant me no harm, after all. "You gave me a start. I'd thought it might be . . . somebody else."

With real concern in his voice, he asked me who, but I told him it was no one to worry about. "I wasn't even sure myself," I said, the truth. I wanted to ask what he'd been spying for – some proof that I was his mother? But it seemed like he might have already believed that. He must've been looking for signs of who I really was. Was it a regular sort of woman who had thrown him away, or was it a strange woman, a broken woman? Where had he come from, really? It was an understandable impulse.

Pretty soon after that he left, asking if he could come back to visit, seeing as he'd moved to a town nearby a few months earlier. Right before he shut the door behind him, he said, "How come you never accepted my friend request on Facebook? I just wanted to see a few things about you. Nevermind – I'm sorry. That was your prerogative."

"Goodbye, now," I told him.

He goes, "I don't like goodbyes, I really don't, so I won't give you one. I'll just see you again." And then he fled with the giddiness of someone who'd finally gotten the thing they'd been desperately wanting. On the entryway table, I found a piece of paper scribbled with a phone number and a message: *Yours faithfully, Marcus, (your son), call anytime.* What a sad little penguin of a man.

Glad to be alone again, I went to the computer with a martini and opened the file labeled "MC." Right away I found it, a pile of secrets. Saved there were a couple of emails from Mrs. Czakowitz from ten years before, and scans of pictures of a little redheaded baby. There was also an article from an online university newspaper, some section titled "Ask the People," and there was a picture of Marcus beneath a quote that said, "No, I don't believe that anyone should be vegetarian. I think it makes you sickly and weak. And then if something happens, you know, a plane crash, a war or something, we'll have to take care of all the vegetarians who probably won't survive anyway because they won't be able to eat the deer or whatever we're killing to survive off of in those dire circumstances." So my son must've gone to college.

I opened the emails from Mrs. Czakowitz. The first one read,

Dear Ms. Heap,

I hope you are doing well. I know it's strange for me to contact you this way, or to contact you at all, but I thought it best for me to keep you informed of things that happen that might affect you and your life. Basically what has happened is this: Marcus has found out that he is adopted. You wouldn't think that it would be such a horrible shock for a boy of twenty-three, but Marky has always been delicate in this way specific to him. Not a physical delicacy, which we were worried about (unnecessarily), him being premature, but a mental one, where he can get fixated on certain slights, or on ways he thinks the world has wronged him. He sees being adopted as a detriment, which you and I both know is not at all true, that being adopted is instead a beautiful miracle sanctioned by God.

Of course, according to your wishes, I have not told Marky anything about you, though he has asked and asked. I pretend like I don't know. He also asks about his biological father, and I simply and truthfully tell him that I know nothing about that person. Anyhow, if you wanted to talk to him, or if you wanted to ask me any questions about this, I would be more than happy to revise our original agreement for the benefit of Marky.

Your acquaintance,
Mrs. Herman Czakowitz

Then, a few months later:

Dear Ms. Heap,

I am writing again to check in and update you on Marky, who has been really quite distraught since he found out that he is adopted and not my biological child. I understand (or think I do) why you did not reply to my last note, and I don't expect you to reply to this one, unless you can find it in your heart to comfort a boy who has started to think of you, though a stranger, as a sort of mother figure to him.

I don't believe that I told you last time the circumstances of Marky finding out about his adoption. In fact, this was quite humiliating to me, since he discovered my old medical records. He is quite the curious boy, always pawing through things he shouldn't, like his Christmas presents. He read over all the things I tried to do to conceive, way back when. It is an ordeal I would never wish on anyone, to discuss one's own fertility with one's son. But of course God did not bless my husband and I in that way, though I am not saying we weren't blessed in many other ways, certainly.

It pains me that, all of a sudden, Marky is putting such weight in being a biological offspring to someone, when we are all children of God. Before he knew anything, it was never an issue. He has begged me for any little tidbit of information about you, but don't worry, I haven't given in. But if you would talk with him, just for a while, then I would be forever grateful. It's difficult for a mother to watch her son suffer, especially when she knows that she has exactly what he wants.

> *Your acquaintance,*
> *Mrs. Herman Czakowitz*

It didn't look like Mrs. Herman Czakowitz had ever received a reply, but obviously Marcus had been burning after his biological mother for the whole decade that followed, seeing as he'd shown up at my door and practically thrown himself on me. I hoped he wouldn't come back, but I knew that of course he would, and then I would have to deal with him. Even though he was technically my son, I felt no desire or obligation to share my life with him. I'd given him up, after all: there was a reason for that. Every mother has her secrets; every mother longs to be left alone. My own mother had been beautiful and cold, not crazy at all, but she had worked so hard to maintain herself for her career that she'd had little time for me. I understood.

Since I was on the computer already, I logged into Facebook and saw that Sallie was on, and she'd posted even more pictures. She must take them every morning, noon, and night.

I typed to her, *Have you ever heard of someone getting an exorcism?*

She replied right away. *no . . . why is that something they do in morocco*

I puzzled over that Morocco for a split second before I remembered I'd told her that I lived there. *Yep*, I typed, *and I'm thinking about getting one. It might be interesting.*

you should do it nothing interesting ever happens around here you should get those while you can

But don't you think it could be scary?

if its not a lil bit scary then probably theyre not doing it right. the whole think is about demons right? so getting them out would be scary

She had a point. I wondered what she'd think if she knew that the demon was her father – really, her father and mother both. Jim Dave and Mary Ellen banished. I warmed at the thought.

tell me about it after, she sent me.

Okay definitely. You really don't think that anything interesting ever happens to you? I thought you said you'd been talking to reporters? Though that sounds like a bad idea really. They are a rotten bunch.

who the hell said ive been talking to reporters

You did, last time we chatted.

i would never say that

I scrolled up through our chat and saw it, right there. *You said reporters had been bugging you.*

oh sure, she wrote, *but i def do not want to talk to them.*

She was like a puzzle with a piece missing; based off all the pictures she took of herself, her goal seemed to be to become two-bit famous, and I doubted she would turn down the chance to sell herself to the tabloids. She had not been this way before; social media must have warped her. *I'm glad you can avoid the gossip and live your life,* I sent her, doing my best. *Reporters are all jerks and liars.*

well life has nothing exciting for me just tragedy

I figured that she was finally going to tell me something useful. Excitedly I typed, *Oh no. What is it?*

She sent a bunch of sad faces and a teardrop. *you dont want to know.*

She was obviously fishing; she'd always been a transparent girl. *I do!! You can tell me.*

But instead of reveal a tidbit about the case, she goes, *nothing much. just that i can never get together tuiton to go to cosmetology school the semester starts soon but I will never get there I should give up now save me the hope*

All she ever thought about was her own self. Lack of funds was the thing topmost in her mind even while her own mother was missing without a trace. I wrote, *How long have you been wanting to go to beauty school?* So far as I knew, this was a recent dream and would likely go the way of her community college plans and her coin collection. Which is to say, in the trash.

ive wanted to be a hair artist forever rmemeber when you mistaked me for one that made me so happy

I figured I might as well try and get something out of her that I was at least mildly curious to know. *Aren't you married though? Doesn't your husband support the family?*

I waited a long time, and then finally she sent, *my man he does his best but dont you think it is important sometimes to be an independent woman or at least know how to be have some sort of ur own life*

I did not feel like giving her advice, seeing as she'd never taken any I'd dished out before, but of course we didn't have at all the same sort of relationship anymore. We were equals now, just two lonely adult women connecting over the net. I settled on some dumb platitudes, *You'll figure it out, pull yourself up by your bootstraps, these things take time*, and she kept sending pictures of crossed fingers and broken hearts. She had always done this, showed her underbelly when it would have been smarter to raise some hackles.

Finally, she wrote something curious: *this is all so stupid too b/c my dad he told me he would help with my tuiton but now he cant and im screwed its so hard to do everythng on your own*

It bothered me that Sallie and Jim Dave had been talking. I'd been under the impression that Sallie and her father had not spoken to each other for months or even a year before he'd died, but I must have been wrong. I didn't like finding out these sorts of things, these secrets about Jim Dave, because they made me worry that I hadn't really known him.

Sallie wrote, *sorry for dumping all this on you i guess i needed to get it out i have no one to talk to here* followed by a sad face.

I figured, I wrote. *Maybe you miss your own ma and so it builds up.*

lol, Sallie goes, *i had my lasst straw w/her years back.*

Before I could think of a milder way to write it, I sent, *What are you talking about?*

Sallie goes, *my mom practically kicked me out my own house she wanted to stick my pa in my old room, so my mom did everything she could to get me to move out w/my bf. like it was unbearable there w/her fighting w/my pa and stuff always breaking and i had to go to a better environmnt*

Sallie had it all wrong, but of course I couldn't call her on it. I'd always tried to keep the house running for her sake, but there was only so much I could do what with my jobs and zero help from her pa. I'd had no idea that she was going to move out until her room was already packed, and by that point of course it made a barrel of sense to put Jim Dave in there. I wrote, *You didn't want to leave home so early?*

it was necessary is what i'm sayin, practically i was asked to leave.

For a moment, I started to feel pretty bad, but then I reminded myself about how manipulative Sallie could be, how she was using these words to trick me into feeling sorry for her for something that didn't happen. Well, I was no fool; I wouldn't be had.

Sallie wrote, *which is why i'm so careful around my own girl let her know home is always a nice safe space*

It dawned on me that the reason I'd rarely seen my grandkid was because Sallie had kept Mae from me on purpose. I had just figured she was too caught up with her family, her goof of a boyfriend, to see me. She never had been good at expressing herself.

With all the fighting you and that boyfriend of yours do that would be impossible, I typed, but then I deleted it; I didn't send it. I let the tiny bit of hurt I felt at Sallie's misunderstanding wash away in the next sip of my martini. It was a blessing, really, to not have to deal with all of the Mary Ellen shit anymore, to step away from it, let it go.

Just like any mother, I would want what's best for my daughter, but as I thought about her, she seemed so distant from me, like she really was just a series of letters typed on a screen. I hadn't seen her for nearly a year, hadn't heard her voice, and all the pictures she posted didn't even look like her, or not the scrub-faced brown-haired kid from my other life. Plus, she was so sad, and a liar. When she'd first come out of me, I could feel the hole she'd left behind, like an actual cavern inside of me, and it pretty much only felt better when I pressed her against my skin. But I didn't have that hole in me, not anymore. I mean, at this point, who I was now, I'd never had that hole to begin with.

THE FORMATION OF CALCIUM

Last night I drank myself down into another brief blink of forgetful-
ness; I got to the point in my bottle where I decided that it would be
more useful to keep going. You see, I'm tired to death lately, and this
blink of a reprieve is so refreshing that it overtakes my headache.
Afterwards, when I awake from the stupor, I don't feel sleepy for
hours and hours, which is worth quite a lot, in my book.

But there is a dangerous side to not remembering. When I awoke,
I checked my phone, and it looks like I called that little shit Marcus
while I was on the blink. I tried hard to recall what I'd said to him,
but all that I could glean was a half-memory of a seashell whoosh in
my ear: the phone breathing. I am not going to panic; I am simply
going to trust in myself that I wouldn't do anything to harm my
evolving life; in any state, altered or not, I am too smart for that.

The whole condo reeks of the cigarette butts that I'd left in wine-
glasses on the windowsill, the kitchen counter, the edge of the tub.

Tomorrow is my exorcism, and all I can think about is sleep and how
much of it I'm going to get in the dead of night, dead to the world,
sleeping like the dead, the eternal sleep . . . I never realized before
how many sayings we have that knot together sleep and death.
Maybe that's why my ghosts inhabit my dreams.

Well, I am raring to recount what happened with my exorcism here.
The outcome was as unexpected as planting a petunia and growing
a frog, truly.

Pastor Maria came to the door alone and wheeling two small

suitcases. I thought that she'd have some kind of entourage, or at least an assistant, but it actually felt better to see her there on her own. I'd smeared half a stick of concealer beneath my eyes and dressed up; I had cheese on little toothpicks arranged on a plate in the kitchen.

But the pastor wanted to get straight to work, so I led her to the bedroom, where she figured the spirits were lurking.

While she dug through her suitcases, I asked her, "How did you get into this business in the first place? Angels and ghosts, it's a strange combination . . . "

She goes, "Not at all; not at all. If I get too close to the devil, dealing with spirits, I'll be pulled back by the angels. You see? It's a balance. *Gracias a Dios*, I see both angels and demons every week. All of life should be a balance. That's one thing they never understood in Cuba."

"Never understood where I'm from, either," I told her. "Probably never understood anywhere." Then I asked her what I had been wondering: if she thought that everyone else had ghosts, too, or would get some eventually.

She goes, "Certainly a greater percentage of the population is afflicted than you would first guess, but all of us? I would say that's a stretch. I wouldn't have time for anything else if that were true."

She wanted to know if I had stuck to my color-coded wardrobe – she complimented me on the burgundy wraparound dress I was wearing – and the reversed sleep pattern, and I told her yes, that I had done an excellent job; I was ready for a blue-ribbon exorcism. I sat on the edge of the bed as Pastor Maria hummed contentedly while she set up her paraphernalia all around me. There were vials of liquid and a camera tripod and crystals and a little elephant carved out of wood. It kind of reminded me of bingo setups, like that day when I'd first met Natalie – first met myself? – and we both had our little lucky setups arranged around our cards to help us win big. My Elvis snow globe – what ever had happened to that? I must have thrown it out when I stepped into this new life, just the way I'd had to get rid of everything else, the tiny "baby's first" spoon with the porcelain handle, my saggy old underwear, the picture of Sallie and Mae that I'd burned in the sink, my relationships, my memories, and now here I was about to get rid of my ghosts. For a weird moment, I felt a pang of missing them, because once they were gone, I wouldn't have anything to remind me of my life before. That is, nothing besides you tapes.

But I didn't need that life.

"When was the last time that the spirits of your parents came to you?" Pastor Maria asked. She lit a bundle of sticks and cracked the window so that the pungent smoke wouldn't set off the fire alarm.

I told her a tiny lie: that the last time I'd seen my ghosts was back when I'd been sleeping during the night. I worried that she'd call the whole thing off if I told her anything different. There was this reality TV show I'd caught when I was trying hard to stay awake, a "weight loss journey," they'd called it, and if the doctor decided that the patient hadn't stuck well enough with their diet plan, he would refuse to do the stomach surgery that would save the patient's life. I wasn't about to screw myself that way. If I didn't get some sleep soon, I'd be more gone than a seventeen-year cicada shell.

"Alright," Maria said, "and the ghosts spoke with you? The way they'd been doing before? And performing disconcerting sexual acts?"

I told her yes. "I got the feeling, this strange feeling – I can kind of sense things about them, you know? But I felt sort of like they hated the idea of the exorcism."

"Really?" Maria's eyes shone behind her glasses as she looked at me. "A hostile undertone about the exorcism, specifically? I did feel an unnatural chill when I first stepped through your front door. A chill as if they were watching me and willing me to leave. But I'm not susceptible to them in that way, which is why I began this profession in the first place."

"Pastor," I said, "do you think the ghosts fear the exorcism only because *I* fear it? I mean, I'm not exactly looking forward to the whole experience, just the outcome, being able to sleep . . . " I pushed my fingers into the mattress until my knuckles cracked.

"It sounds again like you are thinking these ghosts are a part of you, or came from you, but they are not *in* you," Pastor Maria said. "Remember we talked about this? If the spirits came solely from you, then you would be able to banish them yourself – but you can't. The spirits are their own energy, a supernatural force, and you have been caught up within them. I can fix that, though."

"It's your magical power," I said.

"I guess that you could call it that."

For some reason, this made me feel a heap better, probably because a person seemed dumb and crazy if she had made up her own ghosts to torture herself, but being ensnared in their evil ghost plan meant that it wasn't my fault: it was theirs.

"Now," Pastor Maria said, "lie down on the bed, the way you normally do. Yes, under the covers is fine. I am going to ease you into a state – not a sleeping state, but one of deep relaxation, where I can access the spirits through you."

I said, "What if I fall asleep?"

"You won't," she told me. "I've done this dozens of times. You might think that you're asleep, but I'll have control over you. In fact, it might be better if you do think you're sleeping. I will have to speak very harshly to the devil, which is the only way he understands. Now drink this" – she poured a few drops of yellow-tinged liquid from a vial into a glass of water – "and relax." Then she went into this whole relaxing tirade, all this stuff about me floating out into the middle of the ocean on a giant lily pad, and the easeful waves, and me being small and innocent and gently rocked, with my inner turmoil washed away in the tide.

I could feel it pretty well: the rocking waves, the salt on my lips, the fleshy-soft lily pad beneath me. Maria started to prod my body, which felt quite distant from me. The experience reminded me of nothing so much as the time my mother had worked to cast out my mania after that airplane accident. Back then I had felt the same sick but not sick, the same warmth of my bed, the same disconnect between body and mind.

Only, as Maria continued, a marble of panic began to roll around in my chest. The tight, hard, cold thing expanded and rattled against my rib cage. The panic unveiled a different facet to that long-ago memory: my mother had not been trying to help the little-girl me, traumatized and fascinated as I'd been by the airplane crash. She hadn't simply wanted to calm me down. I could see the whole scene as if I were up near the nipple-shaped light fixture in my childhood bedroom: she had been cutting away at my witchiness, making sure I wouldn't have a power that I didn't yet know how to use. She had thought to herself – I could see her thoughts right there, like words scrolling across her forehead – that I would be better off as a regular girl, a girl who didn't have the ability to manifest accidents with her mind.

I think that I was dreaming this, but it felt more like I had traveled back in time, all vividly real, a fever dream, everything three-dimensional and crammed with emotion.

Because my mother had been afraid of what I might be able to do, she'd discouraged me from everything I liked. No make-believe, no more dollhouse, not even any cooking. A recipe was too much like a spell. My mother had schemed to rob me of my powers, but when you got right down to it, she hadn't been able to steal anything: I'd arrived at this moment, my exorcism, because I really was a witch. Still watching from up near the light fixture, I could see the green glow of my powers like an aura around my little-girl body, and I still had that glow – my vision shifted, moving to my bed here, now, in the condo, with Maria ministering to me just like my mother had – a green glow around my body that began to flicker as Maria cussed over me in Spanish.

Was I dreaming? This moment felt intensely real, but then, so did those times the ghosts came to me in my sleep. What had Maria called it? *Lucid dreaming.*

From up near the ceiling, I watched as Pastor Maria pulled a section of the green glow surrounding my body towards herself. Like a string of taffy, it resisted, but she was able to twist one inch, and another, around her finger. It was then I understood that she was trying to steal my witchiness, my green glow, and I saw that she wanted it for herself, that I'd been tricked.

Now I understood why my ghosts were blue and yellow: it was so that they could make green, the color of witch skins and cauldron potions, the color of my powers.

Maria tried to draw my green light around herself, but I knew that I needed to fight back; in the way of dream-logic, doing so suddenly became more important than anything I had ever done in waking life. My slack body couldn't move, of course, since Pastor Maria's potion had drugged me, but I resisted as best I could. My green glow flickered and grew, flickered and grew, as Pastor Maria worked over me.

I cast around desperately for anything I could use against her, now that she'd made me vulnerable, passed out there on the bed, and then finally I hit upon my only weapon: my ghosts. I'd never tried to summon them before, but now I did, I began the stupid breathing techniques I'd learned from the video, and I thought about them intensely, trying to draw them near. To my surprise, they came, all of us floating up near the light fixture. We stared down at my prone body, at Pastor Maria holding her outstretched hands over my chest.

"Is this a crazy dream?" I asked them, but they only shrugged. It seemed impossible that there was any scenario in which this wasn't a dream, even though it felt hyper-real, even though I had control over my lungs. Besides, I'd learned the hard way that what happened in dreams had true-life consequences, could make you sick with sleepiness, could get you into a car accident or provoke a panic attack. Even if this was a dream, I'd be a fool to let Maria win.

I told my ghosts, "Go down there and save me, get her away, break her spell."

"We don't take orders from you," the Jim Dave ghost said.

I go, "Oh yes you do. You told me yourselves that the exorcism would stick you to me forever, and none of us want that."

"She's right," the Mary Ellen ghost said.

"I don't like it." Jim Dave buzzed about angrily. "Not one bit. It's a trick, I'll bet."

"There's not much time," I told them as my green aura shivered violently under Pastor Maria's spell. "Go! It's the only choice; otherwise you're stuck with me for certain."

Then a strange thing happened: it was like my mind and the ghost minds melded together, like our brains were being cooked in the same pot. The ghosts stewed there inside my skull, the broth of our heads mixing. I could smell the rot of them steaming with the life of me. They ransacked my brain for proof that I was trying to trick them, but they found nothing. Somehow knowing that they would obey, I said, "Get down there and save me," and their presence slurped itself out of my mind as they hurried down to my physical body and started flying rapidly around it, moving so fast that their yellow and blue selves became a green blur surrounding me. As soon as they started this, I felt a deadly calm. I would win.

Slowly, I drifted back into my body. In my groggy, half-awake state, I could open my eyes, but not speak or move more than my little finger. It felt very much like I was waking up after a yearlong sleep, and still the weight of my dream, the importance of what had happened, made my whole self shiver. The way a person dreams they won the lottery and awakes ready to buy a mansion, that was me.

"What a session!" Pastor Maria said, holding me against her chest like a baby. I tried to bite her collarbone, but I was still too weak. It dawned on me that she didn't know I'd won. She only said, "It lasted three hours, that's one hour of overtime – we can work that out later. I am completely exhausted. The spirits had a strong hold on you, but I was able to convince them of their place, which is not with you, certainly not, you are no sort of hospitable place."

I noticed that the glass vial she'd doused me with, half its liquid still inside, had rolled behind the alarm clock on my night table.

She said, "Just give yourself a few hours; you'll feel regular soon." Then, she looked at the closet. My limbs trembled slightly; my bladder ached; I was coming back to myself.

When Pastor Maria's hand touched the closet door, my body drenched with adrenaline, but I knew that I had already won, and the trend would continue. With her back turned, I summoned all of my strength and reached for her potion bottle. I hid it beneath my pillow.

She goes, "I got the sense that the spirits felt tied to this place." She gestured at the closet. "Is there any reason that might be? Did your parents store keepsakes in here, or did you put something here that belongs to them?" She opened the closet door, and I thought that my heart just might beat me to death.

But she only looked in, just like I knew she would, and then she began to pack up her things.

Had I really seen her nose wrinkle when she'd opened the closet door, or was that a trick of the light? I'd taken to keeping my clothes in the bureau to the side of the bed because I imagined a stench on anything that came out of that closet.

She tucked a bottle of water beside me and said, "Stay hydrated, and you should be just fine. If you were allergic, we would have seen signs already."

I closed my lips over the lingering aftertaste of the dusty liquid she'd given me to drink. It had been a dirty trick. If she hadn't knocked me out of commission with her potion, she would never have had even a touch of power over me.

All caught up in herself, Pastor Maria goes, "I would say that was another highly successful session for me. Would you mind terribly writing me a review? Just about your experience and our rapport and, of course, how free you feel now, afterwards, since the spirits have quit you. Because it's true that you're safe – they've quit you. Post it to my website." She left her business card beneath my alarm clock. "Now I'm certain that you'd like to get some good rest and good food, so I'll leave you to it. I'll send an invoice, and I very much look forward to seeing you at service on Sunday. You'll feel like a new woman there." She slipped out the bedroom door; her suitcases clattered down the hall.

She hadn't even noticed that I'd stolen her potion while she'd been cleaning up. With her out of my house, I felt immediately better. The glass bottle warmed between my hands. Here was her power, a vial in my fist.

It might sound strange how I only realized now, at fifty-eight, and from a dream, that I am a witch – but the thing is, it's not so far off the mark. For months I've been thinking about my own witchi-*ness*, and it just took this exorcism to tip the idea over. Always I've believed in witches, and I have this theory of life which I hadn't thought about for years: all women have their powers. This wasn't a controversial view in Chautauqua County. All us women knew that we had invisible powers, and that was how we got by. Because if you didn't believe in your power to keep your husband from losing his job, or get away with pocketing some Midol in the long stretch between paydays, or protect your daughter from a C-section because she didn't have health insurance, then you had nothing. Or, nothing but fear. By the by, my theory of life is that Eve was a witch, not from some impossible perfect garden, but from Salem, and if all the women came from her, then we all have the ability to be witches, too. It's my Salem theory. But you do have to cultivate your witchiness a little. It's an easy thing to pass over, that your powers might be more than just abracadabraing the rent that month, and for too long I'd forgotten.

Pastor Maria, though, she'd awoken me to the steady drip that had been forming my strong inner core all this while, just the way calcium builds out of drops of water. You can't see the minerals there, in the water; you can only see that what grows over time is a novel thing, unexpected, but also entirely natural. Now that I have transformed into who I really am, I feel more content than I have in a long while.

After Maria left, seeing as I was already in bed, it was not one bit hard to fall asleep; I just let the warmth of my own body, magnified by the covers, ease me down into it. The sleep was magnificent, better than a hamburger and strawberry milkshake, better than winning the grand prize at bingo: to sleep uninterrupted was heaven. In fact, I think I'll go wade into my pile of pillows again right now.

PLASTIC WASTE IN THE OCEAN

I slept solid for hours, and it was only the end bit that brought me trouble.

My ghosts appeared, and every nerve in my body bristled like hairs raised by static electricity. But for the first time, I felt happy to see them: their presence was proof that my witchiness remained intact.

My ghosts were floating in their corner, just as if nothing had happened, their hands roaming up and down each other's bodies. All the rest I'd just stored up drained away, leaving me instantly exhausted again.

"It backfired!" Jim Dave said, puffing up his already swollen-looking chest. "You bitch, it backfired. Because you let that awful lady do her exorcising, we're stuck with you always. We warned you this would happen, and you didn't listen. We were hoping to retire together up there" – pausing in their handsiness, they both looked skyward – "but now we'll never be able to retire. You've put us in a bind. A real mess. Good job, dumbass."

"You've really gone and done it," the Mary Ellen ghost agreed, sounding more like Mary Ellen than ever.

What kind of person had ghosts soldered to them for eternity, if not a witch? Thanks be I'd finally realized that having ghosts was a sort of power. Even though they were sapping me in one way, through lack of sleep, I was gaining in other ways, in witchiness. These ghosts were my spirit animals, the black cats who rode on my broom.

My ghosts began to pull off each other's clothes, and I stared, and blinked, and finally came to realize that their genitals had switched from the one to the other of them, color and all. Jim Dave had yellow breasts and crotch, and between Mary Ellen's legs dangled a blue penis.

"What happened to *you*?" I asked them.

Jim Dave pulled at his own breasts. "Was how we got around the exorcist," he told me.

Mary Ellen goes, "She was obsessed, completely obsessed, with our haunting sexuality, so all we had to do to evade her was a simple switch."

I must admit that I was fairly impressed by their gumption, that is, until they started sexing in their new way. I just couldn't watch, but they made me.

Tiredness has become my curse. It hurts, it is a physical pain lodged deep inside the right hemisphere of my skull. Tiredness makes me feel stupid and sad. If only I could *know* that it's doing something for me, such as eating a hollow in my brain inside of which can wriggle my witchiness, then maybe I could withstand it better. Because now that I see I am a witch, I need to cultivate this asset which has sat dormant for too long.

Scarcely can I believe all that went on this evening; the insides of my cheeks still taste of blood from where I chewed them up with worry. Like any normal day, I plopped in front of the computer with a cocktail around seven. I sipped very slowly as I scrolled through my social profiles and made up a ditty about a super great hamburger cookout and posted it to compete with all the junk about grand-babies and vegetable gardens and glamour shots of much younger selves.

Then an electronic bell told me that someone had just sent me a message. It was Sallie – she had never messaged me first before, and so I'd assumed I was safe from the bother of her. Now, maybe, I would have to do something harsh like unfriend her. By this point, she was more detriment than boon to me: she hadn't given me anything useful about the police or that stupid reporter, and she got so sensitive at the slightest hint of me questioning her.

Her message was: *i've put down the first quarter payment im doing everyting i can to come up w/the rest or i lose it we start with shampooing im sooo excited*

I rolled my eyes; this girl and her idiot decisions. All she could think about was wasting a down payment on beauty school; no wonder there wasn't any room left in that mind of hers for serious legal matters. *What are you going to do with your kid when you're gone at school all day?* I wrote.

i dunno she is good in front of the tv w/ her dad

Sallie was dumb as a dog and also a hypocrite if her plan to raise up a child right was to leave her in front of the television day after day. I typed, *I thought you were going to do better than your parents.*

oh yeah of course that is a given and not hard either

Wondering what kind of fake history she'd constructed for herself, I asked her what she meant.

for example no matter how angry i would never throw stuff with my child in the room even boiling mad. i wouldnt leave my kid at the car shop w/a creepy uncle or only feed her ice cream for dinner like five nights in a row. i am going to cosmetology school to make a better life for her my daughter which is always my goal in everything i do.

This stuff was lies; maybe I'd given her ice cream one night, but she'd loved it, she'd begged for it. I wrote, *I'm sure your parents tried their best, and as I would wager you know, it is impossible to always make the perfect decision.*

Then she typed this missive: *yeah but i think too that my mom killed my pa*

My first instinct was to close out of the conversation, erase it, so that there'd be no record of what she'd said, and then run off to take a hot shower, but my second instinct was to find out more, since Sallie was finally telling me something valuable. This was what I'd been waiting for, after all. *How crazy*, I wrote, *no way, why would you think that?*

She goes, *not just me. everyone around here does*

My nerves, buckshot, were sounding the alarm. *But WHY?*

even the police have come by and asked after it. they must have some kind of evidence have their suspicions and all. but think about it me growing up in a house where my mom all along was going to kill my pa. that cant be healty and now i've got one of my own im supposed to raise up right

Obviously it's a lie, I wrote, trying to convince her with the power of my mind.

Her: *and the police are always following me around wanting to know this and that, like they came on by my house even in front of all my neighbors. but i had nothin to do with it!!!!*

Me: *Did they say anything, like if they have any leads? Maybe the whole thing is a big mistake because it's just too crazy that your ma might do something like that.*

Her: *you dont know her. this is the woman who gave me a candy bar when i started my period. i was all traumatized bleeding out my vag and she gives me a snickers. what i needed was a tampon and for her to tell me i wasnt dyin*

Sallie is obsessed with herself and always has been. She couldn't even focus for one minute on what I needed to know.

Me: *But do they have any other suspects? There's got to be someone because the other is just too wild.*

Her: *there is some other man the hubs of this woman my mom used to work with, but hes already in jail and denies it and he has an alibi too*

Me: *You never know with those types. I mean, he's already in jail.*

Her: *the police told me if I heard from her i had to let them know straightaway. asked me if i had any idea where maybe she'd gone.*

Me: *And do you have an inkling?*

Her: *i told them florida to get them off my back. plus she had mentioned it a couple times as somewhere cool i never get to go anywhere*

I wanted to scream at her and pull her hair, but I could do nothing through the computer; I was impotent. I wrote, *When was all this? Like when did they come by and you tell them about Florida and all that?*

Her: *just yesterday. i hate it here truly. what's it like in morocco? maybe i could come there sometime but then you need money to travel and ill never have any like if i dont get the rest of my tuiton money i am screwed*

Me: *I would be careful if I were you. It sounds like you basically told a lie to the police. I mean I have heard tell that you should never speculate with them.*

Her: *fo sho.* She spelled it all funny, F-O and then S-H-O, which for some reason infuriated me, her taking it so slangy and light; she had zero idea, the gravity of what she'd done.

I sent, *Take a step back and think over things before they come out your mouth. It just sounds to me like you got too much to deal with every morning, noon, and night.* After I typed this, I waited for a long time, and then Sallie wrote:

MA???????

My heart burned – I knew immediately that I'd made a dumbshit mistake. I wasn't that woman, I wasn't her ma, of course I wasn't, but depending on who thought I was, I could be doomed. As I tried desperately to figure out how to fix it, Sallie was typing, frantic little bursts of half-sentences zinging through the wires to harangue me:

ma come on i know thats you they warned me this might happen
ive been waiting to hear
from you please did you do it for money
i wont tell them never i swear
everyone said there mustve been real money
is that part of all this
did u know they made me id

i need
id the body i have nightmares now
u didnt do it, did u i dont think you could have just let me know
my tuiton is $4500 more this semester
in my dreams i see his drowned face no lips
did u really get urself over to morocco?
its impossible to live this way
ive been telling everyone i am an orphan but its not true is it
is it

Each word was like a small electric shock that built up and built up until I was buzzing all over. I closed out of the browser entirely.

My first thought was that I needed to flee.

But then I mixed another drink and sat down for a true think. Even if she'd told the Chautauqua police about some vague idea how maybe her ma was in Florida, would they take her seriously? Besides, how would they get all the way down here to check things out? Florida was a big state, full of blond-formerly-brunette ladies living solo in condos. Plus, I had nowhere else to go; fleeing would be so much *work*, and it would expose me to getting caught. Things were comfortable here, I had everything that I needed, and actually it might be safer overall for me to hunker down.

But I felt worried, of course I was. Only a crazy person wouldn't be. And if Sallie told the police my name from my Facebook account, and they figured out which condo, exactly, belonged to me, and if they enlisted their Florida cronies to come break down my door, then I don't know how I'll escape. Through the window, probably.

Of course I have to ghost Sallie – isn't that what the young people say? Disappear out of her life for the good of us both.

I deleted my social media. I unscrewed the top screw from the number six on my front door so that it swung down into a nine. I cast a little spell to help keep myself tucked away safe.

I figure that's all a body can do, really.

This morning, I had a new email from Pastor Maria: the rest of her bill. It was a fair amount, and even though my bank account is healthy, a girl never knows when she might need to clear off with plenty of money in her pocket. Besides, I'd paid for a service I hadn't gotten: I was still haunted, still awake all night.

Pastor Maria wanted me to submit payment through her website. I followed the link that led to Pastor Maria's home page, and the first thing I saw was a picture that looked familiar, and then I realized that it was my own bedroom. I clicked on it, which opened a whole album.

There was me, marked as "the possessed," covers up to my chin, looking ghostly pale.

There was me lying down with my arms hovering sort of menacingly in the air.

Me with a glistening cross painted on my forehead in what was probably oil, with crystals circling my skull like a crown on the pillow.

There was the corner of my bedroom with a superimposed arrow pointing at what looked like a large piece of clear plastic hanging from the ceiling.

If that last was supposed to be my ghosts, it was completely wrong. I scrolled through some of the other customers' albums and saw the same nebulous plasticky thing somewhere above each of their prone figures. Was this really what the spirits looked like when Pastor Maria saw them, or was it some trick of Photoshop?

When I was a little girl, I read a book about a dog illustrated with black-and-white pictures to show how the dog saw the world. They can't see color, I guess. And that got me thinking how this dog would have a different view of everything, even if we were standing side by side, even if I got down on all fours and stuck my tongue out like his.

And then that blossomed into thinking about how the same could be true for me and my ma, who always seemed, for example, to notice dust where I saw none, and then I lost the idea for years and years, but it came back to me now, when I think about me and Jim Dave, seeing as we had never noticed the important signs about each other, or me and Sallie, or me and anyone, really. If we all saw so god-damned differently from one another, then how would we ever pick out what was what or who was who or why any of us did anything at all?

I closed out of the website without paying.

I've just had a thought: these tapes are my spell book. Every witch has her spell book – in fact, having a spell book means you're half-way there to witchhood – and these tapes are mine, my special road map for how I became myself. That is why I feel so attached to them, why I carry them with me from place to place even though they could be a detriment. These tapes are alive with me, and so no wonder I can't think to kill them.

Let me explain something here: being a witch does not need to include black clothes, black cats, potions boiling in a cauldron, eating kids, or whatever else. A spell book can be a cassette tape; a black cat can be a blue ghost. Being a witch is more a state of mind – that is to say, a state of empowerment. You need to believe in what you do, in what you can do, and then you focus to make it happen. A little juju here, an incantation there, but it's mostly mind power.

Another *Bang! Bang!* on the door: the most intrusive sound known to mankind. The HOA Nazi just needed to inform me that my address number was broken. I don't know why these ladies are always dipping their spoon in my soup. Don't worry, I told her, the repairman has already been called – like I would need a repairman to screw in one tiny screw – though he was pretty booked up so it might be a while before he comes. That got her to back off, though not without a fair amount of huff.

When my ghosts interrupted my nap this afternoon, I decided to attempt a different tactic: divide and conquer. Once they appeared in the middle of a black dreamless sleep, I explained to those figures that had so plagued me how they worked for me now. The thing is, I have influence over my own dreams; they are *my* dreams; before I didn't realize that. "I don't think you understand," I said to my ghosts, "how my powers are growing. And one of the things you ought to keep in mind is my power over you." They went all fizzy with excitement; they shimmered before my eyes like a mirage I would never reach. I go, "For example, I have the power to bring you back, if I so choose."

The light in the room faded and then brightened – a cloud passing.

"To life?" the Mary Ellen ghost asked, and I said yes.

I explained how I have been making a spell book all the while, *this* book, or rather, these tapes, which eventually will have the recipe to restore them.

"She's joking," the blue ghost said. "She always did this, made promises – oh, I'll help you find another job, oh, we'll convince Sallie to get an abortion, oh, sure we can move to Nashville – but she never kept a one." Jim Dave's impression of my voice was wilted lettuce compared to mine of his.

"Oh yes I did," I said, shifting my focus to the yellow ghost. It was her I could turn first, I felt certain. "You were the one always keeping us back. Never showing up for the interview or letting that Blackburn boy move your daughter in with him."

The yellow ghost bobbed closer to me.

"He always does that," I said. "Turns things around to get his way."

The yellow ghost nodded. "Like when he says us sexing all the time is the best way to haunt you, even when my crotch is sore."

"That's right," I encouraged her. "And I have to say, we need to work together if you ever want to be brought back. Because I'm here, I'm the one in this world, the one with a real body, and so I ought to know."

The Jim Dave ghost looked mad, but he didn't interrupt; he wanted to hear how he could be brought back, too.

I said, "I am using my powers to make this spell book, and once I'm done, I'll know how to rewind you, back to the way it was before. Just like pushing a button on the tape player." The yellow ghost understood, I could tell. "And the reason I am the only one with this power is because I was the one to transform you in the first place."

"To kill us, she means," the Jim Dave ghost said. "She's lying. Even if she could do it, she would never."

"But she might," the Mary Ellen ghost said, her eyes jaundiced and swimming, and I pretended to myself I was drinking them down like chardonnay. I had her, I did, and Jim Dave was a part of her pair. He never had been able to do a thing on his own.

Was I sleeping? This felt nothing like the nightmares I had every time I tried to rest. Maybe it wouldn't be all that hard to convert these ghosts into my bona fide spirit animals. "You are beholden to me," I said out loud to nothing, as I'm saying it again now into here. Beholden, a magical, fancy word. You are beholden to me. You would be nothing without me.

The following Sunday, I skipped church for obvious reasons, and so I was surprised as a lamb sent to slaughter when Pastor Maria showed up at my door. I'd been doing a lot of online research about witches, and I felt torn whether to invite her over the threshold or not. In the end, I did, because one theory is that I would have a home team advantage if we were on my own turf – plus, if we talked out on the stoop, the neighbors might get curious. I sat her in the breakfast nook and brought over a little bowl of salty nuts and some white wine.

"We missed you in church today," Pastor Maria said. "Aren't you feeling well?"

I told her yes, that I was getting stronger every day.

She goes, "Well, you look it. That green eye shadow is an excellent choice."

It seemed to me that she waited until I had a sip of my wine to put the same drink to her lips. If she was worried that I might poison her, then I needed to be extremely careful; it meant that she would be capable of the same and worse with me.

Pastor Maria said, "I'm very glad that I was able to help you. As soon as I walked in here, I could tell that the energy was more positive, that I had really cleared the air for you. Don't you agree?"

She must've taken my noncommittal mumbling to mean yes.

"You know, there are a lot of expenses that go into my business, and I would appreciate it if you would pay that invoice I sent you. So that I can get caught up on my own accounting."

"Oh right," I said, "the invoice. It did seem high."

"Work rendered, work paid," she told me, like this was some universal truth. "We're not communists here."

I let silence take a couple of laps around the room, and then I go, "I have to tell you that the problem is, I agreed to the whole thing under false pretenses."

She looked at me blankly.

"You know what you did," I told her, "so please stop your act. Don't make me bad-mouth you."

"Natalie," she said, "what is it? Just tell me."

I topped off our wine as I said, "Let's be frank: doesn't your witchiness recognize mine?"

She blinked slowly, her glasses magnifying the movement. "I suppose this is my fault." She sighed. "I knew that running a church constructed around angels might bring out some . . . differently wired people, but before they have at least paid their bills. Why won't you?"

"Look," I said, "I know that you were trying to unwitch me, trying to steal the best part of me, so's I just plan to hold on here like a hound with a hare to the truth that *I don't owe you.*"

She stared at me strangely, and I bit my tongue. I needed to work on my conversation, make my words a little more prissy, more refined.

"I never would steal from you," Pastor Maria said slowly, just like that. "I was trying to *help.*"

I told her, "The thing is, you're not the only one with powers. You might have noticed, and stayed away."

She narrowed her eyes. "I see what's going on," she said. "It's even worse than I thought: you're trying to steal my clients, aren't you? If so, then yes, we do have a fight on our hands. That's why you were asking me all those strange questions, right? About if everyone had ghosts? Well, no one will have any confidence in *you,* I'll make sure of that. If you try to hone in on my exorcism market, there will be consequences."

She had it wrong, of course, but I wasn't about to set her mind at ease.

She asked me, "Is that why you pretended to want an exorcism from me? So that you could observe my techniques? Steal them?

"And another thing. Where is my vial? I'd thought that maybe I'd misplaced it, but I see now: you stole it, didn't you? Preparing yourself to start up as my rival. Disgusting. Just disgusting."

"You tried to poison me!" I said. "Why would you think that I'd steal something that made me feel so awful?"

"Unbelievable. That drink just made you a little more giving, a little more relaxed; you didn't deserve it." She stood up, preparing to go. "You will regret this."

"You thought that you were going to snuff me out," I said to Pastor Maria as she hightailed it for the door, "but all that you did was make me stronger, so remember that."

I *must* work harder on embodying myself, fancier language, more precise lipstick, a little head toss every time I down the last sip of a drink . . . Natalie, Natalie, Natalie.

BALANCING THE FAMILY CHECKBOOK

When Marcus knocked on the door, I was already feeling overwhelmed by the burden of society. Maybe that's why the thing that happened, happened.

"Mother!" he said and thrust out a bouquet of purple flowers.

Sallie and now him and Pastor Maria and Lottie and all the horrible people in the world would be the ruin of me. They were evil little tricksters set out to skunk me, but they would see; I wouldn't let them. I adapted too fast.

But – society dictates – I pasted a smile on my face and said, "What are you doing around here?"

"Oh you know. In the neighborhood. Wanted to check on my mother." For a moment, I wondered who that was, and then I remembered: he meant *me*. Ugh. He led the way into the living room and sat down on the couch. I made a detour to the kitchen for a bottle of wine to soften the bother of him, and I stood there with my face in the cool mist of the fridge until he called out, asking where I had gone.

"Yes, dear?" I said, because I'd decided that was what I would call him. Sort of stiff and formal, but just nice enough to deceive him into thinking it was a pet name. I entered the living room with two glasses dangling from one hand, the bottle from the other.

He opened the wine and poured himself a glass almost twice as full as the one he poured me. "How have you been?" he asked me, but in a way that meant he didn't care to hear it, so I just said I was fine and waited.

"I've had another fight with my roommate," he said, and then spewed out an almanac of problems: they'd only been living together for a pair of months, but it was unbearable. The roommate ate Marcus's food, every morsel from the fridge and the cupboard, and the candy bars, too, that Marcus hid in his backpack. Marcus felt sure this roommate was bulimic; they shared one bathroom, which always smelled of vomit, and Marcus would stay up late listening for sounds of the roommate retching so that he could walk in on him and then convince him to get the help he needed.

"Get a new roommate," I said, reaching to refill my glass and wondering idly if this man was somehow drawn to bulimia, since his biological mother – me – had suffered from it.

"But we have a good deal on the apartment. I guess you don't know how hard it is to find affordable housing here. What is this place?" His greedy little eyes roved around. "A two bedroom? Or three? You never gave me the tour."

"Maybe this roommate of yours has chronic stomach problems," I said.

He goes, "I think we need some time apart." He dropped his head into his hands. "I don't want to go back there tonight. It's too depressing."

"Cheer up, it can't be all that bad." I rolled my eyes when he wasn't looking. "Why did you become roommates in the first place, hm?"

He told me that things just happen; they fall into alignment. He said, "The funny part is, he's not fat or thin, not either one. You'd think that he would be fat from all the eating or thin from all the vomiting, but he's just perfectly regular."

I go, "If you haven't ever talked about it, or made any sort of cohabitation rules, I don't think you can get mad at him for eating your food."

He set down his glass and looked at me. "You know, you're right. I can't expect him to do something if it's just in my head. I need to lay it all out. I need to lay the ground rules. Thank you so much for that advice. No one ever gives me advice anymore."

I couldn't tell if he was being serious or mocking me, but I decided to act like he was serious. "You're welcome. Now on your drive home, just think about what you're going to say to him. Plan it all out ahead of time."

"Wow," he said. "Were you a counselor? Before you retired? You retired pretty early, didn't you?"

I said, "I was in business."

"What was your career like?" he asked, again a question he didn't really want me to answer, because he kept talking. "You know, me, I go to the office every day. Sit around in an ugly old chair that hurts my back with this headset clamping my skull, stupidities running between my ears like you wouldn't believe, and I talk nonsense on the phone. It's horrible. At the end of the day, I can barely stand; I'm all stiff and hunched over my computer. It's no way to live. I wish that I could find a construction job, be a forest manager, something that builds muscle."

"People need money," I said.

"Do you have a sweet tooth?" he asked. "I do, I really do. Does our family? I worry about that sort of thing. Disorders, or . . . diabetes."

"Well, don't," I said. "I don't have any issues."

"And what about my father?" he asked. "Did he have any problems, genetic problems, diseases?"

"I wouldn't know anything about that," I said cautiously. "It was a long time ago."

He told me to be careful. "It's hard to say what sorts of problems might crop up. We're weaker than you would think, as a species. And we make terrible decisions, dilute our strengths . . . "

He went on this way for some time, and when he finished the bottle of wine, I said, "It's getting late. I've got to be off to bed."

He looked around with wide startled eyes. "That late already?" he said. "Oh, no. I'm so sorry, but . . . I don't think I can drive. I've had too much." He tipped the last sip in his wineglass down his throat.

"You didn't have much at all," I said and clenched my teeth at him. "We shared *one* bottle."

He goes, "I'm a huge lightweight. I'm really sorry about this, Mother, but there's no way I can drive home in this state. Just this once, would it be okay if I stayed with you? I can even take the couch, if you don't have anything set up as a guest room."

"I don't have a guest room," I said, silently congratulating myself for keeping that room locked at all times. Filled as it was with recyclable bottles and bits of trash, it would make any real guest wonder what was wrong with me.

He flicked a finger against the empty wine bottle. "You know, it's funny that we finished this, because I was wondering if I should talk with you about . . . your drinking."

My patience was running out. "No," I said, "let's not."

"Because the other day when you called me, you sounded a little . . . sloppy."

I resisted the urge to grab another bottle from the kitchen. Of course people's children can grow up to be as different from them as butter and frogs, you just don't know, which is why it's a shame everyone thinks you ought to spend time with your offspring.

He goes, "I only worry about your health. And your safety. It's so much easier to take advantage when a person is inebriated. I wonder if that's what happened to you, before. I spoke with my father's roommate." He paused expectantly, as if I should fall over with enlightenment, but I said nothing. "My father's *cell*mate," he said, spinning his empty wineglass by its stem. "I found him, and he told me what happened. The thing is, Mother, I would really like to be on your side of all this, I really would, but it's difficult."

My hands clenched into fists so tightly that my palms ached

where my fingernails cut into them.

Marcus goes, "I had to come see you to ask. I need to hear it from your mouth: were you working for the police?"

"What?" I said, truly surprised. "No!"

"Well, my father's cellmate told me that you'd gotten into your own trouble, something about selling fake magazine subscriptions to grandmas, and you promised the police to help bring in my father in return for a slap on the wrist. The thing is, my father's cellmate told me that the drugs they caught my father with were *yours*, and that my father was just doing the gentlemanly thing holding them for you, keeping you from temptation."

Once again, Natalie's past had my head zinging loop-de-loos. I go, "You know how men must talk. Being cooped up like that together. They get restless; they say anything."

Deadly calm, Marcus goes, "What I want to know is, was your plan to take those drugs with me there inside your belly? Did you want to *deform* me?"

"Of course not," I said, starting to worry that he was veering towards the ditch. My tongue felt thick. "It was so long ago, the police, you must know how it is, I mean, I was scared."

He goes, "Then you *were* working for them?"

"No," I said, my head pounding, "they made me . . . " I willed tears into the corners of my eyes. "I was so alone . . . "

"Plus" – Marcus thrust a finger into the air – "even worse, the reason Dad was a target in there, in the big house, was because everyone knew that *you* worked for the cops, and so some people got the idea that he did, too. Even though he was a loyal person, they got the wrong picture, and he ended up dead."

How had this conversation flown itself up to Jupiter? Marcus must have planned out the whole confrontation beforehand – I could see from the excited twitch in his cheek that he was enjoying it. In order to give Marcus a few moments of silent mourning for this criminal he'd never met, I sniffled and dabbed at my nose with a tissue from my pocket. I hoped that after he'd gulped his fill of shouting at me, he would leave, and I would never have to open my door to him again.

Finally Marcus cleared his throat several times. "He told me that my father wanted to keep me. That if Dad hadn't been in jail, he would have stopped you from doing what you did. My father, he would have kept us a family unit."

Straight off I knew there was no getting Marcus over to my side, not on this point that had stuck in his crop like a sour old shoestring, so I decided instead to try and hurry us beyond the subject. "You have a more fascinating past that most." I hated touching his moist hand, but I had to appear comforting; I covered it with mine. "I'm glad that you've found me, and we can move on from here."

"We'll see," Marcus said. He yawned hugely; the molars in the back of his jaw gleamed.

I told him that we could call him a cab so he could get some rest at home.

He clasped his hands in front of his chest as if he were praying. "I'm exhausted. Emotionally. The couch is fine for me." He slipped off his shoes and buried his head beneath one of my decorative pillows.

I couldn't believe that he'd buffaloed his way into staying with me. I tried to radiate out my fury when his socked toes poked into my thigh, but he just sighed sleepily and stretched out his legs as soon as I stood up from the couch. If I had known then what he was plotting, I would have shooed him out faster than a milkmaid with her strange stepbrother, but, it's a pity, I wasn't able to see the future.

He woke me in the middle of the night, just after I had drifted off to sleep. He hit my shoulder with the flat of his palm and said, voice wild, "I can't believe it; I can't believe it. How *could* you?" He banged a fist against the wall above my headboard and flicked on the lamp, which threw his features into clownish relief.

Of course I had no idea what he was talking about. I sat up against my pillows and tried to think of the nearest weapon. Maybe my bedside lamp, turned upside down and used as a bludgeon? Maybe the fork from my midnight snack? I could stick it in his crazed-looking eyeball.

He stood over me where I lay in bed. "'Importance of Exact Measurements in Baking,'" he said. "What was that! But who are you? My mother . . . did you kill my real mother?"

It's you, you stupid tapes, the one thing I look forward to making, the few minutes where I feel expansive, telling my story how I want to be remembered – with the *truth* – but the thing is, I'm still here, right? This is my voice on the recording. So's I haven't been ruined, and this is the greatest proof that I haven't, because here's my voice.

Frantically he said, "I should have known – I should have *known* that you weren't my mother, you doing all those dirty things with a foreigner, I didn't recognize your parts and don't you think I would have felt a *twinge* of recognition at the spot that first gave me life? A twinge!"

Well, that's when I figured that he was not only annoying, and perhaps a bit cracked, but also perverted: he must've been spying on me and Thu through those wide-open curtains, just the way Thu had been hoping a body would do.

"Newborns do not remember a thing like that," I told him. "And Thu has lived in California his entire life."

"In any case," he said, "you are a disappointment to my father's memory. Obviously."

I couldn't help it; I laughed, my mirth especially frothy because it was being whipped up by nerves. Of course this inflated his anger.

He goes, yanking at his staticky hair, "It's unnatural! Just entirely against nature for a mother to give up her child like you did me. I should have known that you were slutty, it just proves the underlying anomaly, but for me to see *that* when I went looking for my mother . . . ”

He was acting unhinged, and while it was different than the men of Chautauqua County who went wild when someone dented their new pickup or made fun of their marksmanship, I still figured I could calm him in the same way. "You're right," I said, "you are absolutely right, and it's not fair, and I am sorry about that. What a horrible thing to see."

"It *was!*" he whined.

Of course with him so precarious I could not reprimand him for peeking in windows and especially not for seeking out a mother who didn't want him around in the first place, so I said, "I would have done it all differently, if I could have. You are a remarkable young man."

"I guess some people aren't meant to be mothers, instead they're born with perversions," he said, still thinking that this would hurt me.

I told him that he must be right, and with as much remorse as I could muster, I patted the mattress beside me.

Mumbling to himself, he sat down on the edge of my bed. "But my own mother . . . there would be a twinge . . . ”

"It's very late," I said, "I'm so tired; we ought to talk about this in the morning."

Marcus, his left cheek twitching furiously, jumped up from his seat on the bed. "There is something wrong with you!" he shouted and lurched off, away from me, towards the closet door. He rattled the locked handle. After my scare with Thu and then Pastor Maria, them being so near the closet and all, I'd decided to install a lock on it, just for my own peace of mind.

"She's in here, isn't she!" he said. "My true mother!"

It was as if he were auditioning for a black-and-white movie. He wailed. He fell to his knees. I could practically hear the frantic violin music goading him on.

As he reached up to rattle the door handle again, I knew that I needed a different tactic: I said, "No, no, no. I finally realized what you're talking about. Those tapes. That's right; those tapes were old. They were for a project I was working on once, long ago. An outline for a novel. You know, a kind of suspense thriller thing, a weird murderer story. Mistaken identities. None of that is *real*. Of course not. How could you think that?"

He was breathing heavily, but no longer crying. "What?" he said, and I knew that I'd got him, that I was stronger and smarter and I would come out ahead, I would gather my witchy powers around me, I would be fine.

I said, "You know, a novel. An outline for a novel – people make those all the time. A fake story. Now come here; you're scaring me."

After a few seconds, he crawled on all fours like a cowed dog over to the bed where I still lay.

I said, "Why would you sneak into my things in the first place? That's not very nice."

He goes, "You mentioned those tapes on the phone. Remember? When you called me that night, and I asked if you had any hobbies; they were the one thing you seemed pretty excited about. I just thought I could use them to . . . get to know you a little better."

Well, what a dumb thing for me to have done during my little blink. I have noticed a new impulse of mine, this impulse to talk now that my life is finally impressive; I need to try harder to exhaust that sort of chatter here, on you tapes, and never to any real person.

"You'll be alright," I said. "Try to breathe normally, in through your nose . . . "

"Wow," he said, pulling his knees into himself and rocking his body back and forth on my bedroom floor. "I guess things got a little weird there. I don't know what I was thinking. That was too crazy, you know? Too crazy to be real, but it felt so . . . "

I placed my hand on the back of his head and patted gently to remind him that he was just a dumb little pet. "You seem ready to fall off the tree at any moment. What's wrong, really?" I tamped down my giddiness that I was turning this around on him. I go, "Maybe you're suffering some . . . mental anguish? That you could think such a thing about me? Those tapes, like I said: they are just my hobby. Lots of people have plans to write novels."

He rubbed hard at his temples and said, "Oh no. You . . . you're right. I am going through a bit of a rough patch lately. Okay. Well. You know all that stuff I was telling you, all the roommate stuff?"

I nodded.

"What if I said none of it was about my roommate, but actually my live-in girlfriend?"

Inside, I smiled; he was broken and ready to blame himself. I go, "Why didn't you tell me the truth at first?"

"You know moms." He shrugged. "If I said I had a girlfriend in the first place, you would get all excited and happy that I might make you grandbabies, and then when I told you all the ways that she was messed up, you'd be so worried for me . . . I didn't want to make you worry. My fake mom, you know, she worries so much that she has an ulcer, and you would probably have it even worse because you have the biological impulse, you're a true mother. I don't want to do that to you."

The situation had boomeranged back into my control. I said, "I think that the reason you came to me is because you wanted advice. I have something very deep, and very personal, to tell you. I myself was bulimic, once. My own mother would pinch me with tongs. It's a difficult disease. When someone has it, they need support. Now why don't you listen to your mother?"

He was practically sobbing. "Thank you for telling me that. It's all I've wanted, to just know about your life."

"Of course, dear," I said. He was such a strange little man, crumpled up there on my bedroom floor; I marveled at the fact that, just a few minutes before, I'd worried he was capable of killing me. I said, "Well, you've certainly upset me now. You didn't tell me about your girlfriend; have you told anyone about *me*? Have you told your real mom? I mean, the mom who raised you?"

"No," he said, chin against his chest. "She doesn't understand about the natural impulse. Because of her . . . woman problems, she wants to believe that it doesn't matter who provided the genes and all that. She doesn't understand."

I go, "Does your girlfriend even know that you're here?" And when he shook his head no, I said, "Now what you need is to go back to your own house, and your own girlfriend, and make her a healthful breakfast in the morning and see if the two of you can't talk about it and maybe work something out. I can see how this is straining you; look how you projected that onto me. How you let one silly little thing overtake your imagination. You need to figure it out with her, the girlfriend."

His head snapped up, his wispy hair rising with static. "But it really did feel true. That tape. I mean, the shaky way you were talking, the tone of your voice, kind of miserable and thrilled at the same time, like it had actually happened, the . . . murder. What kind of sick book were you going to write, with those tapes? And the closet – why is it locked? It just felt so . . . "

I sighed, realizing that the incident was not going to float away as easily as I'd hoped, that he would always be questioning me, judging me, checking me against the facts. He would always be dropping by at bad times or peeking in my windows. But that was fine; I knew how to maintain control. "I'll show you," I said, "will that help? I keep jewelry in there, valuable things, so I lock it. Let me open it and you can see for yourself."

He nodded dumbly and started to crawl back towards the closet, but halfway, he must have realized how pitiful he looked, because he rose to his feet. He goes, "I mean, it seems to me that you don't really read. There aren't any books in the house. Wouldn't someone who wants to write a novel have a few books lying around?"

I explained to him, my voice full of patience, that I read books electronically – less clutter. I unlocked the closet with the key from my bedside table, which I hid inside a case for reading glasses – the truth is that I do little reading, since the glasses give me a headache – and I opened the door. Marcus ventured inside.

"The chain for the light is hanging somewhere in the back," I told him. "A bit deeper in." As he groped inside, I shut the door and locked it between us.

"I can't see anything," he said, his voice on the edge of panic.

Breathing calmly, I walked to the hall closet where the stun gun was stored. Back in the bedroom, I flipped it on, touched its metal buckteeth to the door handle, and pulled the trigger. "Dear, I'm so sorry," I called. By now he was making frightened noises, but not quite loud enough to bother the neighbors. "Just open the door. You can find the handle in the dark, can't you? Grab it and twist."

When his hand made contact with the doorknob, I could sense his whole body stiffening with the rigid force of electricity, and then the sag as he finally let go and slumped to the ground.

I opened the door.

At my feet, his body was crumpled like a lawn-mown butterfly, a wing still twitching. I had known that this plan would work even before it had fully formed in my mind, because I was a witch; I had special forces flowing in my favor.

He was out cold, but not quite dead. I popped the top few cheap buttons of his shirt and pressed the stun gun to the skin above his heart. I depressed the trigger again and again, then held it for a long, long time, until I worried that the curls of singed chest hair might set off the smoke detector.

The worst part about a dead body is the final shit. This one seemed explosive; I don't know what the boy had been eating. But maybe it was a fitting result, for me to have to clean this mess, since I'd never changed his diaper when he'd been a baby.

It's exciting, really, to be in my position: that of a woman discovering her essential self. Whenever that happens, it seems like too many others line up to try and take the elemental away from her, but I'd been blasting through the roadblocks, one by one. There was a point not long ago when I figured I might be losing my grip, but it was really society overall causing me to feel that way. Society doesn't make room for witches, and never has – instead, a woman with powers is called crazy. I'm better than them, though. My Salem theory of life is stronger than any Freud. And to anyone who thinks that my Salem theory is bullshit: back in high school, I'd learned all about Freud from this strange teacher, and if millions of people can believe that women at their core are lacking because they have a penis-shaped hole inside them, then what's so wild about believing that all women could be witches, if they just thought to access that part of themselves? It wasn't so far off from Freud's iceberg: witchiness was the huge, submerged foundation of all women, which we could only reach if our bits above the surface were willing to delve a little deeper. Apparently, not many of us are that adventurous.

For a while I left the body like that, just in case lightning was still careening through the veins, ready to zip out and into me, before I went ahead and mummified him. This time, I cast a little spell to keep any of his stink or other bits from leaking out. I gargled with vodka and then spit into the suitcase before zipping the thing for good. This was yet another step towards finally coming into my own. I just need to be careful, always more careful.

SWING SET ASSEMBLY INSTRUCTIONS

Company, seems I can never get away from company. This time, it was Marcus's girlfriend, the bulimic, a short thing with long brown hair done in two pigtails like a little girl, though she had to be thirty-five at least. Before, nerves had plagued me almost every time I'd had to interact with others, but now that I was coming into myself, I felt more or less confident. Right off I invited her in and asked her what she wanted.

She goes, "It's Marcus, have you seen him?" She asked me to please not be mad, but she'd peeked at Marcus's phone the week before – he'd been acting strange, so wired and obsessed – and she'd filed away the information about me "just in case."

"This is all quite a shock," I said. "Meeting you this way."

"So you haven't seen him?"

Not since he was first born, I told her, silently congratulating myself for wasting no time in anonymously calling the towing company. Our HOA has strict regulations on visitor parking, and – no surprise – Marcus had failed to follow them.

"He never came *home*!" she wailed, clearly prepared to open up to me whether I liked it or not.

And since my answer was "or not," I guided her into my kitchen, sat her down at the breakfast bar, and filled the expanse of granite between us with leftovers: half a bacon quiche, a pretty piece of layered German chocolate cake, deviled eggs, shredded roast chicken, peanut butter cookies. "I was about to have lunch," I said. "You must be starving after running around all day looking for him." What I really meant was: you must be incredibly stressed, and I know how you comfort yourself.

"This was only the second place I came," she said around a bite of deviled egg, "after his work, but they said they hadn't seen him either. He'll be fired soon, and then what will we do?"

"Please." I pushed the plate of cookies towards her. "You're helping me out, all this will go bad if someone doesn't eat it."

She did not seem shy to oblige. I tried to remember back to my bulimic days, when food would fill my stomach to bursting, would make me feel more like a bear on the verge of hibernation than a human being. I supposed it was sort of like being drunk, with all the blood pulsing in your digestive bits, leaving your brain cold and open to suggestion.

"I'm sorry," I said when I figured her brain was about starting to freeze over. "I lied to you before." I pushed a gallon of rocky road and a spoon towards her. "I did meet Marcus, briefly, but he begged me not to tell you."

Her face paled as she asked what I meant. A couple of her tears fell into the cookie crumbs.

"I oughtn't tell you," I said. "I've already given away too much. But I can see that you're *distressed*, you're really worried, so I feel like maybe I should."

"Please," she said, "I am *desperate* here, I can't sleep . . . "

I let it out bit by bit, how he felt that they hadn't been getting along, lots of problems had cropped up with the two of them living together, his job was trash, nothing for him here, he'd been considering moving back to the West Coast, and that – he hadn't told me this exactly, I explained to her, though he had implied it heavily – he'd probably just up and go when things got too bad. "When he couldn't stand . . . the relationship . . . anymore. He hates goodbyes, you know."

She dropped her head down into the food mess in front of her and let out a few good sobs. "I was afraid of this," she said. "I pushed him too far, didn't I?"

"Maybe so," I said.

After a while, she got it together enough to raise up her head and take in the devastation around her: the pastry crumbs, marshmallow bits, chicken skin. Melted chocolate smudged her left temple. I've got to admit, I notice these tiny details so much more consciously now than I did before, in my old life. The reason I save up these tidbits from my day is because I know that I'll go off and record them later. I made a mental note that the chocolate smudge on her forehead looked like a penguin only because I thought it would be interesting to say so on my tapes here, and it is, right? It's fascinating how I observe things so much more intensely in order to record them. You tapes have given me a whole new perspective on life; it's like I was sleepwalking before, back in those days when I got eight hours a night.

The girlfriend sat up very straight and asked, "May I please use your bathroom?"

"Oh dear," I said, "I wasn't expecting any company today, and my bathroom is an absolute wreck, not fit for visitors of any sort. I'm sorry."

She nodded as if this were just another tragic fact of her life and told me, in that case, she needed to leave.

"Thank you" – she belched politely into one fist – "for everything."

And now I am here wondering just how big of a problem all this might be for me. I'm hoping that it disappears into the atmosphere like air let out of a balloon. I set it up that way, at least: Marcus's girlfriend ought to feel ashamed when she thinks about our meeting, it will make her feel disordered, what with the way she ate me out of house and home; it will give her the reason Marcus couldn't stand her. She ought never want to see me again for fear of regurgitating that shame.

What I really need to do is sit down and figure out my next step; things seem like they are changing, the eggs have done been laid, and maybe I need to hatch along with them. I'll draw myself a nice bath and have a little think.

It's incredible, truly, the sheer quantity of people who keep coming to my front door. This latest mob was incited by that cookbook witch Pastor Maria, who used social media to enflame the ladies at my old church. I'm not sure what, exactly, she messaged them, but they arrived – six of them, led by the awful Lottie – waving their phones in front of them like torches, though the sun had yet to set.

"Natalie, open up!" Lottie cried, her finger against the doorbell.

When they arrived, I'd just gotten out of the bathtub; I tiptoed away from the window, dripping water, and wrapped myself in a robe. I was about to hide in the bedroom when things got serious.

"If you don't answer," Lottie yelled, "I'll use my key! This emergency justifies it. We *need* to talk to you."

Well, why in the world I'd given her a key, I couldn't imagine. There was no reason for her to stop by if I was off on vacation – I didn't even own any non-plastic houseplants – and we had never been the type of friends to just waltz into each other's houses. It must have been a morbid reason, two women living alone a neighborhood apart; *If I don't show up for church one Sunday, come check if I'm alive . . .*

"Be right there!" I called, glancing quick into the mirror to make sure all my makeup was scrubbed off. I shook my head hard so that my cheeks flapped against my teeth; I needed to get into the right mindset, to change my brain. I hid my hair under a towel and whispered a quick little spell to protect myself. As I opened the front door, I said, "Sorry – I was in the bath."

"Deedee?" Lottie said. "Where's Natalie?"

I shrugged, my skin crawling with strangeness at being another woman so suddenly. "Out."

The group behind Lottie shifted nervously, slipping their phones back into their purses. The street was vacant, but I didn't doubt a neighbor or two was spying through a curtain.

Lottie said to her mob, "We can wait here until she gets back."

My nerves were sizzling, but I kept my face calm as a cow pond. "That won't be until tomorrow," I said. "I'll let her know you stopped by. Any message I should relay?"

Agitation rippled through them, and a few of the ladies started talking over each other, asking when was the next bingo game and why Natalie hadn't been by to sell them new cards and what was going on with that crazy new church, how did the crazy pastor from that crazy church get their Twitter handle anyway, and write them all saying Natalie was growing close with the devil, what in the world could that mean and what were they supposed to do about it?

"Hey," Lottie said loudly, "we don't use that word. Just because another church is different doesn't mean they are crazy. We're tolerant here, remember? Like Brother Dan says."

One woman, who had been silent so far but looked rather weepy, asked why she'd never received the giant teddy bear she'd won at the last bingo.

"I'll get it," I said, grateful for an excuse to close the door in their faces and retreat into the house for a few moments. I knew that I was in a spot if I couldn't call them off.

I hefted the teddy bear and carried it out to the weepy woman.

"Thank you all for your concern," I said. "I'm sure Natalie will be glad to hear it."

Most of the women started to leave, but Lottie said loudly and meanly, "Do you swear to God that you'll tell her?"

The others turned back and pulled closer, as if expecting a fight.

Lottie goes, "Because the thing is, God is always watching us, and He will know if you don't."

The lady holding the teddy bear said, "Brother Dan just hates it when such a devoted member of his congregation falls into darkness."

"It's hard on all of us," Lottie agreed, "especially when her departure feels so strange, as if someone might be keeping Natalie from us, locking her away, filling her head with weird ideas."

I had the door as closed as it could be while still able to peek my face out and keep an eye on them. "How funny," I said, "because that is more or less the way she described *you.*"

I thought for a moment that Lottie might karate-kick the door, but she took a deep breath instead. The lady with the teddy bear said, "So we can call them weird, but not crazy?"

I go, "Natalie has had it up to her skull with your pettiness, always judging people, always thinking you are superior. She got sick of organizing those bingo games for you because you were never grateful. In fact you were downright *shameless.*"

The woman squeezed her giant teddy bear, which sat on her hip like a toddler, so that it folded in the middle and its nose touched her forehead. I could sense the group's humiliation at whatever shameful things they had done shimmering right there beneath their skins – it was a snap to get religious people to feel guilty – but this self-disgust only left Lottie meaner.

"How dare you talk to us that way!" she yelled, and I fretted about the neighbors – the street, thanks be, was still empty. "We are good Christian women, we are *good,* and what are you but a scheming freeloader who probably, if I have ever been right in my life, is filling Natalie's head with your dirty thoughts."

"Yeah," said the woman with the teddy bear, "what were you doing with *my* prize bear anyhow?"

"We all know," Lottie said, "something is not right, and if you are the one keeping Natalie from us, I'll find out about it."

"I would never," I said. "She is her own person."

"And *you*" – Lottie jabbed her finger at me – "are a manipulative one, and though Natalie may not see through you, I certainly do."

Another woman said, "So is she coming back to church? Brother Dan wanted – "

"Let's go," Lottie said. She leaned close to me and winked. "I hope you've got those panic attacks under control."

After they left, my hands would not stop shaking. All of these people – Marcus, his girlfriend, the church ladies – parading by have been a sign that I need to make a change. I fear I've finally reached the point where I must flee this little haven I've created for myself. What if I run into one of the church biddies, me in full makeup, at the grocery or liquor store? It wouldn't end well, I'm sure; those Christians have plenty of experience burning people at the stake. They would never understand what I've had to do in my life; they would never accept a witch. I'm torn up about this turn of events, actually; I had started to enjoy my routines here. I suppose this is a little bit my own fault. I should have figured out a way to gracefully end the bingo games, seeing as there was no how I could go around as Natalie to collect the checks and pass out the new cards, and I should not have made such an enemy out of Pastor Maria.

But everything happens for a reason, and all this has led me to see that I need to focus on Thu. I've been slacking on our phone calls and messages, and of course I had to delete my social media after the incident with Sallie, and I'm not holding up my end of the bingo bargain, which is a dangerous position to be in. I know they like to talk about a woman scorned, but a man whose links to pornography are ignored, and who also doesn't receive the thousands he's expecting in profit from a rigged bingo game, would no doubt have the power to destroy me. A computer whiz like him could send the police a trove of evidence about my business practices, and then they might start looking into other things, prying here and there . . . the end of the harvest is, Thu needs to have a big stake in my crop.

Of course, I have always been good at survival: I'm a changeable sort of woman.

I packed up my tapes and the desktop computer tower and a few clothes. At the store I grabbed cleaning supplies and a new deadbolt for the front door so that Lottie's key would be useless. She hasn't yet stopped sending little missives, text messages pretending concern, that I delete as soon as they hit my phone. Back home, I wiped down every surface and tossed out anything that had my hair or spit or snot on it. I gathered up the empty bottles I'd been hoarding in the spare room and hauled them to the street. After I had packed my suitcases for the trip, I unlocked the closet for the other suitcases, the ones that had caused all this trouble. As I tilted the first suitcase onto its wheels, I felt a liquid shifting from inside, as if I were handling a giant water balloon. For a terrifying moment, I imagined the balloon bursting.

Hefting the suitcases into my car was difficult: I had to wrap my arms around their middles until I was basically hugging the slop inside them to haul them up and over the lip of the trunk. Then I drove to a huge old cemetery situated a few miles out of town and rolled the suitcases along the deteriorating asphalt path. I felt as if I'd stepped into a dreamscape created by my mind, even though I had visited this place once before with the half-buried idea that I might need a hiding place someday. It was early morning and no one bothered me, my only company besides the coffined skeletons a racoon, or something like it, glaring at me from a bush. The chain around the door of the mausoleum I had picked out earlier was so old that it snaked to the ground after one snip of my bolt cutter. For some reason, I stared at it for a few moments, half-waiting for it to slither away.

In the very back of this mausoleum that obviously hadn't been entered in decades, I stored my heavy suitcases. I sat atop one of the two bench-height tombs, which immediately chilled my behind, and I cast a quick hex, just a few words and a gob of spit, then set up a new lock to replace the one I'd broke, to protect them from being found. I have realized that I need these bodies to stay very very still, undisturbed, since their quietness is a part of my transmogrification into a witch. Especially the Mary Ellen body, which is the old powerless me, left behind, and as it decays away into nothing, I grow more fully into my true self. Of course I had been born predisposed to witchiness – the incident with the crop duster making a dartboard of my house had proved that – but witchiness needs to be cultivated to reach its full potential. I've been working to catch up, seeing as mine had languished too long.

I swung by the ATM before I drove myself to the airport, where I bought a ticket to the other coast.

"Here you go, Ms. Heap," the attendant said when she snapped my passport closed over my ticket. "But the flight doesn't leave for four hours."

That's how I found myself in here, the lounge's handicapped private restroom, making this recording. I wanted to get it all down, just the way it happened, while it was still a fresh-cut piece in my mind.

Thu was as surprised as a bitch having her first litter when I showed up at his apartment.

"Bian!" he said, and his eyes kind of rolled back in his head like he was thinking. "I hope you know CPR . . . because you are taking my breath away."

Closely I watched him for any oddities, for any sign that he was trying to fit the whole hog back together, but he hugged me with such simple happiness that I could only figure he truly was glad to see me.

"I missed you," I told Thu. "I wanted to surprise you, you know, for the holidays."

"You missed me?" he asked. "I thought that you might be angry with me."

I told him that I had simply been busy.

He goes, "And then when you deleted all of your social media, I thought it must have something to do with me. I mean, I was shocked, really."

"I just needed a cleanse," I told him. "You know how it is."

For a second, he looked about to cry. "I was worried you were going to break up with me, and now here you are. Oh no, wait . . . are you about to break it off?"

I shouldn't have let Thu roam this far out of my orbit, but I've been distracted. I hoped that he just needed reassurance – his mind was one-track, so I figured it would be easy. Plus, I'd concocted a special plan.

Just the way I had practiced in the bathroom mirror at the airport, I go, "Maybe the holidays are when I feel the most sad, and this year, I was feeling especially vulnerable and alone, because it was this time of year when my mother died, and I was missing her, and thinking you, and I guess I wanted to be around someone I . . . love. It is accurately the opposite of wanting to break up."

Thu's eyes shone; he practically beamed. He hugged me closely and said, "Oh, Bian, I love you too. I've known it for a while, but I didn't want to scare you."

He was clinging to me; he couldn't see the way I was smiling. It was so easy to manipulate a person's emotions, to obliterate from their minds any niggling inconsistencies or doubts.

"So you're happy to see me?" I asked, and he said that he was.

Then I knew that I had come up with the right plan; it was time to set my future in motion.

We walked into his living room, but I didn't really see it. Square brown everything, too low plasticky chandelier in one corner to mark the dining area. I go, "I want to show you something. A surprise."

He looked kind of nervous and excited, just the way I wanted him. He kept fidgeting, pushing his glasses up his nose and nodding for no reason.

"We're going to play a little game." I unzipped the outside pocket of my suitcase, where I'd stored the stuff.

"Bingo?" Thu said. He sat on the couch, and I kneeled on the floor in front of him. I set out my tray that I'd cut short to have just eighteen divots, then I took out the console and began to churn the fifteen balls I'd put inside.

"R!" Thu yelled when the first bingo ball dropped into the receptacle. I put the ball in its place in the tray and churned the hopper again. The balls clicked like a set of fingerless fingernails. "E!" Thu cried.

It went on like this for some time, and once we'd reached: WIL Y U ARRY E?, Thu began to leak at the eyes. I finished up with the final few letters, figuring that would give Thu some time to tie himself together, but once the question was complete, he'd become even more weepy. I began to worry that I'd misjudged matters, and Thu was about to tell me to pound the pavement, but then he dropped to the carpet beside me and grabbed both my hands.

"I'm sorry," he said, sobbing, "I'm sorry."

And I thought, shit. My whole plan is a wet cake.

But then he goes, "I should be the one asking *you*. Will you marry me? Will you?"

Pride swelled up in my chest: never should I have doubted myself. I was a witch; I'd always been able to create my future. "Yes!" I said, and he said it too, and we hot-potatoed this word back and forth until Thu decided it was time to show me his bedroom.

Afterwards, beneath the sheets, the window drapes gaping, Thu said, "When you deleted your social media, I really thought your next step would be to break up with me. It seemed like it was . . . in preparation. But – I'm so relieved – you were only trying to keep the surprise. You have no idea how I was worrying . . . I even put my Sims' house on the market. But you were afraid that too much contact with me would give away what you were about to do. Right? This is the surprise of my life, the most romantic moment I've ever experienced. I only wish that I'd thought of it first."

"I'm relieved," I said.

He goes, "Nothing is forever, and I'm so glad you are my nothing."

He left me to take a nap while he fixed dinner. As I drifted to sleep, I thought about how far I'd come, away from my problems. They had been left in states that touched the opposite sea. I was thinking about ocean waves as I fell into an exhausted sleep.

Pretty soon into my nap, my ghosts appeared; they cooked my brain like spaghetti, then tilted my head to draw the noodle out. "What now?" I asked them.

Jim Dave pressed his yellow breasts together. He goes, "Sure is weird to finally be able to touch these whenever I want."

I said, "How is it that things always turn out just how you like them?"

"I'm a master at gentle suggestions," he told me. "When I'm like this" – he wiggled his ghost body – "I can't personally make anything happen, not in your physical world, but I can target stuff ghostlike, drop a trail of crumbs, encourage you toward the direction I want."

The Mary Ellen ghost, who'd been hovering, silent, in the corner, bobbed a bit closer.

"Get in your head, you know," Jim Dave said, "silently invisibly nudge you my way, and then you put the pieces together, give me what I want. You wouldn't think it, but I can make anything happen. I *can*."

The Mary Ellen ghost poked him hard in the arm. "You," she

said, "did you possibly *suggest* that this monster kill me?"

He stood up from the bed; they both floated a few feet away. He said, "I saw where she was going with it anyhow . . . you were so beautiful . . . I was so lonely . . . "

The Mary Ellen ghost buried her fists all the way through his chest. She said, "Now we're stuck to her forever, stuck *together* eternally, you *wanted* her to kill me, you ruined me . . . "

An oily sweat wove across my skin like a delicate shroud I couldn't escape from; I was so close to getting what I wanted here, too. "You see?" I asked the Mary Ellen ghost. "That's why we ought to stick together. We can't trust him." What I was thinking: divide and conquer. They were *my* ghosts; they needed to belong to me more than to each other. "I'm the one who has the means to help you. Who *wants* to help you."

She bobbed closer to me.

"If you give me room to sleep," I said, "and to think, I'll be able to."

She asked, "With the little problem of being dead, right?"

"Of course," I said. I am finding that the real truth lies in what I make of it, I am my own truth maker, which is the best position to be in.

For the rest of my nap, she hushed and admonished Jim Dave in the corner, and the noodle of my brain cooled so that I could almost sleep.

Who can say why this is bothering me, but I need to set down one thing: I want to make it clear that every time I decided to give another person the truest, most essential part of myself, the gift has been thrown back in my face. I guess that what I'm trying to say is, my marriage proposal is nothing to scoff at. My time with Thu has turned out better because we are not engaged in the dark magic of excavating each other's souls; because I offer him nothing real, our relationship is the calmest one I've ever had.

And another niggling thought, a big bother, really: I wonder if anyone listening to these tapes would ever think to like me? But why is that always something people want out of women? Why can't I fully shake the idea that maybe, someday, after I'm gone, people will listen to my tapes because they find me compelling? The world has engrained in me the idea that women should be like pitiful characters in books, relatable and sympathetic. Well, if you don't like me now, just wait: you might like the next me.

RELAXATION TECHNIQUES FOR THE ELDERLY

I am pleasantly surprised at how easy it is to live with Thu. During the day, he leaves for work, and at night he plays video games and cooks dinner. Last night, after the meal, he brought out a strawberry tart, and a bite of it was already in my mouth when I remembered that I was allergic to strawberries. The walls of Thu's apartment seemed to vibrate and close in, and I worried about what would happen to me as the cloying custard filling expanded in my mouth. Would my throat close up and prevent me from breathing? Would my skin break out in strawberry-shaped hives?

The half-chewed food fell from my mouth back onto my plate, and I wrapped both my hands around my throat. "I'm allergic," I gasped to Thu. "I forgot!"

He brought me a glass of milk that I drank down, and I immediately felt better. I placed my napkin overtop of the red goop on my plate and apologized to Thu. He looked at me a bit strangely, but he just patted my back and put the strawberry tart away.

"Good thing I didn't swallow it," I said, "or my insides might have exploded. It would have been awful."

"Good thing," Thu agreed.

Together we washed the dishes. I had a lot on my mind, but I focused on Thu because I needed him as part of my plan, and so I wanted to make sure that he was happy with me, that he suspected nothing. Besides, it was mildly entertaining and so very easy to turn him bright red with a poke of the finger or a tiny kiss.

After the kitchen was clean, we sat on the couch and I watched as he thumbed through make-believe worlds on his huge TV. Still staring at the screen, he said, "What's the plan?" He hummed a little bit of "Here Comes the Bride" as, with a flick of the index finger, he blasted an ogre thing with what I believe was a sparkling wand.

I told him that I hadn't thought much about it.

He goes, "I guess you were too worried over the proposal to think that far ahead. Damn, I wish I had thought of doing it first, but I was scared."

"That's silly," I said. "I wouldn't have told you no." Tinkling wind chimes from the video game's soundtrack lent weight to my words.

He asked me what our budget should be for the wedding, if we should do it small, or if instead we should blow all our bingo money on something unforgettable.

I'd been waiting for the right time to tell him, and I figured this was it. I go, "Bubbles, we're going to need to cool it for a while with the bingo scheme. The thing is, a couple of the ladies were starting to catch on. Not catch on entirely, but they had some questions. I made a choice to protect our future business ventures. Things are hot right now, but when they cool down, we could start up again, maybe here in Cali, or somewhere . . . else. It's just that things had run their course in Florida. I'd sold too many cards." Finally I paused for breath, afraid what he might say – this was a crucial part of my plan, and though I felt pretty certain that Thu was under my spell, I knew from experience that people could surprise you.

About a minute of silence passed, during which Thu's magic wand entered a dark hall filled with roving-eyed portraits and I fretted like a dove over its egg, trying to figure out what, exactly, I would do if he turned on me. He knows, I thought to myself, he'll figure I'm a danger and matters will go south the way they have before, he knows and my egg is split.

"Tell me this," he goes, his eyes fixed on the game, "did anything in particular happen?"

I told him not in the least, that this was a preventative measure:

I figured it was best to stop while we were ahead.

He cleared his throat; my heart paused. He goes, "Bian, I agree with you completely. You are so smart, because now that we'll be married – we should do it as soon as possible, don't you think? – we won't be able to testify against one another, just in case anything does come down the pipe."

The tinkling video game wind chimes mirrored my soaring confidence. My plan had fallen into place perfectly – though I also wondered just how illegal our bingo scheme really was. *Testify* is a strong word. I told him, "I'm so excited; I can't wait."

"We'll set it up in about a month, then," he said, so unlike himself, so decisive and manly. He smithereened a ghost that appeared out of the wall; its green plasma was the brightest thing on the TV screen. "Right after the holidays."

So: I'm about to get married! That's a big first, for a woman in her fifties.

This morning, I found Thu cracking eggs in the kitchen for breakfast. He asked me if there were any holiday traditions that I was into, like eggnog or church or singing happy birthday to Jesus.

I wanted to try something on him, and so I said, "What if I told you that I was a witch?" My question didn't come out of the blue: I'd been waiting to test out what Thu made of my witchiness ever since I'd come up with the bingo-themed proposal. How many parts of myself would I need to keep hidden from him?

Thu looked down at the bowl of yolks floating like yellow eyes. "Kind of a religious thing?" He picked up a fork and began to whip the eggs, turning the yellow eyes to froth. "Then you're a good witch, with your herb concoctions and potions."

"My herbs and potions?" I asked.

He goes, "Yes, the potpourri that you put everywhere, and the delicious cocktails that you stir up."

"That's right," I said, "I'm a good witch, good for us."

He smiled at me as he dipped a slice of bread into the egg and said how he was surprised that I had talked about church so often — that is, before we'd met in person — when it truly didn't seem that important a part of my life.

"Church is always a fruitful place for business, though," I told him, and he had to agree.

He goes, "It's only that you seemed pretty religious, I don't know . . . not in a witch kind of way."

I tried very hard to remember, but I couldn't. "There was a *before* we met in person," I said, "and an *after*. Things can change from there to here. I might have said things, or even thought things, that aren't accurate now we've met. Because we *know* each other now. And so I can be more myself around you. You understand me?"

"You're incredibly different from what I was expecting," he said, shaking a can of whipped cream. "I mean, sometimes, it's hard for me to reconcile the person I thought I was getting and then . . . *you*. Don't look upset — I didn't mean it that way. I love the you that I've found in person, of course I do. It's good to be surprised in this life."

"That's right," I told him. "Besides, what I'm going for, this is more about being a strong woman, believing in my own power, that sort of thing."

He pushed his glasses up his nose. "Like maybe it means you have multiple wants and desires, all pressurized there inside you, waiting to come out." He tapped a finger against the whipped cream. "Kind of like your many selves are rolled into this one tiny container: you shield your softest, innermost one under a hard shell, and I have to make you pliant before I can reach your core." He sprayed a dollop of whipped cream into his mouth. "It's true! You are whip cream. You taste just like this."

I really didn't care for all this talk of Thu reaching into my core. Of course there was a reason I hid certain parts of myself from him, and the truth is that I want to hide parts of myself from me, too. These tapes are as deep as I'm willing to go. But I have to say, it is interesting, how thrilling it can be to talk through my life, like I'm learning more about what already happened to me. Maybe, some-day, I will be ready to turn over the old earth at my core. "It might be more of a personal thing," I said. "Inner strength and all that."

He goes, "That sounds nice. I've learned most of what I know about witches from my video games. Even if you are a witch, you'll always be my angel."

I rolled my eyes, but he was hugging me so thanks be he couldn't see. Seems like I won't need to entirely guard this part of myself from Thu, which will certainly be a boon to my development. Maybe our relationship has a chance to last for a while, despite the fact that Thu seems to have learned to talk to women from a book titled "Charm Her Pants Off."

When I'm making my recordings like this, it's strange, but all my worries melt away. I wonder if these tapes give me a certain peace, a certain inner quietness, that unease cannot penetrate. After record-ing, I do feel better: all my problems are stored somewhere else.

Well, when I woke up today, I discovered another podcast. I could barely choke down my coffee, anxious as I was to hurry Thu off to the office so's I could play it in peace. Let's go ahead and listen through, though I don't doubt that the content will be worse than a burnt breakfast.

Welcome to NEXT TO MY NECK OF THE WOODS: CORONER BLUES. Since we've been waiting what I would consider an inordi-nate amount of time for the full coroner's report on the body of Jim Dave Washie, your host thought that you all might enjoy a new epi-sode about some curiosities from our subjects' pasts.

Picture Mary Ellen, the crown jewel of her lower-middle-class family. At a young age, she married up, but soon after, tragedy hit.

Her only sibling, a younger sister named Rosie, moved back home under mysterious circumstances after only a few weeks of attempting an independent life. She then committed suicide in the childhood bedroom the two sisters had shared up until Mary Ellen's marriage to her first husband. Your host has to wonder if Mary Ellen's abrupt departure from the family nest caused a rupture between the sisters, something that could possibly have pushed young Rosie to spiral into a depression. Your host herself has felt just how close to the surface depression can lurk, how one small move, one mean comment from a husband, one recently baked birthday cake tossed into the trash can, can break down the brick wall you've built to protect your family, and by that point any little crack might cause the wall to fall.

I wonder what's going on with this silly woman. Maybe her breast implant goo has gone to her head.

Excuse me, back to the subject at hand. Rosie's was no regular suicide, no, but rather a gruesome and unsettling ending of a life. She consumed commercial rat poison, which took three painful days to finish its work.

Look at her, dragging ancient family history into the mix. She must've got her information from the old police report.

Now you may not know this, because your host certainly didn't before researching for this episode, but rat poison is designed with a daylong delay because small children and pets eat the sweet candy-colored stuff by accident so often that the doctors need time to get them the antidote. Well, no one ever brought Rosie the antidote. Another DB.

At the time of her sister's death, Mary Ellen was living a couple of towns away, in Magnolia, with her new husband. Your host wonders what kind of devastation she felt after receiving the news that her little sister was dead. It must have been impactful: scarcely one week after the loss, Mary Ellen started divorce proceedings and moved back home, perhaps even into the same bedroom where her sister had passed. Maybe the shadow of Rosie accelerated the dissolution of Mary Ellen's marriage, or maybe someone like Mary Ellen was never meant to be married in the first place.

Or maybe her first husband was a lying boob who spent more time at the gym than with his new wife.

Actually your host has been thinking quite a bit about the marriage question, and how fair it is that she has spent the majority of her adult life caring for a man and babies, being a complete house mouse, just like her husband wanted, when she might have been able to do all sorts of other things, like possibly becoming an investigative journalist, or a creative nonfiction writer, or any such sort.

Now I see the issue with our little host: she's finally realized that men are fools, poor dear, it took her long enough. No wonder she's fascinated by Mary Ellen, a woman who escaped.

But if ever there was a woman marriage did not suit, I would say it would have to be Mary Ellen. She was a born breadwinner, a get-up-and-goer. For example, when Jim Dave developed a severe hernia after trying to lift a truck in his mechanic shop that had rolled onto a coworker who unfortunately later died, Mary Ellen immediately began working double shifts to support the family. I wonder, though, if this caused a certain resentment within her. Your host believes that all women harbor a secret resentment against their partners, but most of us are able to keep that under control, maybe through a creative outlet, maybe through a little Zumba.

How funny that I would have something in common with a CC-Squared, but I understand her sentiment. Sometimes I feel like if I couldn't whisper into my little tape recorder here, then I would fall right in on myself, fold down into a sad envelope of flesh.

The problem is, when a man decides he isn't one hundred and ten percent happy, he can clock out without looking back. Now I know that it is unbecoming for your host to delve into these sorts of personal matters, especially when HERE IN THE HIGH CHAIR was all about my perfect family, but sometimes I feel like if I don't let it out, then I'll implode. It's not like my husband ever listened to a word I said, so why would he listen in here? That's why, even though he warned me about airing our dirty laundry, your host feels free enough to go ahead and tell you that he's gone and he didn't even attempt to take our children with him. Of course they wouldn't fit into his swank new bachelor pad — which your host's famous intuition and other instances of PC tell her might already be filling up with a feminine touch or two.

Your host would never condone violence, but considering the state of my own marriage, it is not unfathomable to see how it happens that a woman snaps.

Don't miss my next episode; be sure to subscribe! There is plenty more to come on NEXT TO MY NECK OF THE WOODS.

Three hundred and twenty-seven listens, this one. Our little host is striving to make a name for herself. And if the comments are any indication, all the disgruntled women out there love these dips into her disappointing marriage. She probably spilled those few beans just to get herself more listeners. Get a load of these:

HEARME_ROAR: You've got to tell us more about what is going on with you. What if that is the real story here? We all need a space for our voice, to share our story. For example I myself was the victim of an unfare divorce and I am still four years later fighting for my fare share of alimony, it is a never-ending battle. Gather your evidence and be always vigilant.
mamacita4Cer: hun I am so sorry to hear this I know just how you feel men want the newer model no matter we stretched ourselves out giving them heirs not fair :(
XTINAXOXO: I want to know more about the first husband? Is he alive?
mumstheword5: what does she mean PC she's not watching

what she says that much?

eyehartdisney: @mumstheword5 *Probable Cause* PLEASE LEARN TO USE GOOGLE

richardlam: *I would just like to say that your voice is too high to be a podcast host, no wonder your husband left you when he had to listen to that pitch all day.*

DR_WHOEVER: *if you are miserable suicide is an answer*

HPPYMAMA: *i am heartbroke your marriage was so perfect back on the other podcast maybe you can go back to that one and everything will be alright*

SKYNNYMARGE: *You should really provide details to a few suicide hotlines after an episode like this. I would myself but the security settings are blocking me. Be responsible.*

CROSS2BARE: *Does no one else see how this evil washie woman causes everyone around her to suffer? Something must be done.*

SOLESIGH: *How have they not arrested this woman yet for murder? This is why we need more vigilante justice. It is unacceptable that she hasn't been scalped*

twinmama: *the exact same thing happened 2 me he bought an entire condo i didnt know until he had stolen our best silverware you tell me what does he need that 4*

For a few moments, I entertained the idea of chiming in, typing something clever and intelligent that would throw everyone off my trail, coming up with a brilliant username like *ghostgirlgreen* or *whichwitch666*, but then I recalled what had happened when I'd reached out online to Sallie. I'm the sort of woman who learns from past mistakes.

I keep mulling over what happened with Sallie and how worried I ought to be about her throwing my data scraps to the hungry pigs. I am even more convinced that it is necessary to never trust anyone, to live a life of secrecy, to rely only on yourself . . .

Thanks be I am not the type of person who is prone to guilt, who grows an ulcer from biting the inside of their cheek, who is laid low by migraines from thinking over everything they've done, who grinds their teeth in their sleep – hell, I don't sleep at all.

I've just had a jolting thought: Sallie knows that I am Natalie Heap, and because we were social media friends, she might have also seen that Thu is Natalie's boyfriend. I popped open Thu's laptop and checked his social media for personal information, but luckily, a true cyber man, he gives very little of that. The problem is, what all are people able to glean from this stuff?

Maybe Sallie knows where I am at this very moment.

I can't stay here, if that's the case. Obviously I can't. We ought to move up the timeline, me and Thu, have a shotgun wedding, honeymoon somewhere far, far away.

The bottom barrel is, in a strange way, I'm proud of Sallie; I am impressed that she will do whatever it takes to survive, which includes cyber-tracking me down in order to demand her slice of the pie. Who knows how she sensed that I was once who I was, or that I had come into a bit of funds. Maybe that is where her witchiness lies, in her perceptiveness. Maybe Sallie will start cultivating her witchiness someday. Or maybe, like most women, she's a lost cause. I don't plan on us being in a position that I would ever find out.

A HISTORY OF FOOD PROCESSORS

A few days of peace have passed, but now there's a new podcast what is making me feel especially jumpy. Finally Thu has left the house so's I can play it here. If only I could ignore it, but of course it's all I can think about; if I don't listen to it now, I'll go wild, even though I wager the wishbone that I won't like it. Here goes . . .

Your host here with NEXT TO MY NECK OF THE WOODS: UNEXPECTED PROGRESS. It's funny how life is like the ocean, all ups and downs. Well, your host has a feeling that the downtimes are coming for Mary Ellen Washie, the missing Chautauqua County woman. Our boys in blue have announced that they are coordinating with their counterparts down in Florida after a tip about an alleged theft from a sharp-eyed motel proprietor who recognized a picture of our subject when she stumbled upon a certain stellar podcast. I just love it when my work here has real-life consequences!

How could it be, all this time later, that they would connect those dots?

And while the subject of our podcast is sinking, your host is riding the wave up. I know that many of you were concerned for me after my revelation on the last episode, but I am here to tell you that you have no reason for worry: your host has found herself a new beau, or rather, he found her, or rather, they have known each other for years and apparently he had always been mooning for his chance. This man in uniform has already supported your host in myriad ways, not least of which was setting up her podcasting equipment.

I'm cooked; I'm stewed; now they'll start stirring the pot further and further out from that stinkhole of a motel, my stars, who knows what they'll spoon up.

And another thing: for those of you who've heard my ex say that he left me preemptively because he saw this coming, that is pure testilying, because not a thing happened until I was dumped, swear on my mother's grave. Of course I would like to dedicate this episode to him, my new man, Mr. Rock.

That was short – for once no endless blather – maybe she can't say more because they are already deep into the investigation? Or maybe the motel theft is a big plate of nothing and she only needed an excuse to dish about her new man. Let's hope Mr. Rock will keep her busy enough that she'll stop digging into my business, though on the other hand, this clue of hers is rather useful. I already read the comments, a whole lot of junk, so I'll spare the tape this time.

Every day I feel a bit more cornered, a bit more trapped, and even before I knew that they had found out I'd been in Florida, I had been pondering a jaunt to Vietnam with Thu. It did seem a good idea, overall safer, to get away for a while, and now with everyone on my tail, a trip felt even more pressing.

Over supper in Thu's apartment, we talked.

"Bubbles," I said, "I've been thinking about our honeymoon, and how we ought to go big, especially since our wedding will be so small. The honeymoon is a special treat just for the two of us, and I want it to be amazing."

Thu goes, "I'll see about taking some time off work." He carried a pile of noodles to the table.

I explained to him how I'd been looking at tickets, and the moment to buy is now. "I want to inch up our timeline a bit," I said, "head down to the courthouse on Thursday, then Friday we could fly off on our big romantic adventure."

"A bit!" Thu said. "That barely gives me time to clean my shoes. I thought we were planning a month out. My mother won't be able to come from Phoenix by *Thursday*. I was thinking a honeymoon in Vegas . . . "

He was fussing. I told him to sit down, and I swirled noodles onto his plate. I pushed his wineglass towards him; I felt precisely in control of the situation. You see, I'd cast a little spell on our supper, helped along by a drop of Pastor Maria's potion mixed into Thu's wine. It wasn't enough to put him out, but it would leave him susceptible to my suggestions.

I asked, "Don't you love me enough to travel with me?"

His eyes widened; he was a little scared. "You are my universe, the moon and stars and the – "

"Sometimes I worry," I said. If you didn't cut him off, he could babble on like that for ages. "Because I was the one who had to propose, I guess."

"I will always regret that," Thu said. "I mean, it was a wonderful proposal, such a clever concept, but I should have – "

"And Bubbles" – this was my clincher – "I simply don't think I can be here, California, the place of my mother's death, on the day that she actually died. It would break my heart."

His eyes turned heavy. "I didn't realize; I see you're upset. I'm so sorry, maybe we could pay a tribute to her, release a bunch of balloons or . . . "

I said, "I've just got to get out of here before then; I have to go. But I don't want to leave you, of course I don't."

"No," Thu said, blinking, each downturn of his lids lasting a moment too long, "you are my other half, the cream to my coffee, the hanky to my panky, the she- to my -nanigans . . . "

"Yes, but wouldn't it be nice . . . wouldn't it be nice . . . " I chanted this little refrain, and then I waited for the magic to work. It might have also helped that I did whatever Thu wanted for the evening, lights bright, curtains open to the world. He turned on his little Sims and, while they were making a roly-poly ball underneath their zebra-striped bedsheets, he clumsily turned me over on the couch, my face pressed into the cushion so that I could hardly breathe. He stuck his sausage in without gawkily asking my permission first, which was a mildly exciting new development, and even though my potion had left him moving a bit slow, he finished up just as his Sims were squealing with delight, and already he'd slipped out of me by the time their pixelated heads popped out from beneath the bedcovers. As I watched him and his Sims fall asleep, I felt certain that Thu would ease around to my way of seeing things.

For weeks now, starting back in Florida, I have sensed that they would come for me; I'd left too many clues, been betrayed by too many people. And it happened today when Thu was about to leave for work, and I was in the back bedroom getting dressed.

From the way the door shook with knocking, I knew it was some kind of police, some man with a gun strapped to his belt who believed completely in his own righteousness. Immediately I locked the bedroom door and opened the back window; two stories down, the ground pulsed. The sight of it made me dizzy.

Through the locked door I could hear voices, and so I pressed my ear to the wood composite. Formalities over, the policeman said, "Do you know a Mary Ellen Washie?"

I could imagine Thu breaking down, trembling in the shadow of this big man, crying out that I was just a few yards away – but he said, "No."

Which I suppose was technically true.

"Do you recognize this person?" the officer asked, and I could picture him holding up a photograph of a washed-out, unkempt woman with mousy brown hair and a downtrodden roundness to her shoulders.

Though there still might be something about her nostrils, or the shape of her eyes, that kindled Thu's recognition.

"I do not," Thu said, and I finally started breathing again; I would be safe. Already Thu was telling the officer goodbye, he was closing the door, he was rummaging around in the kitchen, and then he was calling out to me that he had to run, he'd be late for work, but he'd see me in the evening for dinner.

All the while he was gone, I wondered. Did Thu have any suspicions about me? Why hadn't the officer asked him about Natalie? Had it been our little host, that clickbait hack, or Sallie, who only thought of her own self, who'd given me up? Somehow they had known to look *here*.

I was as nervous as a wasp stuck in a soda can; I felt sure that any moment, the authorities would park a cherrytop in the lot and march up to the apartment, then break down the front door while yelling that something Thu had said or done had left them suspicious. I stared out of the living room blinds with my martini, watching. If they started up the path, I guessed I would launch myself out the back window. I had this fantasy that maybe I would fly off into the hot blue sky, my two ghosts buoying me up, rather than fall flat on my face against the asphalt. It was a bit superstitious and weird, but I leaned a broom in the corner of the back room, just in case.

But Thu came home this evening as normal. Over drinks, he started off talking about the new water fountain at his office and what we'd cook that night. But then he segued into more cryptic territory, saying things like, "If anyone in a uniform comes a-knocking, never invite them in. Always let them know that you have somewhere to be – soon. And never ever ever tell them more than what they ask for. Remember: monosyllabic is your friend." I nodded along. He goes, "Have you made the appointment for Thursday yet? And bought the plane tickets? I talked to my boss this afternoon: I'm cashing in all of my vacation days."

That he'd come around to my hurried timeline made me feel like an egg being boiled, warm and soft inside, gently rolled on bubbles.

"You wouldn't believe how much I'm looking forward to this," I told him, entirely pleased with myself that things were going my way. I figured that I had done this: Thu was under my spell.

"Me too," he said. "It's just what we need, don't you think? To get away for a while."

Being a witch removes the trepidation from so many things. I didn't worry over whether the county clerk would look askance at my identification documents because I'd cast a spell to help the whole process run smoothly. I didn't fret when the judge asked if anyone opposed our marriage, and I just knew that my passport would not raise any red flags at the airport.

The bottom line is, we made it, we're here now, Hanoi, me safe in the hotel while Thu is off buying supplies. It's magical how you can go to a new place and change your life, shed your old problems like snakeskin left crumpled beside a rock in the desert.

On the morning Thu and I left for the airport, my worries disappeared with each mile we made. I felt a bit nervous for the flying, and I had to remind myself that this wasn't only my second time on a plane, that Natalie had flown all over and that Bian, too, was obviously a seasoned world traveler.

As Thu lifted my suitcase up onto the scale, he said, "Wow, it's so light," and I told him not to worry, that I'd have plenty to put into it soon.

We buckled ourselves in under the flight attendants' supervision. Thu seemed giddy, and he said how surprised he was that we were doing something this wild. He goes, "I feel like a tiger ready to eat your flesh." Since our wedding the day before, he'd turned a bit more bold and handsy.

After takeoff, we knocked together our plastic cups of rice wine and giggled like kids on a field trip.

Thu goes, "Bian – the name really fits you. Did I ever tell you what it means?"

He hadn't, and I told him so.

"My pet name for you," he said. "It's pretty, right? It means secretive."

Just then, my heart took off without me, rolling with that old lethal feeling, but out of self-preservation, I had learned to ignore it. I plastered on a smile; he didn't know a thing. He was taking me to Vietnam to eat pho and lounge on the beach, and I had no intention of going back; I was pretty sure that he wouldn't either, not after I convinced him we ought to stay. Very calmly, I said, "Secretive?"

He blinked excitedly. "Yes, don't play coy. You're a deep, deep woman and you are full of secrets. But I understand. I'm excited for them to come out, little by little. You can tell me; you can tell me anything. You can *trust* me. I know you heard me talking with that detective; I would never betray you. We'll be closer than anyone, once you see that you can trust me. It will be like we've known each other our entire lives."

"Won't that be nice," I said and leaned my head against him. Of course, if he really did find out everything about me, I'd just change myself again, to make sure he didn't ruin me. But in the meantime, it *would* be nice to have him on my side, under my spell. "We're a good team," I said, "in bingo, in life."

His stomach grumbled, and with my ear against his shoulder, it felt like a noise from within my own body. "You know," he said, "I have always wanted to be married, and it's even more special, that we both waited so long to find each other. Our firsts, forever."

A quick wash of confusion suffused me, after which I remembered that it was true, I had never been married before him. "Only call me Bian from now on," I said, "okay? I want to become like a new person for this trip."

"Like we're starting our future together," he said. "You're my wife, and I'll do anything for you."

"Me too," I said.

He squeezed my hand and poured me more wine. "Oh, Bian, I love you. In Vietnam, we'll drink rice wine instead of your martinis. You'll learn to like it."

"I like it already," I told him.

Bian is a strong woman who fortifies herself against the idiocy of the world with rice wine, who whispers all her secrets into a hand-held recorder so that she will never be tempted to say them anywhere else, who will start fresh as many times as she needs. She is a dark pool of mystery, which only adds to her allure. Bian, Bian, Bian – I like becoming her already.

Sometime later, in the midst of a nap, my head resting against the plastic airplane window, a rattle of turbulence disturbed me. Outside in the sky, high above the carpet of clouds, my ghosts – Jim Dave, Mary Ellen, and now Marcus – were flying along beside me. I wasn't really surprised; I waved at them. Jim Dave and Mary Ellen were bickering; Marcus was obviously enjoying the wind in his sparse hair. Maybe I would have a lifetime of collecting ghosts, becoming more powerful with each one, and they would all keep each other company, happily screwing and fighting while they deprived me of sleep. They had once tried to convince me that they were my anchors, but here we all were, up in the sky.

Born in Las Vegas, Nevada, M. S. Coe is an American writer living in Guadalajara, Mexico. After she graduated with an MFA in creative writing from Cornell University, Clash Books published her first novel, *New Veronia*, in 2019. Coe's stories have appeared in *The Antioch Review*, *Cosmonauts Avenue*, *Electric Literature*, *Nashville Review*, *Waxwing*, and elsewhere. She has held residencies from the Herbert Hoover National Historic Site, Petrified Forest National Park, and Ora Lerman Trust.